PROLOGUE

December 1928

'There's somebody coming up the hill.'

Wilf had been told not to talk. Mary, his mother, shushed him. Still, everybody turned to look down the hill, even the vicar.

Two coppers, Briggs and Emerson, were coming up the lane towards the cemetery, looking as if they'd run all the way from the station in Collingford. They stopped when they got to the grave. Briggs, older and fatter, tried to say something but had no breath left. He nudged Emerson's elbow.

'You've got to stop,' Emerson said.

'What?'

Emerson cleared his throat and said, louder, 'You've got to stop the funeral.'

7

The vicar looked at the undertaker, who shook his head. He didn't know what they were talking about either.

Briggs recovered his breath enough to say, 'Perhaps we could have a quiet word.' He took the vicar and the undertaker to one side and they whispered.

Emerson stayed with the mourners. He knew them. Mary Dutton used to come into his dad's shop. Doris, her eldest, was at the same school as his little brother. They nodded embarrassed hellos. Mrs Fellows, Mary Dutton's friend, asked him, 'What's all this about, then?' He said he was ever so sorry, but he wasn't at liberty to say.

The undertaker told the men to put the coffin back on the cart and the vicar braced himself to break the news to Mary.

'This is all very distressing but I'm afraid the police are saying that Dr Willoughby may have made a mistake. There's going to have to be an autopsy.'

'What sort of mistake?'

'I'm sure it's no more than a formality, although I must say that to leave it to the eleventh hour like this shows an inhuman lack of compassion, but rest assured . . .'

Mary wasn't listening. The cart had started back down the hill. She followed it.

'What's going on? What's going on?'

The undertaker turned. 'Somebody's said he was poisoned.'

SKELTON'S GUIDE TO DOMESTIC POISONS

David Stafford

Allison & Busby Limited
11 Wardour Mews
London W1F 8AN
allisonandbusby.com

First published in Great Britain by Allison & Busby in 2020.
This paperback edition published by Allison & Busby in 2021.

A CIP catalogue record for this book is available from
the British Library.

10 9 8 7 6 5 4 3 2 1

ISBN 978-0-7490-2683-7

Typeset in 11.5/16.5 pt Adobe Garamond Pro by
Allison & Busby Ltd

The paper used for this Allison & Busby publication
has been produced from trees that have been legally sourced
from well-managed and credibly certified forests.

Printed and bound by
CPI Group (UK) Ltd, Croydon, CR0 4YY

To Michael, Mary, Sue and John

CHAPTER ONE

January 1929

On the train into Paddington, Arthur Skelton stared at a picture of himself. It was on page four of the *Daily Mail* being read by the man opposite. The same picture, or variations of it, showing him smiling, serious, standing, walking, had haunted him all weekend, in the *Daily Herald*, the *News of the World*, the *Express*, the *Mirror*, the *Graphic* and the *Sketch*. Bloody things.

His wife, Mila, had teased him remorselessly. For a moment he'd thought she was serious when she suggested getting the children to cut all the photographs out and paste them in a scrapbook. For years she'd said that barristers were people who had wanted to be actors but weren't brave enough to stand up against their parents, and here, she said, was the proof. Her husband, the barrister, was a matinee idol. People in the street recognised him. A shy young woman had even asked for his autograph at the bacon counter in Mason's. Mila accused him of loving the attention, of being a slave to fame.

'Look at this one. You're posing,' she'd said, brandishing the *News of the World*.

'I am not posing.'

'You've got your distinguished face on.'

'Is it my fault if my face, in repose, can sometimes appear distinguished?'

Mila laughed so much she ended up dancing.

It wouldn't have been so bad if he hadn't been so conspicuous, but he was six foot three, with a face like a horse and round glasses with lenses so thick that his eyes filled them like moons. And he had a limp. Even though most of the photographs showed him wearing his barrister's wig, he was still horribly recognisable. Some boys had shouted something at him as he'd walked to the station that morning. Not knowing how to react, he'd waved and grinned. Afterwards he wondered whether they might have been saying something insulting or obscene.

The Dryden case – the cause of it all – was already being called the scandal of 1929 and they weren't yet halfway through January. It was a grubby little tale.

A year earlier, Hannah Dryden, rich and glamorous, had divorced her husband, Maurice Dryden, the popular novelist, on the grounds of adultery and desertion. Maurice's next book, *Mistress of Mayfair*, charted the adventures of Helena, an opium-smoking sex-tigress, in London, Paris, Rome, New York and Marrakesh. When he spoke to the papers about the book, Maurice dropped heavy hints that Helena's exploits were based closely on those of his ex-wife, Hannah, who sued for defamation and engaged Skelton to represent her in court.

The usual defence in such cases might have been to point out the dissimilarities between the fictional Helena and the real Hannah: age, appearance, background and so on. But, instead of doing that, Maurice Dryden chose the more difficult but far more vindictive course of claiming that Helena was indeed Hannah and the book a true-to-life account of Hannah's supposed debaucheries.

The trial was an Aldwych farce. Maurice's key witnesses were a grubby private detective who claimed to have kept tabs on Hannah over the course of several weeks, a cashiered colonel in a bad wig and Alejandro Zabala, a self-proclaimed Argentinian fencing champion. Worst of all was a French chambermaid who squeaked, simpered and *zut alors*ed her way through elaborate accounts of Hannah's exploits while flirting outrageously with the judge.

All of them had been carefully primed and rehearsed by Maurice Dryden. They told terrific stories. The *Herald* and the *Mail* published every suffering detail. *Woman's Weekly* put Hannah on its front cover and nearly doubled its circulation. The directors of the Tempolux watch company of Luton made a fortune by producing a cheap copy of the rectangular wristwatch that Hannah had allegedly left behind at the Hotel Negresco, in Nice.

Skelton led the prosecution and found the main obstacle he had to overcome was naivety. Although he was a thirty-six-year-old married man with two children, the witness statements frequently alluded to sexual practices of which he was entirely ignorant. His Latin – *fello*, *lingua* and so on – led him to make some educated guesses, but French – never his strong subject at school – led him to translate *Maitresse de la Douleur* as 'Our Lady of the Sorrows', a misapprehension that was thankfully cleared up before the trial began. Edgar, his clerk, a man much better versed in the ways of the world than he was, helped where he could, although neither of them ever learnt the exact use of the 'haunted mitten', nor why the delivery of eight baskets of fresh peaches to a hotel room might be taken as evidence of lewdness. To help, Edgar tracked down, at a specialist bookshop off the Charing Cross Road, a small but useful library on the subject of sexual deviance.

Marie Stopes' *Married Love* told Skelton that the 'bodily union' of a man and woman 'is the solid nucleus of an immense fabric of interwoven strands reaching to the uttermost ends of the earth; some lighter than the filmiest cobweb, or than the softest waves of music; iridescent with the colours not only of the visible rainbow but of all the invisible glories of the wavelengths of the souls', but made no mention of the strap-on. The works of Havelock Ellis brought revelations about inversion and autoeroticism, while Krafft-Ebing was good on necrophilia, masochism and satyriasis. A less academic approach to the subject came from Emil Rouxel's *Daphne, or the Seven Temples of Rapture* which had been bundled into the bag with the other books.

As it turned out, the success of his defence owed more to his naivety – or at least his naive curiosity – than it did to this lewd scholarship. His first little triumph came entirely without preparation when the grubby private detective claimed, during the depths of a Parisian winter, to have kept a twenty-four-hour vigil standing on the street opposite a hotel in which Hannah was staying. In cross-examination, he claimed to have sustained himself with 'cold, sweet tea from a half-gallon flask and the occasional nip of brandy'. Then, because it had just occurred to him, Skelton asked, 'Where did you go to the lavatory?' The question, and more importantly the detective's stuttering claim to have held it in (a middle-aged man with half a gallon of tea inside him) for the entire vigil, made the following morning's headlines.

A second triumph came when the cashiered colonel swore that he was the model for 'Major Tomkins', the Lothario who, in the novel, spends seven nights of ecstasy with Helena in a shepherd's hut on a mountain in Andalusia. Skelton asked what they ate. The colonel first tried to claim they lived off the land but stumbled over technical questions about the flora and fauna of the Sierra Nevada, so hastily invented some sacks of tinned soup and meat. When Skelton idly hoped they remembered to bring a tin opener, the colonel seemed to crumble. He stared at his feet. His wig slipped.

Banality had brought his flight of fancy – for a moment he had believed that he could truly have been the passionate Major Tomkins – crashing to earth.

Skelton's summing-up lasted more than two hours. The *Express*, *Mail* and *Herald* quoted it in full over several pages. The *Illustrated London News'* account was accompanied by ink and wash drawings, showing Skelton in full flow, stern and dignified. The *Times* described his performance as a 'masterpiece of forensic eloquence'.

It was not a showy speech. His voice rarely rose from his quiet Yorkshire rumble, the flat vowels making the grandeur of the defence barrister – and even the judge – seem so much tinsel.

Instead of attacking the defence case, he praised it. Rather than abusing its inconsistencies, he tried his best to make sense of them. He congratulated Maurice Dryden on his literary invention and his cast of witnesses on their ability to tell spellbinding stories. He apologised for his clay-footed pedantry as he exposed the implausibility of those stories and concluded by repeating the lesson that some of those present had clearly failed to learn in childhood – that we must never let our imaginations run away with us.

The jury was gone for no more time than it took to walk to the their room, go through the formalities, take an initial vote and walk back. Maurice was found guilty and ordered to pay substantial damages and costs.

Crowds had gathered outside the courtroom. They shouted insults at Maurice and cheered when Hannah

Dryden appeared on the steps with Skelton at her side. Skelton lurked in the shadows to allow Mrs Dryden her moment of triumph, but she took his hand and held it aloft, like a boxing referee declaring the winner. She called him 'Her Latter-Day Galahad', as if she'd been a damsel in distress and he her gallant saviour.

Then she took a step back and Skelton found himself – God knows what came over him – beaming and bowing like Gerald du Maurier on an opening night at Wyndham's.

The papers had a field day with the 'Latter-Day Galahad' tag. The name Skelton was forgotten. He was 'Every Gal's Galahad'. He was the 'The Knight in Shining Specs'. They did 'profiles' of him and turned the 'facts' of his life into 'good copy'.

According to the *Herald*, he was a labourer's son, a slum kid from a back-to-back in Leeds. His mum had hated that. His dad was a foreman at Trevis and Nash, the chemical works. A foreman, not a labourer. Corlton Road was a respectable neighbourhood. Their house had a bit of front garden, a bay window and a tiled step.

The *Express* even went on about his limp – the result of his being born with a displaced hip – and tried to claim it was a war wound when in fact it had made him medically unfit for active service. He'd sent them a stiff letter about that, and they'd published an apology.

Most unsettling of all was the way in which the papers turned his life into a well-crafted story with a beginning, a middle and an end: as if his progress from grammar school to university to the Bar had been executed according to a prearranged plan. It never was. Nothing like it. It was as a series of lurches and accidents conducted in a fog of doubts and worries. He'd never once known what he was doing. Not properly. He'd gone from elementary to grammar. His teachers had gone to a lot of trouble to find him bursaries and scholarships so it would have been ungrateful not to go to Cambridge. He did law because it seemed real. His dad knew what it was. You didn't run into many philosophers or classicists on the Hunslet Road but there was a solicitor's office on Church Street. It never occurred to him that he could – or should – make a choice about these matters, and, even if it had, he wouldn't have had a clue how to go about making it. There was just doing what came next and being glad because it didn't involve sweat or grime.

He found himself wishing he had half the substance and certainty that the Galahad chap in the paper had. He seemed, somehow, so much more authentic.

The woman standing next to him on the platform at Paddington Underground station was looking at him. Not wanting to be impolite, he smiled and nodded.

'I know you, don't I?' she said.

'Well, I'm glad one of us does.'

CHAPTER TWO

'I don't know what the problem is,' Edgar said. 'It all adds to your prestige, your reputation. Reputation is exactly what you're supposed to be building; it attracts a better quality of work and much higher fees.'

'I just wish I could have earned it properly,' Skelton said.

'You did earn it properly.'

'No, I didn't. It was a squabble between a privileged woman and her vindictive ex-husband. I don't think there's much prestige going on there. I'm famous, that's all. "Prestige" is what politicians and generals have. Asquith and Haig, they've got prestige. I'm just famous for a bit of fiddle-faddle, same as – I don't know – Dolores del Rio.'

'Dolores del Rio is very good,' Edgar said. 'Have you seen *Ramona*?'

'I'm being serious.'

'I bet she makes a great deal more money than either of them.'

'I don't care about money.'

'Liar.'

Edgar was a dapper, barrel-chested man with a voice that had been compared to that of an outraged duchess. The voice, along with the clothes and the manners, had been carefully acquired and curated for he, like Skelton, was a bootstraps boy, in his case from Stepney. At thirteen, he'd been making a good living in juvenile crime. The police nabbed him, but he argued his case so coherently in court that the magistrate took a shine to him and fixed him up with an errand boy's job at a chambers in Lincoln's Inn. By the time he was eighteen, he was a junior clerk for a 'local' in Birmingham. He returned to London just after the war as a senior and became the *genius loci* of 8 Foxton Row, Skelton's chambers: a calming presence smelling of new suits and pencil shavings.

He and Skelton sat on the easy chairs in chambers, one either side of the low table. Edgar was examining the morning's *Daily Sketch*.

'The resemblance to Dolores del Rio is actually quite striking.' He held up the paper to show yet another awful picture. Skelton remembered it being taken. The photographer had poked the camera into his face and he, because it's what you do when people poke cameras in your face, had grinned.

'D'you think they've painted extra teeth in?' Skelton asked.

'There does seem an unnatural number of them.'

'They're not really that long, are they? It's the angle.'

'Anyway, you are already reaping the rewards.'

The lads, as well as the morning tea, had brought in two hefty document boxes.

'Six cases from Birmingham alone.'

Edgar still had good contacts with Birmingham solicitors and had tipped them off that the Dryden case would thrust his chief into the limelight.

'Three from William Allen, two from Simons and Tinniswood, and one from somebody I've never heard of. They all know your star is rising. They're eager to secure your services before you become too important and too expensive. Although, having said that . . .' With a flourish, Edgar lifted a thick file from one of the document boxes, 'I give you . . . *The Matlock and Ripley Textile Bank versus The Imperial Bauxite Trading Company*. I've had a word with William Allen's managing clerk, and he did not baulk at the suggestion of a thousand guineas.'

The fee was five times Skelton's previous best. Six months earlier, he'd got rid of his old Austin and bought a Wolseley 12-32 saloon for £425. At the time, it had felt like an unwarranted extravagance.

He untied the ribbons and turned the pages of *The Matlock and Ripley Textile Bank versus The Imperial Bauxite Trading Company* brief. The word 'debentures' seemed to crop up five or six times on every page. It made him think of false teeth.

He'd never had a head for business law. The doubts began to clamour. Wouldn't they be expecting somebody far better than him for their moneys? Was he worth that much?

'The other big one is *Rex versus Dutton*,' Edgar said.

'Should I have heard of it?' Skelton asked.

'Mary Dutton, the Collingford Poisoner. The *Daily Herald* has been making a dreadful stink about it for the last week or so. Here . . .'

Edgar had shoved that morning's *Herald* in the document box. He passed it over.

'Defendant's a woman in her thirties, Mary Dutton. Six children. Husband, Ted Dutton, ran a smallholding. Sheep mostly. Some chickens. Ted died, supposedly of gastroenteritis, at the end of last year. The funeral was interrupted, just before the body was interred, by two jolly policemen because allegations had been made that the man had been poisoned and thus the body must be removed for autopsy. The pathologist found substantial amounts of arsenic administered in small doses over a period, possibly of months. Police searched the house, found rat poison containing arsenic hidden in Mary Dutton's pantry. She told the police, and various friends and neighbours have confirmed, that the husband regularly beat her and the children, and generally treated them with immeasurable cruelty. The coroner's court found enough evidence of wilful murder to have Mary arrested and charged. So, means, motive and opportunity. Bang to rights. But the *Herald*'s convinced she's innocent.'

'On what grounds?'

'Mostly, her photograph.'

The photograph was on the front page of the *Herald*.

'She looks like Lillian Gish,' Skelton said.

'Doesn't she just? Del Rio and Gish, together at last.'

'Looking like a film star isn't a line of defence that's been tested in a court of law as yet, but I've no doubt it'd play well with a jury,' Skelton said.

'Of course it would. Lillian Gish could not commit murder. Marlene Dietrich, Gloria Swanson, Anna May Wong, on the other hand, any one of them could have poisoned a husband. Louise Brooks probably keeps a jar of strychnine in her handbag just on the off chance of waking up married.'

'Where is Collingford?'

'A small town that can't make up its mind whether or not it's a part of Birmingham.'

Skelton glanced at the *Herald*. The headline was as big as, if not bigger than, the ones they'd given to the Dryden case. It didn't surprise him. Arsenic was the craze of the moment. A couple of months earlier, there had been reports of a midwife in Hungary who'd been selling arsenic-tainted jams and preserves to women who needed to get rid of husbands, lovers and overbearing male relatives. Thirty-eight corpses had so far emerged in an area about the size of Wiltshire.

This was followed by tales of an American beauty who travelled from town to town marrying in haste, taking out huge life insurance policies and administering bootleg liquor mixed with arsenic.

And now, at last, the British had an arsenic killer all of their own. And she looked like Lillian Gish.

'Where did the police get the tip-off that he'd been poisoned?'

'The woman who laid him out spotted keratoses on his hands and feet.'

'Remind me.'

'A sort of blackening of the hands you get with arsenic poisoning.'

'Why hadn't the doctor spotted this?'

'I don't know.'

'And the laying-out woman reported it to the police?'

'Yes, but not until the day of the funeral.'

'Why did she wait so long?'

'I don't know; perhaps she was shy.'

'So, the police stopped the funeral, sent the body away for autopsy and arrested the wife as soon as they had the results.'

Edgar nodded.

'No other suspects?'

'The *Herald* claims that Mary Dutton was subjected to a thirteen-hour interrogation without food or water.'

'Thirteen hours?'

'I know. Inhuman. The difficulty is that the deceased's late father was himself a policeman.'

'On the local force?'

'A much-loved inspector on the local force.'

'When did he die?'

'Two or three years ago. She killed their favourite boss's

son, so they weren't inclined to be gentle. The *Herald* has compared them to Chicago cops – third degree, bright light in the eyes, lead-lined coshes. The *Mail* profoundly disagrees, of course, on the grounds that our boys in blue are the bravest and most scrupulous men who've ever drawn breath and would never mistreat a lady. The *Mail* and *Express* both think that the *Herald* should be charged with contempt for publishing details likely to prejudice a pending trial, but with both of them it's sour grapes because the *Herald* gleaned the dirty details before they did.'

'How dirty are the details?'

'Nothing Marie Stopes or Havelock Ellis would be interested in – except the husband once tied her to the bed and left her there all day.'

'Why?'

'He was afraid she'd run away. He also beat her with fists, sticks and kitchen utensils; made a pile of the children's bedclothes, soaked them in petrol and set them on fire; and frequently threatened her with a razor and a hatchet.'

'Love's young dream.'

Skelton glanced at the brief, then wandered over to the window and saw Clarendon-Gow, Head of Chambers, turn into Foxton Row.

'He's always ever so nicely turned out, isn't he?' Skelton said.

Edgar joined him at the window.

'Clarendon-Gow?'

'Yes.'

'He has a valet.'

23

'Should I get a valet?'

'Good ones are terribly hard to come by. I expect Mr Clarendon-Gow inherited his.'

'Have you got a valet?'

'I have a sponge, an electric iron and a knack for folding.'

'You do your own ironing?'

'If I trusted Mrs Westing with it, I'd look like a ragamuffin.' Mrs Westing was Edgar's landlady. He'd never married.

'Mrs Bartram does mine. She's not very skilled.'

'I did wonder whether the rumpled look was how trousers were being worn these days.'

'How many children did you say she has?' Skelton asked.

'The poison woman? Six.'

'Terrorised by Dad, then Mum dragged off to prison. Was this before Christmas?'

'She was arrested two days after Boxing Day.'

'Doesn't bear thinking about. Any evidence of adultery?'

'None suspected or alleged. The husband, by all accounts, treated the wife so abominably because he was a brute. No other reason. The *Herald* is making an immense hoo-ha out of the failure of the law to deal with such acts of marital brutality, demanding sweeping and immediate changes. Do you know a man called Norman Bearcroft?'

'No. Should I?'

'He's the local Labour Party candidate for Birmingham East, which includes Collingford. He's taken up the cudgels in Mary Dutton's defence.'

'He's convinced she's innocent?'

'He's convinced the *Herald* thinks she's innocent, and he knows a lot of his constituents read the *Herald*, and he knows there's a general election coming up this year and the Tory incumbent has got a very slim majority. So, he's started a defence fund to buy poor Mary Dutton the best legal representation available. Which obviously is you, the "Latter-Day Galahad".'

'Don't ever say those words.'

'It's going to be a landmark case. Win it and we'll have people queuing up in Foxton Row all desperate for Mr Skelton to take their brief, and every brief they beg you to take will be marked at a thousand guineas. Silk for you by the time you're forty. The only drawback is that the whole thing's a complete mare's nest.'

'The case?'

'Yes.'

'A complete mare's nest?'

'Yes.'

'In what way?'

'This is what will happen. Norman Bearcroft has persuaded hundreds of people to chip in sixpences and shillings to pay for the best legal representation money can buy. You're it. You'll do your best, of course, but there's a formidable case to answer. Means, motive, opportunity all sewn up. And when Mary Dutton is found guilty, all those people who paid their sixpences and shillings, they'll feel cheated. They'll blame you. They'll throw cabbages. All the prestige you earned on the Dryden case will go down the drain. It takes a long time to build a reputation. Terrible thing to squander it.'

'And what if I win?'

Edgar pulled a face.

Skelton turned back to the front of the brief to read the name of the solicitor who had prepared it. 'Critchlow and Benedict. Who are Critchlow and Benedict?'

'No idea. I thought I knew all the Birmingham men. The address isn't even in town. It's in Yardley.'

'Where's Yardley?'

'East Birmingham. I went there once. On a tram. There's nothing wrong with it. Perfectly ordinary sort of place. But you wouldn't want to be a solicitor there. Not if you had any spirit in you. People might pop in from time to time for a chat about voidable dispositions or the meaning of statutory trusts, but you'd never get near a juicy murder. The brief is absolutely useless. No indication at all of a possible line of defence.'

'So why has Bearcroft hired him? Why not William Allen? Or even Aubrey Duncan.' Aubrey Duncan was the top criminal solicitor in London. 'Why Yardley?'

'I've no idea. As I said, the whole thing's a complete mare's nest and we should have nothing to do with it.'

Skelton filled his pipe and lit it. 'We're up Birmingham way next week, aren't we?'

'On Tuesday. The dog case.'

A wealthy Great Dane owner from Solihull was being sued by a Pekingese owner who claimed that the Great Dane

26

had attacked and killed her Peke. She had hired Skelton to defend the dog. To make the case go away, Edgar had asked for two hundred and fifty guineas, got it and wished he'd asked for more.

'Do you think we could find time, while we're up there, to see Messrs Critchlow and Benedict?'

'If you're sure it's not a waste of time.'

'Just to look into it.'

'Oh dear,' Edgar said.

'What?'

'The look on your face.'

'What?'

'You've started caring again. You know what I said about caring.'

CHAPTER THREE

On Saturday mornings Mila, Skelton's wife, taught an archery class at the Lambourn Ladies' Academy. It was not rewarding work.

Before she had started, she had seen in her mind's eye the girls of the academy, under her tutelage, carrying forward the values of the Sauromatians, daughters of the Amazons, observing their ancient customs, taking up arms and hunting on horseback with menfolk. According to Herodotus, no Sauromatian woman was allowed to marry until she had killed a man in battle.

The daughters of Berkshire gentry were not natural warriors. That morning one of the girls had told her she wouldn't be coming any more because her mother feared that archery would give her an unattractive squint, so she'd switched to lawn tennis. Another four had been lost to folk dancing.

Physical exercise, she realised, was regarded by most young gentlewomen, and all their teachers, as having purely cosmetic benefits: gymnastics for grace, PE for the wasp waist, lacrosse for vitality and archery for posture. When Mila tried to point out that the bow and arrow were instruments of death, the girls – rather than facing the target with steely intent knowing that the gold bullseye could one day be the heart of an enemy – giggled.

After the lesson that morning, Mila had been to see Miss Bright, who took charge of Saturday morning activities, and suggested she should teach the girls a little fencing, because there is nothing like lunging and parrying to make the blood run hot. Miss Bright reacted as if she'd been told an unsuitable joke. She reminded Mila that fighting was not ladylike.

Mila replied that the last thing anybody should want twentieth-century women to be 'like' is 'ladies'.

'It is our duty to teach them to fight,' she said. 'I see these girls coming back from a hockey match unmuddied, unbloodied and unbruised, and I despair. When I was their age, the stretcher was never off the field. In Russia, women work and fight alongside the men, comrades together. They load the cannons and pilot the aeroplanes. They are stevedores and stokers. They drive the oxen in the fields and, when there are no oxen, they pull the ploughs themselves.'

Under normal circumstances, at the first mention of Russia, Miss Bright would have telephoned the police, but the girls, she knew, adored Mrs Skelton, not because she was an unpleasantly aggressive Bolshevist but because she was slim and blonde, and had skin like the woman in the Pears Soap advert, and didn't talk to them as if they were nine. Some of them had worrying crushes on her. If she were to be taken away from them, Miss Bright feared there would be complaints, possibly even from parents. So, she did not telephone the police. All the same, feeling a defence of British decency was called for, she tried to make a point about the Russian famine but couldn't remember the details and eventually lost confidence that the famine had in fact been in Russia at all.

Mila walked home in anger, seething with class hatred and cursing the Berkshire bourgeoisie. Why did they have to live in Berkshire? She'd been happy in their little flat in Manchester. She'd been happy in their little house in Clapham. But of course, she had no one to blame but herself. When the children were tiny, she'd read an article in the *Lancet* about the effects of soot, smog and fog on little lungs. The day after, she'd had lunch with a friend who was up in town from Lambourn. The friend said all the usual things that people living in the countryside say to people living in town.

'From Lambourn, I can actually be in the West End quicker than I could when I lived in Chelsea.'

And, 'I always said I had to live in London for the theatres and restaurants, but I never went. Silly, isn't it?'

And, 'You could not believe, when you get off the train at Lambourn station the feeling of peace that positively

30

overwhelms you. You realise that all the time you were in London, your shoulders were up by your ears with the tension.'

And, 'We have two acres at the back. The children spend all day out there, building dens and, you know, having a proper childhood.'

Not long after Mila and Arthur had given in and moved to Lambourn, the friend had gone back to London. Said she couldn't stand it any more.

It was a crisp January day and the air was diamond clear. From the hill, Mila looked back at the academy and saw Miss Bright giving some instruction to the caretaker at the school gates – a range of just over 200 yards. The archers at Agincourt were reckoned to be effective at 240. A sudden gust of wind from the west introduced a note of uncertainty, but she would need only a second of stillness. As the only archer in the county who could make such a shot, she would, of course, be arrested immediately, but, then again, her husband was the best barrister in the country. The *News of the World* had said so just the previous Sunday. Her Galahad would, with one bound, set her free.

Miss Bright finished her business with the caretaker and moved into the quad, behind the wall. Mila consoled herself with the knowledge that there would be other opportunities. At 200 yards, she wondered, would she hear the thunk of the arrow hitting its fleshy target?

Dorothy, who looked after the children, had taken Lawrence off to his piano class and Elizabeth to her ballet. Mrs Bartram, in the kitchen preparing lunch, offered a cup

31

of tea, but Mila poured herself a glass of barley water from the jug in the pantry and took it through to the conservatory.

When Skelton came in from his Saturday morning walk, she was sitting at the rattan table, reading the *Daily Mail*. She had always read at least two newspapers a day. Since the Dryden case, she'd started taking several, the better to tease her husband with his new-found celebrity.

Skelton kissed the top of her head.

'Does Mrs Bartram know you're here?' she asked.

'She said lunch would be about half an hour.'

Calling dinner 'lunch' still made him feel a swank.

He sniffed.

'Is there a smell?'

'You always think there's a smell.'

'I think there might be a smell. There's been a lot of rain.'

'Yesterday there was a light drizzle.'

'Have you checked the Maw of Hell?'

'There isn't a smell.'

Their house – which had been called The Beeches until Skelton and Mila replaced the sign with one that said '24' – was not connected to a main sewer. The Maw of Hell was a manhole cover that gave access to an underground, brick-lined chamber that, in theory, 'digested' waste and allowed the remaining cleanish water to soak away and fertilise the meadows down the hill. Once, after a heavy rainstorm, the tank had overflowed. The smell had been strong.

Wondering if the problem could easily be solved, Skelton had made the mistake of lifting the manhole cover. Some freak of hydraulics had caused it to spurt and he'd had a persecution mania about the thing ever since.

There were in fact three Maws of Hell next to each other, at the bottom of the garden, behind the sheds and the trelliswork that hid the compost heaps. All seemed secure. There was no leakage and no smell other than the usual rot and creosote.

Reassured, he returned to Mila.

'Is there a smell?' she said without looking up from the *Daily Mail*.

'No.'

'I told you so. The *Mail* thinks they'll turn us into Russia.'

'Who?'

'The flappers.'

Skelton considered the words carefully. He worried that sometimes Mila was deliberately obtuse like this simply to see how long it took him to catch up. She liked fast things: hares, sprints, weirs. One day his brain wouldn't come up to her exacting standards and she'd laugh over her shoulder as she ran off with Albert Einstein.

He puzzled it through like a crossword clue. *The* Mail *thinks the flappers will turn us into Russia.*

'Oh, the general election,' he said, and she smiled. He'd passed the test.

In 1918 women had won the vote, but only those over the age of thirty. The move seemed to have done the Conservative Party no harm at all, and their triumph – or partial triumph – at three subsequent general elections gave

33

them the confidence to extend the franchise to everybody over the age of twenty-one who wasn't in prison or a lunatic asylum, adding five million young women – 'flappers' – to the electoral roll. This, according to Winston Churchill, Lord Birkenhead, the *Daily Mail* and practically every fuddled colonel, drunk major and senile brigadier in the Home Counties, was an outrage to human decency. The 'flappers', with their short skirts, bobbed hair and sexual degeneracy, would bring the country to moral and economic collapse and 'usher in the end of civilisation as we know it'.

'If only I shared their optimism,' Mila said. 'If only one – just one – of the girls at the academy would show a scrap of interest in ushering in the end of civilisation as we know it, I would be happy. But from what I can see, they'll all vote Conservative like their mothers, their headmistresses, their vicars and their sweethearts from the tennis club with their little green sports cars and protruding teeth.'

'Ronnie Bunn.'

Mila laughed. Ronnie Bunn was a would-be artist they'd known in Manchester who had a fascinating collection of teeth and an aristocratic squeak.

'He wanted to paint you in the nude,' Skelton said.

'He wanted to paint everybody in the nude.'

Skelton and Mila had met in Manchester, in a room filled with maimed men. This was at the hospital on Whitworth Street where Mila, working with the Almeric Paget Massage Corps, brought war-damaged soldiers back to some semblance of life with her regime of medical exercises.

Skelton, just graduated from Cambridge and serving his pupillage at chambers on St John Street, had volunteered at the hospital, helping the soldiers fill in the endless forms required to ensure their families would be able to make ends meet while they were convalescing and ensuring they'd have a pension when they were invalided out. This had led to a misunderstanding. Mila, having seen him do paperwork with the men, got the wrong end of the stick, assumed he was some official from the War Office and had subjected him to a stern lecture about the adverse effects of petty bureaucracy on the well-being of wounded soldiers. A week later, when she learnt the truth – that Skelton was helping the patients overcome the petty bureaucracy – she sought him out and apologised for haranguing him. Then she harangued him again, this time about the second-rate vegetables her patients were supposed to eat. She'd never lost her passionate advocacy of high-quality vegetables.

The following week, by way of further apology, she offered to take him to see an awful play at the Palace Theatre, her treat. During the interval she criticised the Labour Party's policy on conscription while he ate chocolate creams.

They took bus rides out to Holcombe Moor and up Worsley Woods. Eventually they held hands and went in for a bit of kissing. Neither of them was very good at that sort of thing but they'd always muddled through, well enough to have two children, anyway.

'Are there any biscuits?' Skelton said.

'No.' Mila disapproved of biscuits.

Skelton remembered he had a bag of toffees in his waistcoat pocket. He'd show her what he thought of her biscuit prejudice. Ostentatiously, he took the bag from his pocket, peeled a toffee from the paper and popped it in his mouth. Mila smiled at his mock defiance and picked up the *Herald*.

'This is an obscenity. Why is she accused of murder?'

Skelton looked over and saw she was reading about the Mary Dutton case.

'Oh, that. They've offered me the brief.'

'Have you taken it?'

'Edgar's advising against it.'

'You must take it. She killed him in self-defence and in defence of her children. It cannot possibly be described as murder.'

'If she'd had the good sense to bludgeon him with an axe or stab him with a carving knife in the heat of the moment before she could have a second thought, that could indeed have mitigated the charge from murder to manslaughter. But, unfortunately, the poison was administered in small doses over a period of weeks or possibly months.'

'He tied her up when he went out.'

'That's what she says.'

'Who was the other woman?'

'I don't think there's any suggestion that he had another woman.'

'No. The other woman who was tied up and the judge said the husband had the right to do so.'

'You'll have to be more specific.'

'It's a case from a few years ago. You told me about it when we took the children to the zoo.'

'Oh, that one.'

It was a celebrated case. Skelton mugged it up before every exam. *Rex versus Jackson, 1891.* The defendant, Edmund Jackson, cruelly mistreated his wife, Emily, so she left him. In response, he forcibly abducted and imprisoned her – the defence preferred 'confined her' – in the home. His contention was that 'if a wife refuses to live with her husband, he has a right by law to take possession of her by force and keep her confined till she consents to do so in order to prevent her from permanently withdrawing her society from him'. The court agreed and found him not guilty of cruelty.

'That has no bearing on Mary Dutton's case,' Skelton said. 'Apart from anything else, it was nearly forty years ago, and the judgement was overturned on appeal.'

'And things have changed since then?'

'I should hope so.'

'So, if Mary Dutton had spoken to the police about her husband's cruelty, they would have stepped in, arrested him and she would have been granted a divorce?'

'Well, obviously not, but . . .'

'So, there is the true nature of your task, Sir Galahad. Shout it from the rooftops, this woman was treated abominably by her husband and had no recourse to either criminal or civil law.'

'The difficulty is, you see, that, in court, it would be more diplomatic to soft pedal on the cruelty. Going on about the husband's cruelty would be playing into the hands of the prosecution: emphasising that she had a powerful motive for killing him.'

'But she did have a powerful motive for killing him.'

'Exactly, so the jury will find the prosecution's evidence all the more compelling, find her guilty and she will hang.'

'They wouldn't dare hang her.'

'Oh, I think they would.'

'But she is not the criminal.'

'If the jury finds her guilty, I'm afraid she is.'

'Then the true criminal is the law itself.'

'One could say that about so many things.'

'If the law leaves a woman no escape from a cruel husband other than murder, then the law itself is the murderer.'

'I'd like to see you argue that in the House of Lords.'

'Women are not allowed in the House of Lords.'

'What you're saying is that a wife, if treated cruelly by her husband, should have the legal right to murder him and get off scot-free.'

'Exactly.'

'You can't actually mean that.'

Mila gave him a sly smile.

'Try me.'

CHAPTER FOUR

Outside the Grand Hotel, Birmingham, there was an enormous burgundy Daimler with a liveried chauffeur standing to attention by the open passenger door.

Edgar, when he had ordered a car to take them to the solicitor's offices in Yardley, had anticipated something a little more modest. He was about to apologise when he noticed that his chief's eyes had lit up.

'Is this for us?' Skelton said.

'I'm afraid so.'

In an accent thick enough to stop bullets, the chauffeur said, 'Mr Skelton and Mr Hobbes?' Skelton gave him a smile and extended a hand. The chauffeur looked at it suspiciously. People on the whole did not shake hands with their chauffeurs. Then he remembered reading in the paper that Skelton was from Leeds. Northerners were different.

'And you are?' Skelton asked.

'Keeling, sir.'

Skelton took a trip around the car, admiring the magnificent shine, the enormous headlights and the impressive suspension.

'What is it, a Rolls Royce?' he asked.

'It's a Daimler Double-Six 30 Brougham, sir.'

'I bet the King hasn't got a car as posh as this.'

'Actually, the King's car's the exact same model, sir.'

'Is it really?'

'The Queen's got one too.'

'One each. That must be nice for them if she wants to go shopping and his team's playing at home. Does it go fast?'

'No sir.'

'Could I have a go at driving it?'

'I'm afraid you'd have to ask Mr Patterson about that, sir.'

'It's his car, is it?'

'Yes, sir.'

'Is he on the telephone?'

'Yes, sir.'

'Maybe we could ring him up from somewhere if we get the chance later on and I could ask him. Do you want a go at driving it, Edgar?'

'I don't think so, no.'

Skelton got in the back and stretched his legs. They went

all the way. He could, he reckoned, have garaged his old Austin on the back seat.

'You don't think people will think I'm a terrible swank, driving around in a thing like this, do you?'

'Yes,' Edgar said.

'You have to admire the workmanship, though. Look how they match the grain on that walnut.'

Keeling started the engine.

'Feel that?'

'What?'

'Nothing. No vibration. The quiet purr of precision engineering. Are you all right?'

Edgar was perched on the edge of the seat, looking anxious.

'It's just that I do tend to get a little bilious sometimes in motor cars. I was hoping for something with an open top. I'm all right if there's an open top but, as it is, we may have to stop suddenly.'

'Well, give us as much warning as you can. I can't see there'd be much chance of getting a smell out of this leather.'

'Could we open the windows, do you think?'

The drive up Colmore Row to the law courts took no more than five minutes. Edgar came to no harm; he was a little wobbly but he bore it manfully.

The dog case did not go well. The prosecution produced no less than four witnesses who swore they'd seen the Great Dane make an unprovoked attack on the Peke, together with evidence that the dog had once eaten part of a window cleaner's leg. All Skelton had was two witnesses, a housemaid and a gentleman friend, who attested to the dog's good character.

The dog had not been brought to court, but the owner had brought photographs that, she hoped, gave evidence of its placid nature.

'He's playing with his toy rabbit,' she'd said. 'Can you see? The rabbit is barely chewed. You see how gentle he is. And here he is with my nephew.' The nephew looked terrified.

Skelton lost the case and the Great Dane owner was fined £20 plus costs. She could afford it.

The Daimler was waiting outside the law courts. Keeling told them that the journey to Yardley would take no more than twenty minutes or half an hour. Edgar looked queasily at the car.

'I wonder if there's a tram?' he said. 'I'm all right with a tram. You get a through-draught of air and a jaunty rattle.'

Skelton said he had heard of a man who cured himself of car sickness by sitting with his head out of the window.

'I thought you weren't supposed to do that.'

'That's trains. In cars it's perfectly acceptable behaviour.'

So, all the way from the law courts to the Critchlow and Benedict offices in Yardley, Edgar kept his head poked out of the window. Skelton was right. The fresh breeze with only a hint of smog blowing in his face was just the job.

CHAPTER FIVE

They found the Critchlow and Benedict sign on an anonymous door between a shoe shop and a grocers. Edgar rang the doorbell. There was no answer. He rang again.

'Waste of time,' Edgar said. He turned to find Skelton had already moved on and was looking in the window of the grocers shop next door. After a moment, he went into the shop. Edgar followed.

A woman in a wrap-around pinny was rearranging tins of peas on a shelf behind the counter.

She straightened her tidied her hair when she saw Skelton. She didn't often get gentlemen in nice overcoats and suits coming into the shop.

'Cold out,' Skelton said. 'Nice and warm in here, though.'

'Oh, I couldn't be without my little paraffin stove in this weather,' the woman said.

She stepped aside so that Skelton could lean over the counter and admire the heater. It was green.

'Tiny thing, isn't it?'

'Takes a while. I get it going first thing in the morning when I come in and it's a good hour or two before you start to feel the benefit.'

'You don't happen to stock Trenton's tinned pineapple, do you?'

'Trenton's? No. We've got Libby's.'

'We used to get Trenton's in Leeds. You can't get it down south for love nor money. I thought I might be in with a chance in the Midlands.'

'Trenton's. No. I don't think I've heard of it.'

'It's got a thicker syrup than Libby's. It's very good with cold rice pudding.'

'Cold rice pudding with pineapple, I've never had that.'

'You should try it. It's better with Trenton's though. You don't want the syrup mixing too readily with the milk.'

'No, I can see that. Is that how you like it, then?'

'With pineapple?'

'No, I mean, you'd rather have it cold than hot.'

'Oh, yes. Most puddings are better cold than hot. Apple pie gets a firmer texture when it's cold.'

'Oh, I know. My husband won't eat hot apple pie.'

'How is he on cloves?'

'In an apple pie? He'd spit 'em out.'

'I'm just the same. Cloves are all well and good for toothache but they've no place in your pudding.'

'They can be nice at Christmas.'

'No, just the smell reminds me of toothache. I'll have a quarter of aniseed balls and a box of Swan while I'm here.'

The woman weighed out the sweets.

'We've come to see Mr Critchlow from next door, but there doesn't seem to be anybody there.'

'Oh, I hope you haven't come far. Mr Critchlow was took poorly this morning.'

'Oh dear. Nothing serious, I hope.'

'He has these attacks. It's his heart, I think. Usually they last a couple of days then he's right as rain but there's no knowing really, is there? Rose took him home.'

'His wife?'

'No, his wife went a long time ago. Rose is his daughter. Lovely girl.'

'What about Mr Benedict?'

'He died four or five years ago.' The woman suddenly blushed and waved a finger towards Skelton. 'Oh, it's you isn't it? Rose told me you were doing the thing.'

'The Mary Dutton case.'

'Lancelot.'

'Galahad.'

'Galahad.'

'Skelton. Arthur Skelton. I'm very pleased to meet you, Mrs . . .'

'Pritchett. Call me Vera. Everybody does.'

'I'm very pleased to meet you, Vera. And this is my clerk, Edgar Hobbes.'

Edgar was by the door reading the small print on an advertisement for dog biscuits. 'Very nice to meet you, Mrs Pritchett.'

'You wait till I tell Noreen you was in the shop. She'll kill me she'll be so jealous. Did you ring on the bell for upstairs? Cos it's no good knocking. They won't hear.'

'We rang the bell twice,' Edgar said. 'And it was definitely ringing inside.'

'I'd have thought Rose'd be up there. I saw her come back half an hour ago. Only they've got a woman comes in to look after him when he has one of his turns and he likes it if Rose is here looking after the office. She's most likely gone up the post office. Catch the last post. Shouldn't be too long. You can wait here in the warm if you like. I'd make you a cup of tea only we haven't got the facilities. Noreen usually brings it from her house. All we've got really is pop.'

Skelton looked at the bottles of lemonade, orangeade and dark jaffarade on the floor. He'd never liked orangeade.

'I've got Vimto if you fancy it.'

'That would be very welcome, Vera.' Skelton turned to Edgar. 'Do you want a bottle of Vimto, Edgar?'

'Yes, please, very nice.'

'I'll get one for Keeling as well, shall I? Three bottles, please.'

'Do you want me to take the tops off for you?'

'Two of them, yes.'

'Bit cold for Vimto, really, isn't it?' Vera said.

'Still, it's very refreshing.'

Vera rang up the half-crown and gave Skelton his change. Skelton swigged the Vimto and said, as he always did when Vimto was mentioned, '*In Vimto Veritas.*' Vera smiled vaguely and noticed a spider on the ceiling.

'She didn't do it, did she?' Vera said. 'Mary Dutton. She didn't do it, did she?'

'Well, that's for the jury to decide,' Skelton said.

'And in any case, I don't think the police are being fair on her.'

'Why are the police not being fair?'

'You should talk to Gordon Weatherstone. He knows all about it.'

'Gordon Weatherstone?'

'He's the mobile butcher. He drives round the villages with a van full of meat. He's up Collingford every Wednesday. He says they're not being fair cos of Sid.'

'Sid Dutton. Ted's father?'

'He was a police inspector. And before that he was a sergeant at Collingford police station.'

'So I gather.'

Skelton glanced towards Edgar, who took out his notebook and fountain pen.

'All the coppers thought the world of him. He died two or three years ago. And the thing is, they've all got it in for Mary . . .'

'Who have?'

'The police.'

'Why do you think that might be?'

'Gordon Weatherstone reckons Sid was on the take, and Mary knew he was on the take and the other coppers didn't want her blabbing about him being on the take cos they were all on the take. And so, when Ted died, they set her up with the rat poison and that. And Harry says it's even worse than that . . .'

'Harry?'

'My cousin. He plays football. Not for the Villa nor nothing, just a local team. But they play, you know, Collingford, and the police have got their own team, so Harry gets about and hears things. And he reckons it was one of the coppers who killed Ted.'

'By poisoning him?'

'I'm only saying what I've heard. Harry says one of the coppers killed Ted and they've pinned it on Mary so as to cover up for their own.'

'And why would one of the other policemen have killed Ted?'

'I don't know.'

'This is all very useful, Vera.'

'Like I say, it's Gordon Weatherstone you really want to talk to and Harry.'

'Your cousin?'

'Harry Lawler.'

'I've got it all written down here, Vera,' Edgar said. 'You've been most helpful.'

'To be honest, I was surprised they put Mr Critchlow on it.'

'Why is that?' Edgar said.

'I didn't think it was really his line. He does, like, buying and selling houses mostly, and the what-d'you-call-it . . . when Danny Baines lost his hand at Wilke's and Payne's on the lathe. Got him £1,000.'

'Industrial compensation.'

'He does a lot of that sort of thing. When Mr Steele up at the plating works sacked everybody. When would that have been? In the strike.'

'The General Strike?'

'Oh, there's Rose now.'

A young woman was passing, marching resolutely against the freezing wind in a massive overcoat, a thick scarf and a knitted hat pulled low.

Skelton left the shop.

'Miss Critchlow.' Rose turned. 'Arthur Skelton and this is my clerk, Edgar Hobbes. We're very late, I'm afraid.'

'Oh dear. How long have you been waiting? I'm ever so sorry.'

'You have nothing to be sorry for, Miss Critchlow. We've had a productive five minutes chatting with Vera. She keeps it lovely and warm in there.'

'She's got a paraffin heater.'

'I know. She showed me.'

'I telephoned at about a quarter past four,' Edgar said.

'I was with Dad. You see, Dad . . .'

'Yes, Vera was telling us about your father. Poor man. Has he seen the doctor?'

'The doctor came straight away, and Mrs Carberry. She's trained as a nurse. She's very good.'

'And it's just you and your father in the office, is it?'

'Yes, so I'm holding the fort.'

Rose had her keys out.

'Er . . .' Skelton was about to say that under the circumstances it would be best if they left Rose to look after her father and made another appointment for a more convenient time. In truth, he thought it unlikely that another appointment would be made because he would do what he could to get a more competent solicitor appointed to the case.

But then he caught a look of desperation on Rose's face. She had guessed what he was about to say, and possibly what he was thinking. Her father had been given the most important case of his life. He had had a heart attack – possibly as a result of taking on the most important case of his life. Rose felt it was her responsibility to 'hold the fort', to keep things ticking over as normal even if that meant somehow dealing with an important meeting with important men from London, one of whom had had his picture in the paper. The prospect of going home and saying to her father, 'They came all that way, I was late getting back from the post office and kept them waiting, then they said not to bother and left,' was unthinkable.

'Lead the way,' Skelton said.

Edgar, who was well on his way back to the Daimler, turned with some surprise and followed.

Rose took them up lino-covered stairs to the outer office. The furniture was cheap and old, the Anaglypta coming loose here and there. But Edgar saw beyond the shabbiness. He noticed that the blotters had been changed that morning and the labels on the drawers of the big cabinet had been freshly written by somebody with a beautiful copperplate hand.

Most impressive of all were the bookshelves on which all the legal texts had been 'faced', which is to say that the volumes, irrespective of size, had been pulled to the front of the shelf so that the titles on their spines stood in identical prominence, with none lurking in the shadows of its neighbours. Edgar wished he could photograph these details to show the lads and junior clerks at 8 Foxton Row. 'You see, this is how it should be done.'

Rose took off her coat and hat. She was dressed as if for an afternoon's hard rambling in tweed skirt, plaid stockings and brogues. The fire had been banked up. She gave it a poke and added a shovel of coal.

'Should I make you some tea?'

'No, we have Vimto. We got an extra bottle for our chauffeur, but you'd be very welcome.'

'No, no, that's all right. Would you like tea, Mr Hobbes?' Edgar raised his Vimto bottle with a smile.

'Dad did want me to apologise very particularly knowing you'd come all this way.'

The voice was a mix of hockey sticks Roedean and backstreet Brum. Skelton wondered if she, a solicitor's daughter, had been brought up speaking posh but had roughened up the accent the better to fit in with school friends, just as he'd tried to go the other way – from common to posh – when he'd first gone to Cambridge. He'd never managed it, and had frequently made an idiot of himself, particularly on the long 'a' sound; saying he was going to 'halve a bath' or talking about his 'marths master', before giving it up as a bad job and sticking with the 'a's he was born to.

'And he wanted me to tell you how honoured he is to be working with such a celebrated legal mind, and how glad he is you've accepted the case.'

'Mr Skelton hasn't actually accepted the case,' Edgar said.

Rose sat back in her chair.

'Oh,' she said. 'I thought it was settled.'

'I'd just like to know a few more details,' Skelton said.

'Mr Skelton has many other commitments and needs to be sure he can give every case – and especially this one – the time and the attention it deserves.'

Rose frowned. Not only had she to hold the fort, it was, it seemed, up to her to persuade the celebrated legal mind to take the case. Never one to shirk her duty, she sat upright and held Skelton's eye.

'Mary Dutton deserves the best,' she said. There was steel in her voice.

'There are some excellent barristers in Birmingham.'

'Not like you, though. What details do you need?'

She had what looked like a school exercise book on the

desk in front of her and flicked through the pages, every one filled with the artistic copperplate.

'I'm sure I can help. I'll certainly do my best, anyway. I'm doing my articles and Dad kindly took me through the various case notes and files.'

'You're doing your articles?' Skelton said. Lady solicitors were no longer the novelty they'd been five years earlier, but all the same they were thin on the ground in London and this was Yardley.

'I've wanted to be a solicitor since I was eight years old,' Rose said.

When Skelton was eight, he'd wanted to be a pirate. Or, failing that, a jungle boy, raised by wolves. And when he was nineteen, which he guessed was about Rose's age, he was up at Cambridge, studying law. His ambition then ran to a bike and a girlfriend.

Skelton noticed that Rose's notes seemed to be rather longer than the brief her father had provided. He took out his own 'notes' – a quick list of topics he'd scribbled on the back of a receipt from a hardware shop while riding in the car. It was crumpled. He smoothed it out on the edge of Rose's desk. Rose watched, fascinated. Was this really how top barristers went about preparing their defence of a woman's life? With scribbled notes on the back of a bill?

'There are just a couple of things I need to get clear,' Skelton said.

'Yes?' The 'yes' came out rather more school-marmish than Rose had intended. Skelton looked up. Rose boldly stood by her tone of voice and smiled magisterially.

'The original report was signed off by an Inspector Dunford,' Skelton said, 'and yet there's no mention of him in subsequent reports or statements.'

Rose was relieved. She could field this one dead easy.

'Inspector Dunford was in charge of the investigation but then he got transferred to the Warwickshire Police, and since then it's as if it's been somebody different every other day. At the moment it's an Inspector Vokes, brought in from Leicester, but I think he's only a temporary replacement.'

'So, effectively, there is nobody in charge.'

'Effectively.'

Skelton looked down at his notes.

'Have you had much communication with Dr Willoughby, who attended Ted Dutton?'

'Yes, and with Dr Russell, the pathologist who did the post-mortem. Dad asked Dr Willoughby whether any of the medicines he'd given Ted could have contained arsenic. Dr Willoughby replied that they didn't.'

'He's an elderly gent, isn't he?'

'Dr Willoughby has been practising medicine for almost fifty years.'

'Could he have made a mistake? Muddled his pills?'

'If he was that clumsy, wouldn't he have killed half the population of Collingford by now?'

'Good point. What about Dr Russell? Was he able to tell whether the source of the arsenic was definitely the rat poison rather than weedkiller, say, or some such?'

'I don't think so, no.'

'Have the police explored other sources of the poison?'

'I don't think they have. Dad sent in a list of questions and requests for information. The replies weren't very satisfactory. The police seem to think their work is done. Part of the difficulty is that the Collingford Borough Police Force is yet to be absorbed into the Warwickshire Force and comes under the jurisdiction of the local watch committee, which Dad says is not very good.'

'I get the impression that Ted Dutton was rather a pugnacious chap. Presumably he made many enemies.'

'I expect he did.'

'Have any particular names cropped up? Have the police interviewed many people?'

'No.'

'Have the police, as far as you know, even considered other suspects?'

'I don't think they have, no.'

'Do you know the town of Collingford at all?'

'No, I'm afraid not.'

'There are six children in all, I believe.'

'Yes.'

'Have they gone to an orphanage?'

'No, they're being looked after by . . .' Rose turned the pages of her notes. She had it there somewhere. '. . . a Mrs Enid Fellows. A friend of the family.'

'She must be a very good friend to take on six children.'

'I suppose she must.'

'Do you know much about the other principals in the case?'

'The . . . ?'

'Ted's mother?'

Rose looked again at her notes.

'Jessie Dutton,' she said.

'What kind of woman is she?'

'I'm afraid . . .'

'I believe Ted Dutton had a brother, Billy.'

'Did he? I'm very sorry, Mr Skelton, you've ventured into an area of questioning I'm not prepared for. I can tell you what's in Dad's notes and so on, but I know very little about the background to the case. As I say, I've never been to Collingford.'

'It's really not very important.'

Rose looked relieved and a little ashamed.

'I'm very sorry Miss Critchlow,' he said, 'if my tone is sometimes a little abrupt. The habit of cross-questioning dies hard.'

'Don't mind me,' Rose said. 'I'm fine.'

Skelton nodded. 'It takes great strength of character to stand up to cross-questioning. It does you credit.'

'I practise,' she said.

'You practise standing up to cross-questioning?'

'Yes. In my head. I imagine myself in court. D'you know about Pelmanism?'

'I've heard of it.'

'It's a system for training the mind. I've been doing it for more than a year now.'

'Perhaps I should try it.'

'The brain and the will, they're both like muscles. The more you exercise them the stronger they get. If something's worrying you, then you must spend a little time every day imagining the worst that could happen and training your brain and your willpower to cope with it. A lot of famous people do it.'

'I know, I've seen the advertisements.'

'Sir Robert Baden-Powell recommends it and so does his sister, Agnes.'

Baden-Powell was the founder of the Boy Scouts. His sister had started the Girl Guides.

'Are you a Girl Guide, then?' Skelton asked.

'Ranger Captain. Silver Fish. Been to Foxlease twice,' Rose said, like a soldier repeating his name, rank and number. Skelton had no idea what 'Foxlease' or 'Silver Fish' meant but got the general idea.

There was a Girl Guide troop attached to the Lambourn Academy. Mila had been camping with them once and had been impressed by the girls' resourcefulness but, as an atheist republican, she was put off by the amount of God and King involved. Also, the singing.

'They sang,' she had complained, 'endlessly and incomprehensibly.'

The Scouts had never held any attraction for Skelton. To him it seemed tasteless for people who have houses and kitchens to sleep in tents and cook on campfires when there were people in the world – in England, even – who had no option but to sleep in tents and cook on campfires. It was like Bright Young Things going slumming in Whitechapel for a jape.

'I've been to Foxlease, Waddow Hall, Gilwell and Brownsea,' Rose said.

'While I have been to none of those places,' Skelton said. 'Have you ever been to Waddow Hall, Edgar?'

'I don't think I have, no.'

'There you are, then.' Skelton stood. 'Well, I can see you must be very busy, Miss Critchlow and we really mustn't impose on your time any more.' He and Edgar put on their coats.

Rose stood but did not move.

'So, you'll take the case,' she said.

Edgar interrupted. 'As I said before, Mr Skelton has to decide whether he could give the time and attention such an important case deserves. There are many factors to consider.'

Rose ignored him and concentrated the full force of her Pelmanistic will on Skelton.

'It would mean a very great deal to people knowing she's got somebody as good as yourself to take her side. Dad is a marvellous man, very, very good at his job, very thorough, but he's only ever done one murder before. And, of course, he's not a barrister anyway. And it is a marvellous honour, not to say a long-held ambition . . . and . . .' Rose moved without pause from persuasion to harangue, '. . . I just think it's wrong. If she killed him at all it was in self-defence. Defending the children as well. I know the legal definitions – murder and manslaughter – but for pity's sake, surely you of all people can't just stand by and watch a poor woman like that go to the scaffold and leave her children orphans. He beat her. He took a gun to her. You've read the accounts. They're going to hang her. She needs your help.'

Skelton and Edgar, standing in their coats, had adopted identical poses, like Tweedle-Dum and Tweedle-Dee, both holding the fingers of one hand in the palm of the other watching Rose's performance with patience and concern.

Rose noticed. 'Oh, I shouted. I shouldn't have shouted, should I? I'm ever so sorry. You must think I've got a blasted cheek talking to you like this.'

'The four things a lawyer needs,' Skelton said, 'are an exhaustive knowledge of the law, stubborn persistence, the gift of the gab and the cheek of the devil. Cultivate that blasted cheek, Miss Critchlow. It'll be a friend for life.'

CHAPTER SIX

Breakfast at the Grand Hotel had provided neither of them with much in the way of comfort. The hotel restaurant was a cathedral with cruets. Wondering whether it might do a better dinner, Skelton popped his head around the door and found the acres empty but for a solitary waiter who looked as if he might have seen service with Raglan at Inkerman. Heroes who have been nursed by Florence Nightingale are commendable fellows, but you wouldn't want them bringing your whitebait. Not if you were hungry.

Edgar suggested the Lyons Corner House at the end of New Street. Skelton hadn't realised they had Corner Houses in Birmingham. He thought they were just a London thing. He liked a Lyons. Always reliable.

They ordered the *menu de souper*; soup, fish, mutton and profiteroles – half a crown.

When they'd finished, Skelton opened a fresh tin of Balkan Sobranie and spent a moment sniffing it before filling his pipe. Edgar took an ashtray from a neighbouring table and lit up a Gold Flake.

'Should we pass, then?' Edgar asked.

'On the Dutton Case? What do you think?'

'The prosecution has one of the most watertight cases in the history of jurisprudence,' Edgar said. 'Our solicitor's ill and the police are being, not to put too fine a point on it, uncooperative.'

'Rose is very capable.'

'I'm sure she is for a Girl Guide, but as a solicitor I'd say Vimto Vera at the corner shop has the more professional approach. And anyway, I suspect that the reason Mr Critchlow has been unable to provide us with a foundation on which we could build a defence is that there is no foundation on which we could build a defence.'

'You don't happen to know much about sheep, do you?' Skelton asked.

'What?'

'Ted Dutton kept sheep. I'm just remembering a case from ten or twenty years ago. Something to do with sheep dip.'

'Sheep dip?'

'They dip the sheep. They have this bath of stuff and they dip the sheep in it one by one. I remember seeing it up near Horsforth when I was a lad.'

'To wash the wool?'

'I thought it was to kill the ticks on the sheep.'

'I'm sure you're right.'

'The case was *Rex versus Weston*. *Winton*. Something like that. A man was caught by neighbours trying to drown his wife in a vat of sheep dip. The woman didn't drown but died some weeks later of arsenic poisoning.'

'The sheep dip contained arsenic?'

'Exactly.'

'So, you think Mary Dutton tried to drown him in sheep dip?'

'No. I think we might be able to sow sufficient doubt about Mary Dutton's guilt by suggesting that he may have not taken proper precautions when dipping his sheep.'

'And that's it?'

'What?'

'That would be the cornerstone of your defence?'

'It's a possible line of argument.'

'Sheep dip?'

'Yes.'

'So, let me get this right, in court, the prosecution would keep repeating cruelty, rat poison. Cause, effect. And we'd be bleating on about sheep dip. She'll hang, and all that wonderful prestige you earned on the Dryden case will melt away like snowflakes in a furnace.'

The coffee came. They smoked and sipped in silence.

Edgar's attention was drawn by a commotion in the street outside. A cinema commissionaire was berating a group of rough-looking lads who had stolen a full-size cut-out picture of Janet Gaynor from outside the West End Cinema and were dancing with it suggestively. It was a windy night. A particularly fierce gust blew Janet out of the youth's hands and sent her sailing over the traffic. The same gust removed the commissionaire's maroon topper. The lads gave chase to both. One of them intercepted the hat just as it was about to roll under the wheels of a bus and kicked it out of the way. His pal headed it into the arms of a third, who played goalkeeper, saved it magnificently, dusted it off and, smiling, returned it, only slightly the worse for wear, to the commissionaire. At the same time another lad had climbed halfway up the side of a shopfront to save Janet, who had lodged herself above the shop's sign. He kissed her in triumph as the rest of his gang applauded.

Edgar, laughing, turned back to Skelton. Skelton wasn't laughing. He hadn't been looking at Janet at all.

'She has six children.'

Edgar sighed. He'd suspected that something like this might be brewing ever since he'd warned his chief about 'caring' back at 8 Foxton Row. The ghost of Elsie Grace was back.

It had been Skelton's first experience leading the defence in a murder trial. The Oxford assizes. Elsie Grace was a seventeen-year-old up for killing her own baby.

The doctors who had examined her had found her 'feeble-minded' but *compos mentis*. She had been raped by a soldier and left pregnant. Her parents – she lived in Mansfield – had thrown her out. An aunt had taken her in for a while, but that arrangement came to an end when the aunt's lover came to live with her. The girl had given birth in some sort of doss house and then, hoping that another aunt might help her had tried to walk with her baby to Aylesbury. Along the way the baby had drowned.

Skelton spoke to Elsie twice before the trial and both times it was all he could do to stop her weeping. She was worried that the baby had not been baptised so it couldn't go to heaven. Skelton assured her that all babies, baptised or not, go straight to heaven. He told her how important it was in court to speak clearly and tried to assure her that, if she took his advice, there would be a very good chance she would walk free.

Several times she had come out with a phrase she'd got from somewhere, a clergyman or relative perhaps.

'Better that God should have taken the baby that way than let the poor thing starve to death because I couldn't feed it.'

It seemed to give her some sort of consolation. Skelton stressed that she must not say such things in court because it might give the impression that she had deliberately drowned the child and even though that might seem an act of mercy on her part, it would not to the judge or to the jury.

They were wasted words. In court, the girl barely had the sense to know where she was or why she was there. In those days, infanticide was still a capital offence. She knew she might hang. And she trusted Skelton to make sure she wouldn't.

He thought he did well. The prosecution case was sloppy. They produced a witness who claimed that Elsie had been to a bath house in Sutton-in-Ashfield with a bottle of gin to try and get rid of the baby. Skelton pointed out that there was no bath house in Sutton-in-Ashfield.

Another witness, who claimed to have seen Elsie in the doss house trying and failing to pluck up the courage to cut the newborn's throat with a razor, muddled up her story several times and clearly should have been coached more carefully.

A third maintained that Elsie had been to see a woman called Daisy Groves, a baby farmer who 'adopted' unwanted children for a fee, but that Elsie could not afford the twelve shillings that Daisy demanded. The briefest glimpse at the records was enough to establish that Daisy Groves, the baby farmer, had been tried and hanged for infanticide long before Elsie had fallen pregnant.

The prosecution counsel, a sneering man named Grisby, ignored the evidence and concentrated instead on convincing the jury – as if they needed convincing – that killing babies was very wrong. He left them in no doubt that finding Elsie not guilty would put them on the side of child murderers.

Guilty. The judge put on the black cap and passed sentence. Elsie understood that. She was dragged from the court screaming, and all the time staring at Skelton. He had failed her. She knew he had failed her.

Back in London, Skelton did what barristers do. He put the matter behind him and moved on to the next case. A week later Edgar, working late, was surprised to find his chief still at his desk. When Edgar spoke to him, he didn't answer. The haunting had begun.

Edgar had pulled a chair aside so as to make a bit of clatter.

At that, Skelton came to and began to shake. Not like somebody having a fit, just like the sort of shivering you get when you're cold. Edgar called his name a couple of times and in the end had to grab him by the shoulders to stop the shaking.

Edgar had seen his youngest brother, Arnold, who'd been in the trenches, get like that sometimes. Arnold used to blub. Skelton didn't blub, but he came close. Fresh air usually helped Arnold if you could get him out of bed.

Edgar helped Skelton into his coat and took him for a walk down to St Paul's and onwards. Near the Shadwell Basin he bought a couple of pies and they sat on a wall and ate them. That seemed to help. Then he took him into a horrible docker's pub and got a round of B&Bs and glasses of whisky. Edgar had been talking all the way about anything. In the pub he babbled on about some performing dogs he'd seen the week before at the Islington Empire. This made Skelton laugh and start talking again. He told Edgar about a smooth-haired fox terrier he'd once known in Leeds who could pickpocket handkerchiefs like the Artful Dodger and, if everybody put their hats in a pile, could pick them out and bring them to the right person.

Edgar's brother Arnold was never cheered up so easily, but then Edgar often had the feeling that Arnold didn't want to be cheered up. Difference of temperament.

Nevertheless, the ghost of Elsie Grace could still blindside Skelton whenever she wanted.

He could see why Skelton cared so much – more than other barristers, anyway. Other barristers – the Charterhouse and Trinity brigade – hadn't usually known anybody like Elsie Grace. Not outside the gaol and the courtroom, anyway. Edgar had and so had Skelton. At St Saviour's Elementary in Leeds, Skelton had known a lot of Elsie Graces. Elsie Grace had been the girl from up the road who wasn't all there. One wrong turn and any one of his sisters could have been an Elsie Grace. One of Edgar's sisters – he never spoke of this – had fallen pregnant when she was fifteen. A friend took her to a woman who said she could get rid of it. Whatever the woman did resulted in an infection. His sister died.

The waitress arrived and asked whether they'd like more coffee. Skelton shook his head.

'Are you sure you wouldn't like a brandy or something?' Edgar asked.

'Let's give her a decent show, shall we?'

'With the sheep dip?'

'There must be a thousand other suspects.'

'And the police aren't interested in finding any of them.'

'All the same, I think we should give it a spin.'

Edgar pinched his nostrils. He made a point of never directly contradicting his chief once it was clear that a decision had been taken, but he saw no reason to deny himself a sharp intake of breath now and then.

Skelton relit his pipe. 'It's a while since I've been in touch with Alan and Norah.'

CHAPTER SEVEN

Alan and Norah were Skelton's cousins, Uncle Gilbert and Auntie Mildred's twins. When Skelton wrote to them, he addressed the letter to Gilbert and Mildred, as he always did, asking them to forward it on because he never knew where his cousins might be from one week to next. They roamed the country on the Lord God's business.

Their most recent stop was in Evesham, so that's where Uncle Gilbert forwarded the letter.

They always liked hearing from their cousin, not least because he invariably tucked a couple of pound notes, and sometimes a five-pound note, in the envelope.

His letter arrived at an opportune moment. Only the previous day, Norah had said she reckoned their work in

Evesham was done and it was time to be moving on. Their last meeting at the chapel where Alan had been preaching was a triumph. The crowd spilled out into the street. When Norah took out her accordion and led the celebrants in 'The Old Rugged Cross' there were tears. And that night the Angel came again to Alan in his sleep.

He'd been thirteen when the Angel first spoke to him and just about to embark on the terrible adventure of puberty, so things did tend to make an impression. The Angel had told him he had to do God's work. It was his calling, his vocation. The difficulty was that the Angel had been vague about what kind of work this might be.

Alan had asked his dad about it and his dad, to his credit, hadn't just dismissed the apparition as silliness, instead saying that medicine was very much God's work but if Alan wanted to be a doctor, he'd have to study fearful hard at school because the qualifications were punishing. Alan said he didn't think he was up to it. And wouldn't God know better than to single him out for a calling he wasn't up to?

Alan was a worry to his parents. A lumpy, clumsy boy who didn't seem to have any talents or interests. He'd do a bit of this, a bit of that, a bit of reading, make a model, but there was never any excitement in him. Not about things, anyway. He loved a chat, liked to listen, and had a frank and open nature that drew people to him. Charm would be an overstatement, but it was something going in that direction. Some people thought it was odd that a boy of his age should be so interested in other people and some even wondered if he might be a bit simple. He'd stand on a street corner and gossip with old women, and do it so well they'd forget he wasn't one of them and tell them things about their insides that thirteen-year-olds aren't supposed to hear. Other than chatting, he only really knew how to mooch. He'd mooch around the house and then go out and mooch around the town, or mooch on the beach.

They lived in Rhyl, so it wasn't as if there was a shortage of things to do. You could swim in the sea, play football on the beach, go up the pier. There were amusement arcades, parks, pleasure gardens, all sorts. His dad ran the Pavilion Theatre so he could have watched a different show every week without paying a penny if he'd wanted to, and sometimes he did, but most of the time he liked to be backstage, watching the acts from the wings and chatting with the men who moved the scenery and the poor acrobats who were always so aching and bruised.

His twin sister, Norah, was a different kettle of fish entirely. She was shy and stammered in company but sit her at the piano and she'd play for hours. She could dance, too, draw pictures of horses and dogs that broke your heart, and she could sing. By God she could sing. Loud and pure and beautiful her voice was. Alan had mastered a few chords on the banjo which he strummed with vigour enough to wear out a tortoiseshell plectrum in a week but his singing voice, though loud and generally in tune, was not altogether pleasant to listen to.

After a bit, his parents decided that perhaps he should

go into the Church. Perhaps that's how it worked. When God wanted you to enter the ministry, he eased the way by making sure you were no good for anything else and blessed you with a mediocre singing voice.

Gilbert and Mildred were not religious people. They were Methodists and intended to go to service every Sunday, but something nearly always cropped up, so they were only able to manage perhaps one Sunday in four. They'd sent the children to Sunday school more regularly, though. Anyway, when it came to it, it was the Methodist Minister, Mr Hughes, they turned to for advice about Alan's future.

Mr Hughes was helpful and tried to be encouraging, but he'd known Alan since he was a toddler and found it difficult to summon much enthusiasm for the boy's prospects.

Afterwards, Alan said he wasn't sure he wanted to be a Methodist minister anyway.

'Why not?'

'It's too obvious. It's too easy.'

'It's the church you were brought up in.'

'That's why it seems wrong. Those who follow the word of God should never take the easy road.'

'Become a doctor, then. Like I said. That's very hard.'

'No. I know now that the ministry is the right path but feel I should explore other possibilities.'

'Well, you must do as you please.'

Alan started with the Roman Catholic church on Ffynnongroew Road, where the Irish and Italians went. God did not speak to him there, or if he did it was in Latin. At school they'd only got up to the Third Declension (*Rex, Rex, Regem*). Alan could not believe that God would speak to him using declensions and conjugations he was yet to learn, and anyway the smells made him sneeze and some of the Italian and Irish people looked at him funny because he didn't know when to cross himself and when to kneel.

He tried, though, even to the extent of attending a couple of classes for converts. At one of these he asked about missionary work, wondering whether Catholic missionaries had difficulty making converts among cannibal tribes on the grounds that the cannibals, having tasted real human blood, might be able to form a more informed, and possibly more sceptical, view of transubstantiation. The priest suggested that he was being facetious, and when he said he wasn't the priest said he was and maintained that being facetious about such matters was dangerously close to blasphemy. Alan asked how a question, innocently put, could be blasphemous. When he didn't get a satisfactory answer, he stopped going.

The Church of England was at least in English, but it was in a form of English, poshly spoken by a very English vicar with a voice like an oboe, that was alien to him.

He tried the Presbyterians, the Baptists and the Congregationalists, and at the library he read up on the Mennonites, the Plymouth Brethren, the Seventh Day Adventists, the Jehovah's Witnesses, the Greek and the Russian Orthodox Churches, the Quakers, the Shakers and the Latter-Day Saints. He read of Emanuel Swedenborg, who, like him, was plagued by strange and wondrous dreams and he read of Mary Baker Eddy who warned against the dangers of malicious animal magnetism.

Eventually he went off the idea of being a minister altogether and looked round for something else he could do. Nothing to do with religion. He wanted something crisp. Something attainable and straightforward, like the civil service or accountancy. You take the exam: if you pass you get the job, and that's who you are. So, when he left school, he got a job at the head office of E. B. Jones in Water Street where they taught him clerical skills including book-keeping. He stuck it for three years and learnt how to keep ledgers nice, but all the time the Angel's voice – or rather the feel of the Angel's voice – kept coming back to him.

He had, he realised, certain fundamental difficulties with the Christian religion – or at least the way it was practised.

If God was so great and so glorious, if the gifts he gave us were so bountiful, if his love was love divine all loves excelling, if his glory filled the skies, why was everybody so miserable about it? Even the Italian Catholics – the ones he'd seen dancing with continental abandon in the ice cream parlour – as soon as they went to church looked as if they'd lost a shilling and found a penny. And he'd seen happier faces on dead fish than he saw on the Congregationalists. Did they really think that smiling was a sin?

And, my goodness, they were judgemental. Nothing they liked more than finding a sinner and blackening his name, often in whispers; or not even whispers, they'd mouth the words.

They'd mouth them in Welsh.

Alan couldn't be doing with any of that. He liked the God that was slow to chide and swift to bless. He liked the Jesus that loved the prodigal son, the tax collector and the fallen woman.

He planned his next move very carefully. It took courage. He told nobody, not even his mum or dad or Norah. He got a couple of beer crates and nailed them together. On the back of a showcard they were throwing out at work, he painted, in big red letters, 'God Loves Those Who Laugh'. The following Saturday afternoon, he set up his crates and his sign on the beach by the old pier and started playing his banjo. A little crowd – ten or fifteen people – gathered in the hope of having something to jeer. He put the banjo down and in his strong, clear voice told a joke about St Peter at the Pearly Gates which went like this:

The souls of the dead are queuing up at the Pearly Gates waiting to get in. And St Peter lets the virtuous in through the Pearly Gates, and the sinners he throws into the fiery pit of hell. But some of the sinners he puts to one side to wait. And one of the virtuous asks St Peter, 'Why do you cast those sinners into the fiery pit of hell but put those others on one side. And St Peter said, 'Oh, they're from Wales. They're too wet to burn.'

It wasn't much of a laugh, but it was enough. When the crowd jeered and heckled, he addressed them, not to shut them up or to belittle them but with a genuine interest about what they thought. He engaged them in conversation.

'I'm learning about this stuff the same as you are, see. And so long as you stay curious and don't get stuck with fixed ideas about these things, you can stay lively, can't you?'

At the end he picked up his banjo and sang, to the tune of 'They Didn't Believe Me', 'And when I told them / How glorious you are / They didn't believe me / They didn't believe me / Your mercy, kindness, care and grace / Puts this big smile upon my face / You brought joy to the world / And made laughter a prayer.'

By the end, the crowd had grown to thirty or so. They applauded. Afterwards some of them wanted to chat and he was only too glad. They took him to the ice cream parlour, treated him to sundaes and they all had a grand old time.

The next Saturday he did it again with different jokes. His mum and dad came and were astonished. Who'd have thought it? He was good. He didn't have much in the way of flash or proper showmanship but he what he did have was that rare ability to stand on stage – or beer crates – and be absolutely natural, absolutely himself.

The crowds grew. After a couple of months, he was getting a better turnout than the churches. At the Congregational chapel, the minister denounced him from the pulpit, and this caused a flurry of letters in the *Rhyl Journal* and another big increase in the crowd sizes, so he had to talk much louder to be heard at the back. Thankfully, he had been blessed with a very loud voice.

Norah got a little collecting box and took it round. One week they made thirty-two shillings, which was more than a week's wages at E. B. Jones. They gave the money to the Blind Children and to the Waifs and Strays.

Alan was seventeen when the war started.

When he reached his eighteenth birthday, he asked his dad whether he should sign up for the army and his dad had told him not to be so daft.

'Won't girls give me the white feather if I don't?'

'Only the stupid ones and you wouldn't want anything to do with them, anyway.'

When he was nineteen, the army came for him. It was time, anyway. There wasn't much taste for a God of Joy among people who'd lost a husband, a brother, a leg or a lung. They stuck Alan in the Royal Army Service Corps and moved him about doing this and that all over the place but never within forty miles of a trench.

He liked the moving about. He liked sitting on his kitbag on a dark station platform in the cold waiting for a train. He liked sitting on the train, marvelling at the way you could fall asleep in the dark and wake up in the light a hundred miles away from where you started. He met people who'd been on boats and trains for days and days and woken up in places like Mesopotamia and Thessalonica.

Once the travel bug had got him, there was no losing it. He even liked marching. The distances you could go were wonderful. You could walk thirty miles in a day, forty if you pushed yourself and if you didn't stop for a rest between dawn and bedtime. He'd been to Bangor a few times on the bus, but now he realised you could walk it. You could walk from Rhyl to Bangor in a day easy. He could probably have walked from Rhyl to his grandma's house in Leeds in a couple of days – less than that if he kept walking all night as well. Set off after breakfast one day, arrive in time for breakfast the next.

He looked on a map and found Mesopotamia and reckoned he could walk all the way there in a couple of months, except for one bit where he'd have to swim.

Not long after he was demobbed, he saw an advertisement in the *Western Mail* for a sale of ex-army stock including greatcoats, cooking utensils, building materials and vehicles. The vehicles included old Rover Sunbeam ambulances. He went to Wrexham on the train to look. The ambulances had all seen service in the war and had suffered, but Alan was sure that his dad, a man who could turn his hand to anything, would be able to fix one up.

The army just wanted rid of them, so they were dirt cheap. Even so, Alan had to use all the money he'd saved up out of his army pay and borrow money from his dad to buy one.

One of the army chaps in Wrexham showed him how to change the gears and put the brakes on and once he'd got the hang of the steering he managed quite well. Wrexham to Rhyl in six hours without a single breakdown.

His dad helped him strip the engine down and put it back together. They did out the inside of it like a little ship, with a bed and cupboards for clothes and cooking pots, eating things, the bedding, the books, the tools and the banjo. Two bits of wood held the tin opener in place. Bottles were stowed so they wouldn't ever rattle.

On the side, Norah painted 'The Joy of Jesus Mission'. That's what he was going to do. He was going to drive around bringing the joy of Jesus to people first in Rhyl, then Prestatyn, then perhaps to South Wales and all over. Perhaps he'd go to see his aunties and uncles in Leeds.

Then Norah, who'd recently broken up with her fiancé, said she wanted to come with him, so they put in an extra bed for her and a curtain across the middle to allow for a bit of privacy. It was cramped but ever so neat.

'Are you sure you want to do this?' their mother asked them nearly every day before they went. And both of them said, 'Oh, yes.'

They'd been on the road pretty much ever since and had acquired a tent and a lot of other bits and bobs to improve their living arrangements. The old Rover Sunbeam ambulance was a faithful friend.

Prayer and the newspapers directed their steps to where they were needed. They'd learnt that their message was best received where there was trouble, a mining disaster, say, or an epidemic, so they always welcomed the little tip-offs they got from their cousin Arthur – a murder here, a robbery there, pointing the way to fertile ground where the joy of Jesus could best flourish.

When he directed their footsteps, he liked them to write every day or so, telling him about who they had met and what they had been told. Sometimes, Arthur would use this information in his legal cases, and it was right that he should do so. Arthur was a good man. He had once told Alan that he was an atheist, but Alan knew that people only said that sort of thing for effect. Arthur, whatever he said, was doing God's work. He was a seeker after truth, and they were as glad to help him in his mission as he was glad to help them in theirs.

'*Whatsoever things are true, whatsoever things are honest, whatsoever things are just, whatsoever things are pure, whatsoever things are lovely, whatsoever things are of good report; if there be any virtue, and if there be any praise, think on these things.*'

The prayer meetings in Evesham, they knew, would carry on without them under the auspices of Mr Inch, a local builder who played the mandolin, and Mrs Floyd, who worked the harmonium. So, they packed everything up, set off early in the morning and were in Collingford by teatime. They found a place on the edge of a pasture, close to woodland, and walked to the nearest house to find out who the landowner was. Alan was good at the next bit. When asking a favour he had a way of approaching the matter from the side and leading towards it, so that by the time he got there it was the landowner offering rather than him asking.

This, Norah had once said, must have been the way Joseph had talked to the innkeeper in Bethlehem.

CHAPTER EIGHT

Edgar had made several attempts to get in touch with Norman Bearcroft, the Labour candidate for Birmingham East, by telegram and telephone, but Mr Bearcroft, it seemed, was a busy man. As well as the Mary Dutton Defence Fund, he was involved with a long-running industrial dispute at the Sheldon Coach Works, a cokemaker's strike in Saltley and a struggle to prevent the closure of the Washwood Heath orphanage. He sat on Labour Party policy committees on disarmament, slum clearance, education and foreign affairs, and he was producing Jerome K. Jerome's *The Passing of the Third Floor Back* for the Co-Operative Players at the Solihull Little Theatre.

A week after their trip to Birmingham, Bearcroft at last returned Edgar's calls. He said he was in London and would be free for twenty minutes if they could meet him at 12.30 that afternoon in a pub called The Albion in Limehouse Basin.

'Why Limehouse Basin?' Skelton asked.

'Because he's on a committee to do with canal transport, because Limehouse is the kind of working-class district in which he likes to be seen and with which he likes to be associated, and because – I'm assuming – The Albion is a vile place in which men such as you and I with no grime on the collar nor gravy on the waistcoat will feel uncomfortable and thus find ourselves at a disadvantage. He is a very calculating person.'

'You don't like him.'

'No.'

'You've had one conversation on the phone.'

'It was enough.'

The Albion stank. Mostly it was unwashed flesh, but there was stale beer in there, too, vomit and faecal smells from a lavatory and, of course, the cold stench of the Thames. The panelling, the floor, the ceiling, the people and the drinks were all the same shade of greyish-brown. It was old. Dickens could have drunk here, maybe Shakespeare and Marlowe, and possibly Chaucer, but none of them would have, because they were all too choosy.

Oddly, none of the clientele seemed to have London

accents. Skelton heard Welsh, Lancashire, Yorkshire, a lot of Birmingham and Black Country.

'Off the canal boats, come into Limehouse Basin,' Edgar explained. He was whispering, the same way you would at the zoo in the presence of tigers.

They had arrived a few minutes early and there seemed to be no sign of Bearcroft. Or, at least, none of the company looked as if he might be a prospective Labour MP, then again, as Edgar pointed out, still whispering, there was no telling these days.

Skelton knew from experience that drinking beer in a place like this led to diarrhoea and he was fairly certain that ordering a bottle of lemonade might lead to accusations of cissiness and subsequent death. Already, as Edgar had predicted, their clean collars and gravyless waistcoats were attracting attention. Skelton asked for straight gin and Edgar did the same. It was dispensed from a glarney bottle with no label. Skelton gingerly sipped, wondering, as he did so, whether the rumours that home-made spirits caused blindness were true.

It wasn't bad.

Edgar agreed. 'I used to know a bug hunter in Stepney had a still at his gaff. Said it's all in the botanicals.' Edgar rarely returned to his roots but, when he did, he revealed a fluency in street slang and criminal argot that would have impressed Diamond Annie.

'Is a bug hunter somebody who hunts bugs?' Skelton asked.

'You looking for a job with the monkeys?'

'I've no idea what you're talking about.'

'A bug hunter is somebody who cheats or steals from drunks – which is a description that probably applies to every other person in this pub.'

They sat at a table next to a family – man, wife, several children. The father took from his coat a cold leg of lamb wrapped in moss, produced a clasp knife and cut off strips – one for him, one for his wife and one for the children, several of whom scampered on the floor in the spit and sawdust.

Edgar kept his feet on the rungs of his chair. He'd just had his shoes soled and heeled.

Bearcroft came in as if his arrival had been prepared by a town crier and trumpets, bursting through the door and posing for a moment flanked by two supernumeraries. He was a burly chap perhaps in his forties, his hat on the back of his head, his tweed overcoat unbuttoned and flapping to reveal a blue suit made of fabric so stiff it bent like cardboard. Though nobody seemed to know him or to recognise him, he nodded and smiled as if they did, looked around, spotted Skelton and Edgar and approached like a pike stalking prey.

'Mr Skelton and Mr Hobbes, I'm very pleased to meet you. This is Muriel and this is our Stanley.' Skelton was a little confused by the 'our Stanley'. Bearcroft was not a working-class socialist. He was – you only had to look at him – the product of one of the better public schools. Did he seriously believe that the odd northernism might lend credence to his pose as a 'man of the people'?

Did he?

Bearcroft found a chair, pulled it over to the table back-to-front and sat on it with his arms crossed over the chair's back. Muriel, an improbably tall woman and Stanley, a sixth-former bristling with self-importance, stood behind like caryatids.

'Now, what are you drinking?'

'It's gin,' Skelton said, 'and it's very kind of you to offer but I'm afraid a second will have me pie-eyed.'

Bearcroft laughed as if 'pie-eyed' was a cue for it. 'And I've been swimming in tea all morning,' he said, 'so I don't think my bladder could stand another drop of anything.' And he laughed again because he'd said 'bladder', which, he thought, topped Skelton's 'pie-eyed'. 'Now, what can I do for you gentlemen?'

'I don't know if you've heard, but Mr Critchlow is ill,' Skelton said.

'I have heard, yes. But he does have these little attacks now and then, and I've no doubt he'll be back at his desk in a couple of days. He's a very good man. Very sound. The best. Very experienced.'

'I'm sure you're right, but I do wonder whether he has the right experience for this case. I believe he's only ever worked on one murder before.'

'He's the right man for the job.'

'William Allen in Birmingham, a solicitor I can highly recommend, did some quite remarkable work on the recent Stirchley Shootings and helped secure the acquittal of Beatrice Nichol in the face of a very strong prosecution case.'

'I know him.'

'I'm sure that Mr Allen would . . .'

'He stood for the council a couple of years ago.'

'I wasn't aware . . .'

'As a Tory.'

'I can't imagine how his politics would have any bearing on the matter.'

'Politics, Mr Skelton, has a bearing on everything.'

'I'm sure you're right, but in a case of this nature . . .'

'Politics has a bearing on everything, especially in a case of this nature. Let me speak plainly, Mr Skelton. Mary Dutton was for years subjected to beatings at the hands of her husband. Her only escape was to kill him.'

'My job is to establish her innocence.'

'Either way it makes no difference. The Mary Dutton Defence League, of which I am founder and chairman, is dedicated to bringing justice to that poor woman and to women all over the country who find themselves in the same iniquitous position. We have the *Daily Herald* behind us and in a week or so, you'll see, the marches will begin. Young women, wearing white frocks with sashes in purple for dignity, white for purity and green for hope, will, like their suffragette mothers and aunts twenty years ago, take to the streets and march – this time not for the vote but for Mary Dutton. There is to be a general election in May. Five million young women have been added to the electoral role. Do you think those young women are going to vote for the party that leaps to the defence of Mary Dutton or the party that hangs her?'

'Yes, of course,' Edgar said, 'if she hangs that could give you a huge electoral advantage.' He tried to disguise his contempt, but his voice went waspish halfway through the sentence.

'If she hangs it will be a tragedy, Mr Hobbes. A terrible tragedy. An obscenity. A crime against all decency. But let's make no mistake about this, her blood will be on Tory hands. But if she gets off – and we all hope she does with every fibre of our being – we must be sure that there is no doubt at all that her victory, your victory, our victory will be a victory for the Labour Party. Critchlow's a good man. There are widows of men killed at the Vicar Lane Explosion who would be in the poorhouse if it hadn't been for the sterling work he did to get money out of those hard-faced criminals around the board table. Back in 1919, when the boilermakers came out at Stannings and the bosses called out the specials, Critchlow was there on the picket line shoulder to shoulder with the men, taking careful note of every outrage and assault, shouting the legal odds at the enemy. Make no mistake, Critchlow is the best there is.'

'Yes, I'm sure Critchlow is an excellent solicitor in those sorts of cases,' Edgar said, more waspish than ever, 'but the difficulty we have here is that Mary Dutton isn't a boilermaker.'

Bearcroft ignored him and turned to Skelton. 'You're sound enough, too,' he said. Skelton didn't want to be 'sound'. 'You're from a back-to-back in Leeds—'

'It isn't a back-to-back.'

'—and your wife was out with the suffragettes in

Manchester and . . . is she actually a card-carrying red?'

'How do you know anything about my wife?'

'We check these things.'

Skelton was proud of his ability to remain calm under provocation, but now he raised his voice. 'That is a flagrant invasion of privacy, and an outrage.'

Bearcroft raised his louder. 'No. I'll tell you what the outrage is, Mr Skelton. The prospect of five more years of Tory government – that is what the outrage is. Do you know, in Newcastle, one in five children is medically malnourished, and in Aston, on my own doorstep, families of five and seven have to live in one room? Unemployment's up, vast areas of the country are derelict. The Tories give tax cuts to the rich and at the same time they rob the health insurance societies, cut dole and throw thousands of workless men and women onto the Poor Law. So, please, don't talk to me about outrage.'

Skelton pushed his gin away and looked at his watch.

'We really—'

'You see, Mr Skelton' – Bearcroft had stopped haranguing and now had on his 'common sense and hard facts' voice – 'Mary Dutton's life, much though it's precious to us, and much though we wish with all our hearts and souls to preserve it, is not the only life that hangs in the balance here. There are the lives of a hundred thousand miners in the pits of South Wales, of Yorkshire, Derbyshire and Durham, there's the hundred thousand shipbuilders on the Tyne and on the Clyde, there's the million – think of that, Mr Skelton – the million and more children who will go to bed tonight hungry and who will die before they're grown of want, starvation and disease.'

The man at the next table, the one with the leg of lamb, said, 'Shut your bone-hole.'

Bearcroft turned to his entourage and said, 'Hand out the pamphlets, Stanley.' And Stanley began to do so.

The clientele of The Albion pub took the neatly folded leaves of paper and examined them uncomprehendingly.

'They're off the canal boats,' Edgar said. 'I'd be surprised if one in twenty of them can read.'

Bearcroft stood and addressed the pub. 'A Labour government will make universal literacy its highest priority.'

An old man, very drunk, approached him, put one hand on his shoulder and said, with great menace, 'Are you the man that married my sister?' At which Muriel drew herself to her full six foot four, took Bearcroft by the arms and almost carried him out of the building. Stanley, spotting with alarm that his companions were retreating, dropped his pamphlets and ran to keep up.

The barman called over to Skelton. 'Was he with you?'

'Never saw him before in my life,' Skelton said, which was substantially true.

Skelton and Edgar sipped their gins in silence for a while. Then Edgar said, 'We should do this more often.'

CHAPTER NINE

Monday 28th January, 1929

My dear cousin Arthur,

It has turned very cold up here in Collingford, so cold that I've had to get my balaclava out, which I have not had to do for, I think, three years. Norah had stored it neatly away with mothballs, so it stank a bit, but it had no more than its regulation number of holes. Did you have the gale last week on the Monday night? It blew something terrible here.

We got here on Friday and are camped in a place called Brannock Woods, just on the outskirts of Collingford. We'd barely settled in when the wind came. All that night we could hear great crashings of branches being flung about. We were afraid that one of the great trees in Brannock Woods would blow over and crush us in our van, but the Lord saw fit to spare us and, in the morning, we found that He had blessed us with a great bounty of fallen wood for the little stove we have. Chopping the wood keeps me as warm as the stove itself.

Collingford seems a very pleasant town. More of an overgrown village, really, but the Market Square and the High Street have every sort of shop you could want and there's even a little cinema showing a Harold Lloyd film that Norah says we saw in Llandudno about five years ago. We buy most of our provisions – milk, eggs and so forth – from farms as we go along so have little need for shops, but it is nice to look. Norah got some soap and pins for her hair, and buttons to replace the hooks and eyes that had gone awry on one of her frocks.

Everywhere you go, you run into sharp-faced men in brown soft-hats and raincoats. They are newspaper reporters. We popped for a moment into the King's Head, which is the big pub in the Market Square, and it seemed to be full of them in various stages of insobriety. This was at about two o'clock in the afternoon. It is clear that the Mary Dutton case is regarded as something of a *cause célèbre*.

On the Tuesday, we sought out and made friends

with the local Methodist minister, the Rev. Pusey. He was a little stiff with us at first but eventually I learnt he had an interest in moths and I happened to have a book called *The Romance of Insect Life*, signed by the author Edmund Selous, a gentleman who came to one or two of our meetings when we were in Dorset. I presented him with the book as a gift, and he invited me to preach at his chapel next Sunday.

On the Wednesday, going door to door, we came to Hinckley Lane, the address you gave in your letter for Mrs Enid Fellows and found Mrs Fellows hanging out her washing in the garden. Six children, Mary Dutton's children, were running about her garden.

A round, cheerful lady, she seemed to me, very quick in her movements; the sort of capable person who finds it hard to sit down for a moment's peace during the day but must be on the go all the time. Watching her hang out the washing was like watching a precision drill in the army. The sheet comes out the basket, fold here, fold here, tuck here and here and throw it over the line. Pull it straight, in go the pegs and on to the next one. And all the time she was watching the children, chatting with them, telling them off.

We didn't go in the garden but stood by the gate.

The question of mendacity is one that we have been over many times, but still it bothers my conscience. To have gone straight in there and told her that we were the Joy of Jesus Mission, but we were also cousins of Arthur Skelton who had directed our footsteps towards Collingford, would, of course, have been self-defeating. Although morally and ethically I see no difference between your work and God's work, others might. Christ Himself never told direct lies, of course, but there were occasions when He concealed the truth.

And as they did eat, He said, 'Verily I say unto you, that one of you shall betray me.' And they were exceeding sorrowful, and began every one of them to say unto him, 'Lord, is it I?'

But He did not tell them, did He? He did not tell them that His betrayer would be Judas, even though He knew it to be so. Because if He had told them, it would have defeated His greater purpose.

Treading the fine line between concealing the truth for the greater purpose and telling lies can sometimes be tricky, and I pray for forgiveness if now and then I fall into error.

'They're very fine children, missus,' I said to her. 'They do you credit.'

You see, although the implication was there, I never said outright that I thought they were *her* children. All the same, she took the implication. She told me they weren't hers. She didn't have any of her own. Her husband had been killed at Cambrai. These were the children of a friend, she said, who had had to go away for a while.

Norah told her she was from the Joy of Jesus Mission. Enid said in that case we were wasting our time. She got all the church she wanted from the vicar already. She'd had the Band of Hope round just before Christmas and she'd seen them off in less than a minute.

So, I started singing the song about Grandpa's wooden leg. I'm sure you know it.

Peeping through the knot-hole, in Grandpa's wooden leg
Who will wind the clock up when I'm gone?
Why did they build the shore so near the sea?
And a boy's best friend is her mother.

This made the children laugh. It's the volume, you see. I don't think they'd ever heard anybody sing quite as powerfully as I do. You'd be surprised at how easily that can make people laugh. I also make faces, but it is mostly the loudness that they laugh at.

The children wanted to learn the song, so I sang it again and again until they had it off pat and could sing it with me.

Enid asked Norah whether I was a bit tapped, and Norah told her I probably was but that I was all the better for it. Enid had finished pegging out the washing by this time and she invited us into the garden asking if we wanted a cup of tea. We said yes, so she went indoors and watched from the kitchen window while she fussed around with the kettle, pot and cups.

Norah took out her penny whistle and played some tunes on it and we chatted.

The children are all bright as little buttons, particularly Doris, the eldest. Doris is wise beyond her years. Talking to her you could be talking to a woman of forty or fifty. She has seen too much and knows too much, I suppose, poor little soul.

Anyway, Mrs Fellows brought the tea to us, outside. When we had had that, it clouded over and started to spot with rain so Mrs Fellows very kindly invited Norah and I to take shelter in her parlour, which offer we gratefully accepted. We were able to keep the children entertained while Mrs Fellows got on with a bit of housework. I did the disappearing coins, the pencil levitation and the indiarubber egg for the older children. Norah told Bible stories for the younger ones.

She showed them the pictures of Jesus we have in a book. One in particular excited them which is a picture of Jesus as the Good Shepherd, carrying a sheep on his back, while other sheep flock around him. John 10:14, 'I am the good shepherd, and I know my sheep and I am known of mine.'

One of the little boys, whose name is Wilf, said that he had seen his daddy carry a sheep like that, and Norah remembered that you mentioned in your letter that you were wondering whether the poison could have come from sheep dipping. So, Norah turned to a picture showing John the Baptist baptising Jesus (Matthew 3:13–17) and Wilf said his daddy used to do that with the sheep just like in the picture. His daddy used to get in the water with them and give them a 'really good wetting' and give himself a 'really good wetting and all'. Then Doris told the little boy off in no uncertain terms for talking about their father. She said she did not like thinking about her father at all.

The incident cast a solemn mood over the company, so I sang, 'I'm an airman, I'm an airman, and I fly, fly, fly, fly, fly.'

Then Mrs Fellows offered to make us another cup of tea, but Norah pointed out that the rain had stopped and the sun was coming out, so we had best be on our way. Mrs Fellows asked us to drop by another time and we said we would be glad to. Norah told her that I would be preaching at the Methodist Chapel on Sunday, and Mrs Fellows said that she would come along and bring the children with her.

They were as good as their word. The children behaved themselves impeccably without fidgeting or talking all the way through the meeting. Even the little one did not cry.

Thanks to our knocking on doors in the week, we had an excellent turnout. Norah brought along her accordion and I brought my banjo, the easel and the cards on which Norah has written the words of the songs with her paints. Her lettering is magnificent. I am sure that she could find a job making shop signs and advertisements at the drop of a hat if she ever wished.

And when I told them, we sang, *how glorious you are*
They didn't believe me, they didn't believe me,
When, in my prayers, I see your face
It shines with glory, joy and grace
You brought light to our lives, so the world could see.

You should have seen the scowl on the Rev. Pusey's face, when we started. We see it all the time. The dark looks when we start. They think we are turning their chapels into places of entertainment, you see, into music halls. Which, of course, is precisely what we are doing.

Why are music halls more popular than churches? Is it because people have turned their faces against the Lord? No, it is because churches have turned their faces against the joy of Jesus, which the music halls still embrace.

Some of the clergy are not converted to our way of thinking. More than one has said, 'It's just a concert party.' To which I reply, 'So was the Anglican Mass four hundred years ago with all its singing and chanting. The only difference between what we do and what they do is that we're much more up to date.'

Several have accused me of blasphemy (and I trust if such a charge were to be taken to court, I would be assured of the best defence counsel in the land), but I have never known one turn his back when the collecting plate goes around.

This evening we had sprout pie for supper. It is an invention of Norah's, like shepherd's pie but with sprouts instead of mince. Sprouts are very cheap. Some people do not care for sprouts, but I cannot get enough.

I am ever yours faithfully in the joy of Jesus,

Alan

CHAPTER TEN

'Did you hear about the riots?' Edgar said as the train pulled out of Euston.

Skelton had. Mila had shown him the *Daily Mirror* at breakfast. Page five had a headline – MARY DUTTON – RIOTS IN BIRMINGHAM – and three photographs, one large and two small. The small photographs were the now-familiar image of Mary Dutton looking like Lillian Gish and one of Skelton, taken on the courtroom steps during the Dryden trial. The large photograph showed a group of women outside Winson Green prison, looking rather less riotous than the headline suggested. Their banners announced that they were members of the 'Mary Dutton Defence League'.

Just as Norman Bearcroft had predicted the week before, the flappers were taking to the streets.

Mila was impressed as she always was with the threat of civic unrest, especially where women were involved.

'I think "riots" might be labouring the point,' Skelton said. 'But I've no doubt the *Mirror* already has plans to encourage a few of them to chain themselves to railings or deface a public monument.'

Keeling was waiting with the Daimler at New Street. Skelton looked longingly at the driver's seat.

'I had a word with Mr Patterson,' Keeling said. 'Unfortunately, there would be a problem with the insurance if third parties were to drive the Daimler.'

'I'd be happy to sign a document saying that I'd personally be liable for any damage or injuries.'

'Yes, sir. Mr Patterson considered that possibility, but then it occurred to him that you are a lawyer.'

'What – and he'd be worried I could get round any promises I made with legal wrangles?'

'Not in so many words. But . . . you are the country's most celebrated legal mind, sir. It's in all the papers.'

'I'm not that good.'

Keeling opened the door and they climbed in.

'Law courts first, is it, then on to Winson Green?'

'All right, Edgar?' Skelton asked.

Edgar made a face and rolled down the window.

Although Skelton had taken *Mrs B. D. McKillop versus*

The London, Midland and Scottish Railway Company only a few days earlier, the case itself, in one form or another, had been running for the best part of two years.

Mrs McKillop's husband, Brian, was a Scotsman who had moved, with his wife and three children, to Birmingham just before the war. In 1927, while visiting his sick father in Dingwall, Mr McKillop was run over and killed by a train. Mrs McKillop sued the railway company claiming that their negligence had been the cause of her husband's death.

The letters filled a thick file.

The company first claimed that the man was trespassing at the time of the accident and therefore the company was not liable for his safety.

The plaintiff claimed that the snow was so heavy that the man could not have known he was trespassing.

The defendants claimed that there were signposts and fences along the whole length of the line.

The plaintiff claimed that the snow had drifted so deeply that the signs and fences were either buried or otherwise obscured.

The defendants claimed that, because of the snow, the train was moving so slowly that if the man hadn't seen or heard it in plenty of time, he must have been drunk or deaf.

The plaintiff argued that if the train was going so slowly then the driver must have been drunk or blind or both not to have seen the man on the line in plenty of time to stop.

Skelton had a brief word with Mrs McKillop outside the

court. She had been reading about some mining disaster where the widows had got ten bob a week in compensation and reckoned she was entitled to at least the same amount. Her kids were all grown up so there was no claim for them. She also told him – it is extraordinary what you can glean in a short time if you're a chatty sort of person – that she had sugar diabetes. Skelton knew this meant she was unlikely to live for more than five years and probably a lot less.

He met the defence counsel and solicitors in the corridor. Defence was Gilpin, a pleasant chap he'd once had dinner with when they were both at a loose end during the Gloucester assizes.

The defence solicitors said that the company was very against paying any sort of compensation because a principle was involved. They didn't want to set a precedent.

Skelton wondered if they really believed that paying a few pounds to a woman whose husband had been run over by a train would encourage other women to push *their* husbands under trains. And even if they did believe such a thing, would a full public trial with headlines in all the newspapers make it more likely or less likely that other women would be inspired to push their husbands under trains. Gilpin persuaded the company that, given the additional attention that Skelton's celebrity had brought to the trial, it would be better to settle out of court.

Skelton started the bidding high. He said he believed that Mrs McKillop would settle for £5 a week and added that her diabetes would mean this probably wouldn't cost the company any more that £1,300 over five years, or £780 over three.

After a hurried, whispered conference with his solicitors, Gilpin said he doubted whether the company would agree to anything over £2 a week. Skelton said he might be able to get the widow to agree to £2 10s if the company would swallow costs. Hands were shaken. The judge was informed. Skelton told Mrs McKillop that the railway company had agreed to pay five times as much as she'd been expecting. The dance she did probably shortened her life by another six months, which would save the company £65. The whole process had taken not much more than half an hour.

CHAPTER ELEVEN

Prisons always reminded Skelton of the infant's cloakroom at St Saviour's Elementary; the same enamel-painted brick walls, the same smell of disinfectant and sick.

They were ushered into a room furnished with a plain wooden table and four chairs. The wardress who'd shown them in said she'd go and get Mary, and left them. They sat listening to the prison noises: echoing feet, the odd shout, the clang of iron doors.

The table wobbled. Edgar looked at the legs, located the one causing the wobble, tore off a bit of his Gold Flake packet, folded it and jammed it under the defective leg. It made no difference.

The wardress came back with Mary Dutton. Mary was tiny,

less than five feet, and bore herself with a glamorous frailty. She wasn't in prison clothes. Custody prisoners were allowed to wear their own. She had on a grey skirt, a good bit longer than was fashionable, and a faded blue and white blouse.

The wardress told her to sit down and, at Skelton's nod, left the room.

'Good afternoon, Mrs Dutton,' Edgar said, 'My name's Edgar Hobbes and this is Mr Skelton, who's been asked to defend you in court.'

'I've seen your picture in the paper,' she said. Her voice belied her appearance. It was deep, almost manly. 'You haven't got a cigarette you could spare, have you?'

Edgar offered her the mangled Gold Flake packet. She took one and cupped her hands to protect the flame as Edgar lit it. He dithered with the dead match, looking around for an ashtray.

'There's a couple up there,' Mary said, indicating the high windowsill. Edgar fetched them over.

'So, how are they treating you, Mrs Dutton?' Skelton asked.

'It's a prison,' she said. Stupid question. 'Have you brought news of the kids?'

Skelton had heard all about the children in his letter from Alan but, since it would be imprudent to reveal, even to Mary, that he and Alan were in cahoots, he said, 'I'm afraid not.'

'If you see them, tell 'em I miss them.'

'I most certainly will.'

'Jean had a bit of a cold when they took me. Enid says she's all right, but Enid could just be saying that to stop me worrying.'

Skelton looked down at his notes in the file to remind himself of the name.

'This is Mrs Enid Fellows,' he said.

'She's a very good friend. She writes nearly every day to tell me how they're getting on.'

'How old is Jean?'

'She'll have her first birthday on the 28th March. Will you get me home by then?'

'We'll do our best, Mrs Dutton.'

'Some of the women have got babies in here.'

'I think they'd be very small babies, newborns.'

'They said. I can hear them crying at night.'

'I can imagine that must be very distressing for you.'

'One of them's called Jean.'

'It is a lovely name. My sister Amy's got a girl called Jean. It's a long time since she's been a baby, though. They grow up so fast, don't they? Amy's Jean was fifteen last birthday. Your eldest is . . . what?'

'Doris'll be twelve in April.'

'Still in school?' Mary nodded. 'How's she doing?'

'She doesn't get on with the teachers. But she's not dense or anything. She likes facts.'

'What sort of facts?'

'What?'

'What kind of facts does she like?'

'I don't know. Funny ones. She came home one day and said a whale wasn't a fish.'

'A whale?'

'It isn't a fish.'

'It's a mammal,' Edgar said.

'He knows, doesn't he?' Mary said. 'There aren't any numbers with a "b" in them.'

'What about a billion?' Edgar said.

'Until you get . . . no, the way you say it is if you started counting now and you counted for the rest of your life you'd never get to a number with a "b" in it. That's what Doris says.'

'She's right. She's a smart girl.'

'She gets them out of *Peg's Paper*.'

'I didn't know they had things like that in there.'

'You can learn a lot from those magazines.'

'I thought it was just stories.'

'No, there's other things, too.'

'My daughter's a bit young for them,' Skelton said.

'What's her name, then?'

'Elizabeth.'

'That's nice. How old is she?'

'She's eight.'

'Same as our Susan. Have you just got Elizabeth?'

'No. There's Lawrence. He's ten.'

'Same age as our Wilf.'

'What's Wilf like?'

'He's the devil incarnate.'

They laughed. It was going to be all right.

When he was a pupil, Skelton had been complimented by an elderly silk for having the 'common touch'. But Skelton knew he didn't have the common touch at all. He was just common.

'Right. Edgar's going to get his pen and his notebook out now, and he's going to ask you a lot of questions, some of which might be a little delicate.'

'Why don't you ask the questions?'

'Because Mr Hobbes is better at it than I am, and I find it more useful to listen. It is important that you answer the questions as honestly and as fully as possible. Tiny details can become very important in the courtroom.'

Mary nodded.

Edgar took her through the basic biographical facts point by point. Born Betton Strange, near Shrewsbury, 1897. Mother died giving birth. Father died sixteen years later. Went into service as a housemaid. Met Ted Dutton in Shrewsbury where he'd gone for the market.

'He was the most handsome man I'd ever seen. Ever so shy, though.'

'He was a shy man?'

'He could hardly speak for blushing. At the start he could barely stand to look me in the face; he said he was afraid his heart would burst open. It was me had to propose to him in the end.'

Somebody walked fast along the corridor outside. A door was unlocked, opened and locked again. A woman, sounding outraged, shouted, 'Boiled potatoes?'

'Was it a big wedding?' Edgar asked.

'No. We got married in Shrewsbury. Just me, Ted, the vicar and a few people from the house where I worked.'

Skelton, who had been rummaging through the notes, looked up and said, 'Ted's parents didn't come?'

'No.'

'Why was that?'

'It was a war wedding. All done in a rush. Ted had his call-up.'

'This was in . . . ?'

'20th May 1916.'

'So, he was in uniform?'

'No. His papers had come through but, one thing and another, they didn't actually take him until the November, so we had the summer.'

'This was in the house in Collingford?'

'That's right.'

'Where you were still living at the time of your arrest?'

Mary nodded. 'Rained nearly all the time, but we were ever so happy.'

'And Ted was good to you?'

'Couldn't do enough. Used to make me daisy chains. Some mornings we'd get up before dawn, go down and sit with the sheep, watch 'em drinking the dew off the grass.'

Skelton smiled, nodded at Edgar to continue and busied himself with his pipe, which wasn't drawing well.

Edgar finished writing something in his notebook, turned back a page, studied it for a moment and asked, 'And what dates were the children born?'

'They took Ted in the November,' Mary said, 'and he came home for Christmas and then they sent him off to France in the March. Doris was born on the 15th April. I didn't know if Ted was dead or alive. Same as everybody. Then I got the letter saying he'd been gassed, and I thought that was terrible, but they all said it was good news cos it meant he'd be coming home. He was blind for a bit. That got better before he came home. And then he had the cough, but that went away after a bit an' all. He was different when he came back from the war, though. You could see it in his face. Everything about him. He had moods.'

'What kind of moods?' Edgar asked.

'One day, not long after he'd come back, I said something that crossed him and he took his belt to me. He was sorry afterwards, of course. God, he was sorry. He got down on his knees and begged me to forgive him and swore it'd never happen again. So, I forgave him. And I believed him. Two days. Two days later he punched me in the face and, when I fell back on the table, he punched me again.'

'Had you done anything to provoke this?' Edgar asked.

'I must have done something, I suppose, but I can't remember what. Some little thing.'

'And was he sorry again?'

'I didn't wait to find out. I ran away. I got Doris and I got out. Though I didn't know anybody in Collie, so I started walking back to Shrewsbury. Somebody had told me it was fifty miles, but I knew if I just kept walking long enough I'd get there. Me and Doris. Somebody must have seen me, and they told Ted and he came after me on a bike. He said he was sorry again. More sorry than the first time. And he said I should feel for him cos he didn't know what came over him. Some sort of madness he said it was. So, I believed him again. Then the day after that he locked me in the outhouse, and he had a pistol and he said he was going to kill me if I tried running off.'

'A pistol?'

'This table wobbles.'

'I know,' Edgar said. 'I put a bit of cardboard under the leg, but it doesn't seem to have made any difference.'

Mary wobbled the table while Edgar looked. He bent down shifted the wedge he'd made. The table still wobbled. Then Skelton, who had disassembled his pipe and was holding the pieces in place, bent down to have a look himself.

'It's the tile that's wobbling, not the table,' Skelton said.

It was true. The floor was tiled. The tile that the table leg was standing on wasn't bedded properly.

'We should move the table to a different tile,' Mary said.

They did so. This cured the wobble.

Shelton took his little penknife out and started reaming the bowl of his pipe into the ashtray.

Edgar studied his notebook for a moment and said, 'We were talking about the pistol. Did Ted threaten you with this at other times?'

'Are you sure this is how we should be going about things?' Mary said.

'In what way?'

'It's no use me going on about how horrible Ted was, is it? I been thinking about it. In the court, if I go on about how cruel he was, that just makes it look more likely I killed him, doesn't it? I mean, I didn't kill him, but I can imagine people thinking, *If he'd treated me like that, I'd have killed him*, and that makes them think I must have killed him. And it isn't going to do me any good if they start thinking like that, is it?'

'It's very clever of you to see that, Mrs Dutton,' Skelton said.

'And I'm fed up of talking about it, anyway. I told the police and I told the reporters from the papers. I know I didn't poison him, so I know somebody else must have done it. But nobody seems interested in who that might have been.'

'Did Ted have many enemies?' Edgar asked.

'Well, he didn't have any friends.'

'Was he a drinking man?'

'No.'

'Never drank at all?'

'Never had a taste for beer or nothing like that. He loved sweets, though. He loved Everton Mints. You know the striped ones?'

'I know, like a humbug,' Skelton said.

'Or a bullseye,' Edgar added.

'No, bullseyes are round,' Mary said. 'And they're nothing like humbugs, either.'

'I thought they were.'

'No, Everton Mints have got a toffee centre.'

'Have they? I don't think I've ever had one, then. I've seen them in shops, but I never knew they had a toffee centre. Did you, Edgar?'

'So, they're chewy?' Edgar said.

'You get the hard, minty bit, then the inside's chewy,' Mary said.

'And Ted was fond of these?'

'Oh, he'd do anything for a quarter of Everton Mints.'

'That was his only . . . could one call it a vice?' Edgar said. 'He had no lady friends?'

'He had no friends at all, men or ladies.'

'And he never went to the pub? Did he go out at all?'

'He'd be out all day with the sheep. Markets. All over. He'd go out. He wouldn't tell me. He'd say it was none of my business. Sometimes he'd be out all night.'

'But you never suspected he might be seeing another woman?'

'I wouldn't have thought so. He wasn't interested in that sort of thing at all.'

Edgar looked up at Mary, and then at the wall behind her head. He pulled back the cuff of his shirt and scratched his wrist, unsure how to word the next question.

Skelton weighed in for him. Using his broadest Leeds to defuse any squeamishness, he said, 'Six kids is going it a bit, isn't it, for a chap who wasn't interested?

'Six times. More or less,' Mary said. 'He was shy, like I said. Or . . . what d'you call it? . . . prudish. He was prudish about anything like that. Got that from his mother.'

Edgar, relieved, turned over a couple of pages of his little book and made a cryptic note in very small handwriting. Skelton looked over, wondering whether he was recording the number of times intimacy took place and calculating the approximate dates.

112

'Did you get on with his mother?' Skelton asked.

'Jessie? She hated me from the start.'

'Why was that?'

'He'd married beneath him.'

'Because you were a servant girl?'

'And I come from Shrewsbury.'

'And she held that against you?'

'And because I'm pretty. She used to be beautiful. Have you seen photos?'

'No.'

'She was beautiful and now she's striking but, you know, an old lady.'

Skelton sucked on his empty pipe. Edgar held his fountain pen poised in mid-air like a bone-china teacup. Both looked at Mary, waiting for her to continue. Did either of them know the first thing about women? It didn't seem plausible.

'Some women are like that,' Mary explained. 'When they're beautiful and then they get old and they're not beautiful any more they get sour. Jessie's a very sour woman. A very cold woman. And religious. I don't know whether she was always religious or whether it's just something she turned to when she got old, because the sourness of it suits her.'

'When you say she's religious . . .?' Skelton said.

'Very, very religious. Knows whole chunks of the Bible by heart. Especially the bits about burning in hell.'

Skelton nodded. He knew the type. He took out his Balkan Sobranie, filled his pipe and, having discovered that a leg of his chair had landed on the wobbly tile, rocked himself

113

gently. Edgar allowed him three rocks, then gave him a look to say it was getting on his nerves. Skelton stopped rocking. Edgar took over the questioning.

'Did you have much to do with Ted's father?'

'Sid was all right. He was a police inspector.'

'He died . . .'

'Three years ago. I looked after him towards the end.'

'In what way?'

'When he got so he couldn't get out of bed. Ted's mum couldn't look after him, because she's never been well herself. So, he came to live with us, and I looked after him.'

'Was Ted's mother grateful for that?' Mary pulled a face. 'How long was he there for?'

'At our house? Not long. Six weeks or so. It was his lungs, then his heart, his stomach and his kidneys. He just got worse and worse and worse. The doctor said there was nothing he could do for him.'

'And the name of that doctor was . . . ?' Edgar asked.

'Dr Willoughby.'

'This is the same Dr Willoughby as the one who attended Ted in his last illness.'

''S'right.'

Skelton was looking through the file.

'You didn't mention looking after Ted's father in your police statement,' he said.

'I didn't see the point. They all knew anyway.'

'The police all knew about this?'

'They knew all about Sid. Course they did. He was their boss.'

114

'Inspector Dutton.'

'They all thought the world of him.'

'What about Ted's brother?' Edgar said.

Mary prompted again, 'Billy.'

'Could Billy not have helped when his father was ill?'

'Billy? You don't hardly ever see Billy. He's off on his motorbike all the time. He does racing and the Wall of Death.'

'What's that?' Skelton asked.

'The motorcycles gradually climb the sloping walls of a circular room,' Edgar said, 'until, taking advantage of centrifugal force, they're horizontal.'

The woman in the faraway cell yelled, more outraged than ever, 'Boiled potatoes?'

'The police say they found rat poison in your pantry,' Edgar said. 'Was it you bought the poison?'

'I'd never seen it before. Ted must have bought it. But I don't know why. We never had rats in the house. They wouldn't dare come near. Ted had his dog, you see. Gyp. I think it was Gyp's passing that did for Ted in the end.'

'His dog died?'

'Last summer. Ted took it bad. Nobody could do nothing right after that.'

'He liked animals?'

'He loved his dog. He loved his sheep. He'd walk ten miles through the snow if he thought one of his sheep was in trouble.'

Skelton sat up. Now they were on to something.

'Did he dip the sheep?' he said.

'What?'

'Sheep dip sometimes contains arsenic.'

'Oh, right. You're thinking that's how he might have got poisoned. Yes, he did dip the sheep. You have to.'

Skelton sat back and gave Edgar a 'told you so' look.

Edgar wrote *Sheep dip???* with three question marks in his notebook.

'And might there be other sources of arsenic around the farm?' he asked. 'Weedkillers, perhaps.'

'I wouldn't know. He had things in the sheds.'

Edgar wrote *Weedkillers* in his book and, spotting that Skelton was looking over his shoulder, added no question marks but went so far as to underline the word.

'Did Ted ever take his meals elsewhere?' Edgar asked.

'In what way?'

'I'm wondering whether somebody else might have had the opportunity to poison his food. Did he ever eat at his mother's house?'

'He didn't like going to his mother's house.'

'Or at a pub or a cafe?'

'No.'

'You say he was often gone all day and sometimes all night. Did he miss his dinner?'

'He used to take pies.'

'What kind of pies?'

'Meat and potato. I used to make him meat and potato pies with a lot of pepper.'

Edgar wrote *Pies* and underlined it twice.

The wardress knocked and popped her head around the door.

'They're having their tea now.'

'Yes, of course.'

When the wardress had gone, Mary said, 'Sometimes in the evening I'd see him walking home through the fields towards the house and there'd be something in the way he was walking – with his head down and swishing at the grass with his stick. I'd know I was for it when he got home.'

As they came out of the prison gates, they were confronted by a group of twenty or thirty young women, shop girls, factory girls and two older women, better dressed than the others, in fur coats. Some of the women carried signs declaring their allegiance to the Mary Dutton Defence League.

They spotted Skelton.

'It's him. It's Galahad. It's Skelton.'

'Have you been to see Mary, Mr Skelton?'

'Does she know we're out here, fighting for her?'

'You must be freezing cold,' Skelton said.

'We were planning to do an all-night vigil but with the weather like this we'd all catch our deaths. I can't feel my feet as it is.'

The Daimler, with Keeling standing to attention, was parked a little way along the road.

Edgar tried to quicken the pace.

One of the older women said, 'If you had some words of encouragement for the ladies, Mr Skelton, I'm sure they'd be delighted.'

They had reached the car. Skelton, not nearly as abashed by the attention as he felt he ought to be, stood on the running board and addressed the crowd.

'All I can say, ladies, is that I promise to do my utmost to ensure that Mary Dutton receives a fair trial and is treated throughout her ordeal with decency and humanity.' This got a cheer.

'There were reporters here when we were up the law courts yesterday, taking photos,' the older woman said. 'I wish there was one here now.'

'Vi's got her Brownie.'

The one called Vi produced the camera.

Edgar watched disapprovingly as Skelton, trying hard to look dignified, posed for photographs with various combinations of the women. When they were safely in the car, he said, 'Sterling performance, Dolores. You do realise that those are the people who, when you lose, will be at the front of the queue to throw cabbages.'

'Stick your head out the window or you'll be sick on me.'

Edgar rolled down the window and exposed his face to the freezing wind.

'Murder house, at Collingford, is it?' Keeling asked.

'Is that what they're calling it?'

'It's turned into a bit of an attraction. People like to look, don't they? They've had to put special buses on from Old Square cos the 14 only goes as far as Kitts Green. Running a Sunday service and everything. Packed, it is.'

* * *

The drive from Winson Green to Collingford took longer than expected. Though Edgar kept his head out of the window all the way, somewhere in Washwood Heath he spotted a public lavatory and asked to stop.

Skelton got out of the car to stretch his legs. Keeling did the same. He took out a rag and polished the Daimler's bonnet.

'Do you always drive this car,' Skelton asked, 'or does it vary from day to day?'

'Mr Patterson's got four cars altogether, but I usually get the Daimler.'

'You're very lucky.'

'Oh, I know. I like the uniform, too, and the great thing is I get it all provided. Shirt and everything. So, I can keep my own clothes nice. I've got three suits hanging in the wardrobe at home.'

'Have you really?'

'Blue serge, heather mixture and black for funerals. A good suit's an investment, really, isn't it?'

'That's exactly the way I look at it.'

'You don't mind me chatting, do you?' Keeling said.

'Of course not.'

'Only Mr Patterson said I shouldn't cos some people don't like it.'

'Oh, I like a chat.'

'Yes, so do I.'

'We'd better find somewhere for lunch, I suppose, at some point. I wonder if there'd be somewhere in Collingford,' Skelton said.

'I don't really know the town.'

'You'd be very welcome to join us.'

'That's very kind of you, Mr Skelton, but I've already got my dinner.' Keeling fetched his snap tin from the driver's compartment. He opened it and lifted the ham sandwiches that his wife had made fresh that morning to show he had fruit cake underneath and a bar of Dairy Milk. He had a flask of tea, too.

Skelton admired the warmth of the tea.

For a minute, neither could think of anything to say.

'I've got some snapshots of Mr Patterson's other cars,' Keeling said, 'if you'd like to see them.'

'Yes, please.'

But Edgar returned before they could get to the snapshots.

CHAPTER TWELVE

'The Murder House', Mary Dutton's house, was a mile or so outside Collingford, at a place called Farrier's Cross on the road towards Hinckley. It was a more substantial building than Skelton had imagined; a proper farmhouse, dishevelled but sturdy – with a brick extension on one side, roofed with corrugated iron.

Two distinct crowds were at the gate: the first, a mixed bunch of gawpers chatting amicably with the policeman on duty; the second, a group of fifteen or so young women, all in home-made 'Mary Dutton Defence League' sashes. The young women had discovered, as protesters often do, that there is a limit to the amount of shouting, chanting and waving you can do. They had leant their banners against the hedge and were now chatting and giggling. One was demonstrating some new dance steps she had learnt.

On the other side of the road from the gawpers and the flappers, two newspaper reporters were trying, by their indifference and the manner of their smoking, to distance themselves from the other groups in the way that professionals do when amateurs are present.

The arrival of the Daimler caused a stir. The gawpers looked, the protestors picked up their placards and banners, the reporters straightened their hats and took out their notebooks.

Edgar introduced himself and Skelton to the policeman who opened the gate to let them into the garden.

A woman with no teeth, at the front of the crowd of gawpers, asked, 'Who's that, then?'

'He told the copper he was from London,' her friend said.

'I seen his picture in the paper. He's famous.'

'Which one?'

'The skinny 'un with the glasses.'

'Who is he?'

'Can't tell you who he is but I can tell you who he i'n't.'

'Who i'n't he, then?'

'He i'n't Douglas Fairbanks, is he?'

'It's Mr Skelton,' one of the young women called from the safety of her group. 'Three cheers for Mr Skelton.' The young women cheered, and Skelton acknowledged their support with a smile and a wave of the hand.

'Have you spoken to Mary Dutton?' the journalists

asked. 'Does she have a message for our lady readers? Do you have a message for our lady readers? Did you fall in love with Hannah Dryden? Have you fallen in love with Mary Dutton? Are you upset by the thrashing Huddersfield gave Leeds United on Saturday?'

The policeman beckoned a burly-looking chap standing among the gawpers.

'What's your name?'

'Tug. People call me Tug.'

'Right, Tug, I'm putting you in charge of this gate,' the constable said. 'If you let anybody through, you'll have me to answer to.'

Tug turned to the crowd. 'You hear that? My gate now.'

The policeman, who said his name was Briggs, led the way into the kitchen. Everything was clean and tidy. The lino was patched but looked as if it had been scrubbed every day since the house was built.

Briggs had clearly made himself at home with a loaf of bread, a hunk of cheese, butter, tea things and a newspaper turned to the sports page.

'There's usually a dozen or so gawpers out there. But if you think that's a lot, you should have been here on Saturday. Fifty or sixty there was. They love a murder round here. They have to put special buses on for the Saturdays. Out of Birmingham.'

'Yes, we heard.'

'They were coming in from Coventry and all. Had to have two of us on duty to keep them orderly.'

'D'you get overtime?'

'Do we heck, if you'll pardon the French. Villa was at home for the cup match on Saturday and all. Nil-nil draw so didn't miss much. I'll put the kettle on, shall I? Is your driver all right?'

'He's got sandwiches and a flask of tea,'

'Oh, ar. Got a missus who looks after him, then?'

'Yes, indeed. Bar of Dairy Milk and everything.'

'I'm lucky if I get a glass of water with spit in it out of my missus.' Briggs' face fell as he considered the woman, then, as another thought struck him, his expression changed to one of thoughtful yearning.

'I love a Dairy Milk,' he said. 'Mind you, have you tried the Fruit and Nut?'

'I'm a Five Boys man,' Skelton said.

Edgar was fond of Charbonnel et Walker's violet creams, but he decided to keep quiet about it.

'Have you had your dinner?' Briggs asked.

'Not yet, no,' Skelton said.

'You must be starving. Help yourself to bread and cheese.'

'You're very kind.'

Skelton cut himself a doorstep and a hunk of cheese, then offered the knife to Edgar, who shook his head.

As he washed up the teapot, Briggs saw that some gawpers had found their way round to the yard at the back of the house. He tapped on the window, and at the same time, Tug appeared and chased them away.

'They can get quite nasty when they find out there's

nothing to see. Hundreds of people must have walked past this house and never given it a second glance, but just cos it's been in the paper they run special buses. It's the same house, isn't it? Dusty – that's my mate who was on with me last Saturday – he said we should splash a bit of red paint around, make as if it was blood. I don't know why you'd have blood at a poisoning, but they wouldn't think of that, would they? Just be pleased there was something to look at. I'll show you round when we've had a cuppa.'

Skelton was already looking. He'd found the little pantry with the meat safe and bins.

'Is this where the poison was found?'

'Yeah, it was up on the shelf at the back, hidden behind all them jars.'

'Very sensible. I'd imagine that if I was keeping rat poison in a house with six children running about, I'd want to keep it on a high shelf.'

Briggs joined Skelton at the pantry door. He noticed a jar of pickled onions, unscrewed the lid, popped one in his mouth and offered them. Edgar looked away. The jar was nearly empty. Skelton had to fish around but got two.

'Thanks.'

The kettle boiled.

While Briggs busied himself with the tea, Skelton and Edgar went through to the parlour. This was neater even than the kitchen. There was a table, chairs, a bench and a dresser, but no clutter or ornaments or pictures. Even the candlesticks, lamps and fire irons had gone. Edgar opened a drawer at the end of the parlour table, took it all the way out and held it up to show it was empty. They went back into the kitchen.

'Has the house been cleared?' Edgar asked.

'What?'

'There's barely anything in the pantry and the parlour looks as if nobody's ever lived in it.'

'A lot of stuff was taken away as evidence.'

'So, it's at the police station, now?'

'I expect so. Except the perishables. Obviously, you couldn't expect us to hang on to the perishables. They'd smell.'

Briggs poured the tea.

'Did you know Mary Dutton personally?' Skelton asked.

'Not really, no. I mean, I saw her around and I met her a couple of times at the Christmas parties. She used to bring the kids to them at the Victory Hall.'

'She's very worried about the children.'

'If she was that worried, she wouldn't have killed her husband, would she?'

Skelton was about to say something about the presumption of innocence but didn't want to put Briggs' back up.

'Did you know Ted?' Skelton asked.

'Oh, everybody knew Ted Dutton. And I knew his dad, of course, cos he was a sergeant at Collingford nick when I first started, before he got bumped up to inspector. Gone nearly three years. But he was poorly a long time before that. His lungs give out. Sadly missed. It's not been the same since he went.'

126

'What's different?'

'The spirit. We were Sid's lads, weren't we? You knew you'd always be looked after.'

'In what way?'

'You know. If you were in trouble, or your kids were sick or something, you know, Sid'd always have your back.'

'Financially?'

'Yeah, wonderful man. Mate of mine's house got struck by lightning. Practically had to be rebuilt, new roof cost nearly £150. But he was on the force, so Sid sorted him out. You know, out of the benevolent fund.'

Not wanting to sound too interested, Skelton sipped his tea before saying, 'And where did the money come from for the benevolent fund?'

'Oh, you know. Bring and buy sales, raffles, dances.'

'Must have been very successful to raise £150.'

'Oh, they were.'

'And there were just the two boys?'

'Eh?'

'Sid just had two sons?'

'Ted and Billy.'

'And neither of them wanted to become policemen?'

Briggs laughed. 'Billy and Ted? No. They were barmy, the pair of 'em. You know how some kids are just like their dads and others are the opposite. They were bang opposite. I mean, they were the nicest blokes you could want to meet. Both of 'em. But daredevils. One or the other had always got some great gash or a busted arm, you know, from where they'd fell out of a tree or something. I've seen the two of 'em pick a fight with a threshing machine.'

'You knew them well?'

'I was in the same class at school as Billy. Ted was a couple of years older, so I didn't know him so well. Used to see Billy down the pub sometimes but these days he's away such a lot. Goes all round the country with his HD Super 90, racing and one thing and another. He did the TT last year. You know the TT? Big motorbike thing on the Isle of Man. I don't think he won nor nothing, but he had his name in the paper. It's kept him out of trouble, anyway.'

'Was he in trouble much?' Skelton asked.

'He used to run with the Collie Boys, didn't he?'

'What's that?'

'The gang, you know. There was no real harm in it. Just a bit of rough and tumble, you know. Collie Boys against the Brummies. I mean, most of the stuff you read in the papers was made up.'

'What was that, then?'

'Eh?'

'In the papers?'

Briggs seemed astonished that Skelton didn't know the story. 'The bloke outside the Troc in Birmingham.'

'This was in the papers?'

'Oh, it's ten years ago now. Collie Boys nearly killed a bloke outside the Troc in Birmingham. The Trocadero. It's a pub.'

'And was Billy Dutton involved in that?'

'He was flash, you know.'

'Billy?'

'Dressed flash, you know. First bloke I ever knew to get a spearpoint collar. Women liked him. Carried himself. This madman just come at him. I mean, really serious. And Billy saw him off, but the bloke was one of those cocky types and didn't know when he'd had enough. So, then Billy had to get serious and all, didn't he? Same with the bloke here.'

'In Collingford?'

'In the Bull. Bloke called Stamford from the pump works goes berserk over losing a game of shove ha'penny and goes for Billy with a glass, so Billy had to sort him, didn't he? Did a bit of damage. Bit of scarring.'

'Was Billy ever arrested?'

'He was arrested in Birmingham, but he was never charged. His dad sorted it. Give him hell when he got home but he was never charged with nothing. You want to see the upstairs?'

The three bedrooms – one for the boys, one for the girls and one for the parents – had been stripped as clean as the parlour. The beds were made up but the cupboards and drawers were empty. Edgar, wanting to be thorough, got down on his hands and knees to look under a bed.

There was nothing to see except an enamel po.

The wardrobe was the sort with recesses either side of the door. It looked as empty as everything else but, on the floor, deep inside one of the recesses, Skelton found an old tweed jacket and held it up to show. It had a big tear down the back seam.

'Must be one of Ted's,' Briggs said. 'I'd better take it down the station and put it with the other evidence.'

Skelton handed it over.

The window of the main bedroom overlooked the backyard. 'What's in the outhouses?' Without waiting for an answer, Skelton took the stairs two at a time and went outside.

Briggs and Edgar joined him.

There was a lavatory, a coalhouse, and two sheds for tools and sacks of feed.

Skelton examined the sacks and found bonemeal and other fertilisers, some sort of feed supplement for chickens and a big bag marked 'Faridge's Bluestone (Copper Sulphate)'.

'What is it you're looking for?' Briggs asked.

'Do you happen to know if any of these sacks contain sheep dip?'

'Sheep dip?'

Edgar was reading the label on a rusty can of Jeyes Fluid. 'Or weedkiller?'

Briggs cottoned on. 'I can't see why she'd keep the poison in the sheds when she already had it to hand in the pantry.'

'That is, of course, assuming that Mary Dutton was the poisoner,' Skelton said.

'If you don't mind me saying so, sir, I think she'd save everybody a lot of time and fuss if she just pleaded guilty and accepted what was coming to her.'

'You're so sure she killed her husband?'

'I don't see who else could have done it.'

'Norman Bearcroft is fairly convinced she's innocent, and so are all the people who contributed to her defence fund, and the journalists who write for the *Daily Herald*, and their readers.'

'Yeah, well, there's always some, i'n't there?'

Back in the kitchen, Briggs poured a second cup of tea and Skelton got his pipe out. Edgar flicked through the paper that Briggs had been reading and came to a picture of Mary.

'She looks such a sweet little thing, don't she?' Briggs said. 'Wouldn't hurt a fly. You don't know the half of it, though. She's not from round here, you know. She's from Shrewsbury.'

'I don't quite see the significance . . .'

'Jessie never took to her.'

'Ted's mother? Why not?'

'You know . . . she didn't fit in.'

'Because she was from Shrewsbury?'

'That and the conniving. That's what really got on their nerves.'

'Conniving?'

'Oh, yes. Mary Cross is a conniving little madam. She knew how to get her way, didn't she? I mean, you know, we've all heard about Shrewsbury women, haven't we?'

'No, I don't think I have.'

'And you don't want to. Take it from me. Make your hair curl.'

There was a ruckus outside. Briggs went through to the parlour and looked out of the window. A boy, no more than seven or eight, was standing perilously on a high branch of a beech tree, singing 'Bye Bye Blackbird'. The gawpers, the protesters and even the reporters seemed to be enjoying the performance.

'I'd better see about that,' Briggs said.

He went to the front door and shouted to the man called Tug: 'What's going on?'

'I caught him trying to crawl through the hedge,' Tug said, 'so I put him up there to keep him out of trouble.'

'Is he quite safe?' Skelton asked.

'Course not. I wouldn't have put him up there if he was.'

In the car on the way back to New Street, Skelton pulled a bag of sweets from his pocket and offered them to Edgar.

'What are they?'

'Everton Mints.'

'Where did you get them?'

'Ted Dutton's jacket I found in the wardrobe. I sneaked them out when Constable Briggs wasn't looking.'

Skelton took one and sniffed it.

'How long d'you think they've been there?' Edgar asked.

'The packet looks newish and there's no traces of mould or fluff. I don't think I ever had an Everton Mint.'

'Please don't.'

Skelton popped it into his mouth and sucked.

'It is like a mint humbug,' Skelton said, 'but then, when you bite, you get a completely different change of texture.'

'You're eating a dead man's mint.'

'I'm not sure I like it much.'

'It's disgusting.'

'It's the toffee centre. It's all wrong. The hard mint and the soft toffee are two entirely different sensations, aren't they? This is a sweet that can't make up its mind. Trying to offer the best of both worlds. Are you sure you don't want one?'

Edgar turned his head and stuck it a long way out of the window.

CHAPTER THIRTEEN

Wednesday 30th January, 1929

My dear cousin Arthur,
The bird life in Brannock Woods is quite magnificent, particularly over by the pond across the way. I must start making a list. Just today I have seen blue and great tits, greenfinches, goldfinches, blackbirds, robins, sparrows, jays, a reed bunting, mallards, teal, tufted duck, shoveler, lapwing, coots and probably six or seven other kinds that I cannot remember. I even saw what I thought might have been a waxwing, but when I looked it up this seemed unlikely. Norah said she thought it was a starling. I told her it definitely had

a crest. She said starlings sometimes have crests, but I do not think this is right. The starling in my book does not have a crest. Norah says they only show their crests when they are angry; the one in the book must be in a good mood. These disagreements usually blow over in the end.

This last Monday our door-knocking took us to the east of Collingford and to Summers Hill, which, as you know, is where Jessie Dutton, mother of the deceased, lives.

Her house has its own road going up to it, a carriage drive I suppose you'd call it. It is a very grand house indeed, or at least it is compared to the other houses in Collingford. It is cream-coloured, with three stories if you include the dormer windows at the top, and columns at the porch.

We pulled the bell. It did not seem to work, or if it did work the bell was at the back of the house somewhere and could not be heard from the front. I was all for leaving, but Norah said we should have a look around the back and was off up the side passage before I had a chance to argue. The back garden was beautifully kept. At the top, a neat arrangement of cinder paths divided off the flower borders – no flowers at this time of year, of course. Down at the bottom there was a vegetable patch and beyond that fruit trees and blackcurrant bushes from which a leather-aproned gardener appeared, pushing a wheelbarrow.

He didn't seem unfriendly. Norah apologised for troubling him and said we did not seem to get any answer from the bell on the front door. He told us that the cook and the maid were probably off somewhere gossiping and had not heard. He rapped hard on the back door to summon Minnie, a maid properly turned out in a black dress, white apron and cap. We told her our business. She said she did not think the mistress would be interested, but she would ask anyway and went off. A minute later she came back and told us that her mistress did wish to speak with us after all. She showed us into a parlour – a drawing room it would probably be called in this sort of house – which looked just like Great Auntie Flo's parlour in Leeds where you had to keep stock-still for fear of snagging on a bit of lace and bringing all sorts of china dogs and tinkly glass ornaments crashing to the ground, except this one was even more stuffy, if you can imagine that such a thing could be possible. There was a huge fire in the grate and the big velvet curtains were drawn, and there was another thick curtain over the door with a draught excluder at the bottom that the 'mistress' asked us to replace as soon as Minnie had left.

The 'mistress' was dressed all in black bombazine and some of the framed photographs on the sideboard had black ribbon tied around them. We introduced ourselves and she, with a sort of wounded defiance, announced that she was Jessie Dutton, the mother of

Ted Dutton 'whose murder you have probably read about in the newspaper'.

So, there you have it. We have been here for not yet a fortnight and we've met the children and were sitting in the drawing room of Ted Dutton's mother.

She might once have been beautiful. Norah agrees with this and says you can see it in her eyes and in the bones of her face. She has good posture and sat very upright, very dignified. There was a trace of Birmingham in her accent, but she spoke so slowly and so precisely that it all but disappeared.

News of our meeting at the Methodist chapel had reached her, she said, and although she was not sure of our methods, in general the reports had been favourable, and this was why she had invited us in. Other door knockers – particularly religious ones – are given short shrift, she told us. Worst of all, she said, she had been having a lot of trouble from newspaper reporters who had taken to trampling the front garden and trying to peek through the windows. So persistent had they been that she had had to call the police who had threatened dire consequences if they troubled her any more.

The maid brought in tea things which included some very small cakes covered in pink icing.

Mrs Dutton asked how well we knew the Methodist minister and I told her that we had met him only the previous week so barely knew him at all. She told me he was not a compassionate man, took the tiniest bite out of one of the little cakes, pulled a disgusted face and flung the rest of the cake into the fire. I found them delicious.

Then she went through all the other clergymen in town starting with the vicar at St John's, the church by the Market Square. I told her I had not had the pleasure of meeting him. She said she doubted whether there could be any pleasure in such an encounter, the Reverend Eales was a selfish man who thought more of his dogs than he did of his parishioners. I asked what kind of dogs they were. She said she didn't know the name of the breed but that they were of medium size and very ugly.

In the same vein she told me that the Congregationalist minister was so ignorant of religious matters that he barely knew his New Testament from his Old and that the Baptist church smelt strongly of ammonia.

We thus realised that she is of an unfortunate breed we encounter everywhere we go on our mission. Some people, especially if they have a little more money than their neighbours or an inflated sense of their own importance, believe that ministers of the Church and possibly God himself should afford them preferential treatment. If they do not receive it, they become vindictive.

This sometimes, but not always, goes hand in hand with a tendency to expect other forms of attention from the clergy. A good preacher, you see, can excite a religious fervour in a congregation and there are those – thankfully few in number – who confuse this with baser passions.

Once, in Newbury, a large lady called Winifred pressed me against the glass of a Sunday school door and asked whether I had urges. Luckily, Norah chose that moment to put in an appearance, without which I fear my only escape would have been violently to push the woman away or perhaps even, God forbid, to strike her. Once again, when these individuals do not receive the attention they think they deserve, they become vindictive.

Jessie Dutton is certainly of a religious turn of mind. I was sitting next to a little glass-fronted bookcase and glanced at the titles. *The Pilgrim's Progress* was there, Charles Kingsley's *Town and Country Sermons*, Catherine Booth's *Papers on Aggressive Christianity*, many other works of a similar nature and three or four Bibles in various bindings. She had her scriptures by heart. Talking about what she expected from a minister of God, for instance, she was able to recite Malachi 2:6–7, which even I had trouble identifying. You find three or four people in every congregation who have the Psalms by heart and often long passages of the New Testament, but there can't be three or four people in the entire country who have learnt the Book of Malachi. Although I did once come across a man who could recite the Book of Nahum backwards. He said he'd learnt it for a bet. I asked how much. He said five shillings. I asked how long it had taken him. He said about four months. I suggested that, if he had devoted four months of his life to some other enterprise, he could possibly have made a great deal more than five shillings. He said he had never thought of it like that.

Jessie Dutton asked me what I thought of the Catholics. I told her that I had met some good ones and some confused ones, and that I feared that an over-strict dependence on dogma could sometimes get in the way of natural Christianity. She asked me whether I thought, when the Catholics go to confession, it really wipes the slate clean in the way that they say it does.

I said I thought it depended on what was in the heart and not what was in the words, but that sometimes the tongue has to speak – or even better to sing – the words before the heart can know its own truth.

She seemed to like that. We talked more – in general terms – about sin and redemption. It would be very fanciful indeed for you, dear cousin, to imagine that her interest in these matters suggests that she has some great sin, possibly connected with the death of her son, weighing on her conscience, and she certainly gave no indication that her interest in these matters was anything other than theological. We certainly did not press her to talk about Mary Dutton and the supposed 'murder'. I know that for your purposes it would have been useful if we had done, but one cannot, as I'm sure you will understand, force these things.

After half an hour or so, she said she was tired, so we made our goodbyes.

I said that I would let her know when we were having another meeting and that she would always be welcome. She said that she had enjoyed our chat.

Afterwards, Norah made two pertinent observations. The first was that although, on the sideboard, there were several framed photographs, presumably of Sid, Ted and Billy, nobody in any of the photographs was smiling. I do not set great store by this because they all looked to me as if they had been taken in a photographer's studio. I have only been in a such a place once in my life and the proprietor's insistence that I smile made me more melancholic than I ever remember feeling.

Norah's second observation was that Mrs Dutton was drunk. She thought that she could smell it. She has a better sense of smell than I do. She said that she has known people in the past who speak slowly and with precision – just as Mrs Dutton had been doing – so as not to slur their words. When I thought over the matter, I realised that Norah might well have been right.

Did I mention by the way that we are having trouble with our old Rover Sunbeam? On the way from

Evesham to Collingford it developed some steering problems. Closer inspection revealed worn bearings in the rear-end axle differential. I can probably do the repairs myself, but the spare parts could cost between fifteen and twenty-five shillings. I might also need to purchase some extra tools, but I am sure it would still be cheaper than getting the repairs done at a garage.

Ah, well. These things are sent to try us and I'm sure the Lord will provide.

It is half past ten now. Norah has already turned in and I fear I am keeping her awake with the scratching of my pen so . . .

I am ever yours faithfully in the joy of Jesus,
Alan

CHAPTER FOURTEEN

It had been a cold January, but the start of February was almost balmy. Warm enough anyway to remind you of the almost unimaginable days of last September, when you could walk about without scarf or coat and not for a moment hanker for indoors.

Skelton noticed in the local paper that there was a Greta Garbo film showing in Slough. He had decided long ago that, because her grandfather was Swedish, Mila was obliged to like Garbo on the grounds that she was a fellow countrywoman. When Mila protested that she had no feelings for her one way or the other, Skelton would say, 'Yes, you do like her. You know you do.' It was one of their many, complicated jokes.

They didn't often go to the pictures, so it always seemed a treat. They took the Wolseley and parked on the High Street.

A crowd had gathered outside the Crown. Ronald Parker-Ellis, local MP and Skelton's neighbour, a Conservative, was making a speech. He had, Skelton assumed, thought that Saturday night was the time he'd be most likely to get an audience of the new voters, the 'flappers', but the young men and women passing, on their way to a dance at the Drill Hall barely gave him a second glance, so he had to make do with the usual crowd of Tory diehards wearing their rosettes, and a couple of old men from the pub.

Parker-Ellis fancied himself as a skilled raconteur with a ready wit. He wasn't. He was a self-important and ill-informed bore. He had two anecdotes, both inconsequential, both about golf, and both trotted out, word for word, at the drop of a hat, in speeches, at parties and during meetings. And the most remarkable evidence of his self-centredness was that he had never once noticed, when he reached the 'punchline' that, though his own laughs were hearty, his listeners could barely manage a few embarrassed snorts. In the previous year, he'd been part of some delegation to meet Mr Mussolini in Italy and no doubt believed that Il Duce still chuckled every time he remembered the 'wonderful story' about the sliced ball bouncing off the tree at the fifteenth hole.

Parker-Ellis was wearing a distinctive homburg hat, taller than usual – almost the height of a topper – with a curly brim. A group of lads started chanting, 'Big black hat, big black hat,' which they thought was funny. After the twentieth or thirtieth repetition, Skelton thought it was funny, too, especially when Parker-Ellis fingered his hat, nervously calculating the most politically advantageous course of action. If he took it off would it make him more popular with the younger voters or would it make him seem a weakling, at the beck and call of the mob?

Eventually a policeman, that stout defender of democracy, moved the lads on. They went without a fuss, having spotted a proselytising vegetarian who often set up his soapbox outside the butchers and wore tweeds and a beard. The lads joined his crowd and started chanting, 'Big brown beard, big brown beard.' Parker-Ellis spotted Skelton in the crowd.

'And we are indeed privileged to have among us, ladies and gentlemen, Mr Arthur Skelton,' he said, 'who, I'm sure you know, has recently distinguished the legal profession by his masterful advocacy during a much-publicised case which earned him the acclaim of the nation and the soubriquet' – slight snort of not-quite laughter – '"The Latter-Day Galahad". Perhaps you'd like to join me, Mr Skelton, and enlighten these ladies and gentlemen with the benefits of your understanding of some of the problems that face our constituency and our great nation.'

Parker-Ellis' portly cohorts with their big blue rosettes were applauding, pushing Skelton forward. This was barefaced cheek. He was damned if he was going to endorse Parker-Ellis.

It did occur to him to take up the offer, go up and say what he really thought about the constituency and the country, except that would require the sort of coherent opinions that he could not summon, not at a moment's notice, anyway. And he had Mila to think of, too. As a good, if sometimes sullen, neighbour, she had put up with Parker-Ellis in her drawing room and endured glasses of sherry in his, but if Skelton went up on those hustings and appeared to support the Tories, he knew she'd do for him with the coal hammer.

Mila saved the day. In a voice louder than the cheering crowd – God, she had a pair of lungs on her – she proclaimed, 'My husband has promised to take me to see Greta Garbo, and I don't want to risk being one second late.'

This got a big cheer. Everybody knew that Garbo took priority over politics; and the idea that The Latter-Day Galahad was ruled by a bossy wife was marvellously entertaining.

Skelton gave a theatrical eyes-to-heaven – 'You see what I have to put up with' – and allowed Mila to take him by the arm and drag him away.

'He made me think of Miss Pennington,' Mila said when they were clear. Miss Pennington had been Mila's boss at the hospital in Manchester, a terrifying woman who'd been arrested in '05 along with Annie Kenney and Christabel Pankhurst for 'spitting at a policeman' – she'd actually kicked the copper in the testicles, but the law didn't want that made public – outside the Free Trade Hall.

'What about Miss Pennington?' Skelton asked.

'Something she used to say when she had to deal with people like Parker-Ellis.'

'What was that?'

'She used to say,' Mila did an impersonation of Miss Pennington's cultivated hoot, '"Ladies, it would appear we are campaigning for the wrong thing. It's not the vote we should be demanding, it's guns."'

Just as Skelton was preparing to leave the house on the Monday morning, there was a ring at the doorbell. It was Parker-Ellis standing there with a fixed smile on his face, just as if he was welcome.

'Good morning, Skelton, glad to have found you're still here.'

Skelton checked his lines of escape. 'I catch the 8.32 into town, so . . .'

'Yes. I'm on my way to a constituency meeting in Maidenhead.' Parker-Ellis was wearing his big black hat and a fur-lined Ulster. 'My driver's outside. We could give you a lift to the station, if you like. I wonder if I might come in for a moment?'

'Yes, of course.'

Skelton took him into the drawing room. It was a calculated move. The fire was never lit in there until the children came home from school. The alternative was to take him into the dining room, but Mila was finishing her breakfast in there with a butter knife in her hand which she would not be afraid to use.

'It's about these houses,' Parker-Ellis said. 'You must have heard. Old Tommy Northwood's sold half his farm to Tutton and Grant as building land.'

'I thought that had all been thrown out by the county council eighteen months ago.'

'And now the decision's been reversed. Have you seen the plans?'

'No.'

'An "estate" they call it. Villas. Tudor revival. Turn the whole place into Wembley Park. If we get enough local people to lodge complaints, I'm sure we could get it stopped.'

'Isn't there . . . ?'

'Yes, I do realise there's a housing shortage, particularly for lower paid workers, but not here. There's no shortage here. Lower paid workers don't want homes here. There's no work. No, they want homes in Reading or . . . the trading estate thingy in Slough. No, these are homes for Mr and Mrs Buggins, clerks and drapers and coal merchants.'

'Gosh I'm going to miss my train,' Skelton said, and began to usher the politician towards the front door. 'I won't take up your kind offer of a lift. It'll be much quicker to take the shortcut down Brickett's Path.'

'I take it then I'll have your support in opposing this "estate"?'

'I can see it's a matter that needs to be taken very, very seriously.'

Skelton had manoeuvred him back into the hall and had a hand on the latch when Parker-Ellis said, 'Oh, and one other thing.'

'Yes?'

'These riots are very worrying.'

'Which riots.'

'The women.'

'The women?'

'The women rioting about your woman. The murder woman.'

'Mary Dutton.'

'Exactly. Isn't there anything you can do?'

Skelton could have mentioned that he'd seen the 'rioters' with his own eyes and found them quite charming but life's too short.

'I'll give the matter my closest attention,' he said. 'Must dash.'

He ran towards Brickett's Path.

CHAPTER FIFTEEN

Saturday 9th February, 1929

My dear cousin Arthur,
Your contribution to the repairs of the Rover Sunbeam was very gratefully received. After many enquiries, I discovered that, rather than going to Birmingham for the spare parts, I would be better to go direct to the Sunbeam factory itself, in Wolverhampton. It was quite an adventure, involving as it did two buses, a train and another bus and taking the best part of three hours, but I did get into one or two very interesting conversations. One of the bus conductors told me a lot about racing

pigeons I did not know before. A man at a bus stop said the tides in Morecambe Bay come in faster than a man on a galloping horse and many people, walking across the sands, have been engulfed by the advancing waters and drowned. I said, 'Like Pharaoh's army in the Red Sea,' and he laughed a lot at that even though I meant it more as a pertinent observation than any sort of joke. To be honest, I still cannot see what was funny about it, but he did seem a little bit simple-minded, poor soul.

The people at the Sunbeam factory could not have been more helpful. Though they stopped making that model not long after the war, they managed to sort out the parts I required and charged me next to nothing. I have quite a lot of change left over from the money you so kindly sent me which I will happily return to you should you so wish.

Otherwise I will put it towards the general work of the mission and bless your generosity.

I was two days under the van making everything good again, with an old eiderdown on the ground and a couple of Tilley lamps so as I could keep going after dark. It would have gone quicker except one of the parts didn't seem to bed properly and I was the longest time filing it and fitting it, filing it and fitting it, over and over until it properly bolted down. The time spent was well worth it, though. We gave her a test drive and she ran sweet as a nut and had lost all the uncertainty in the steering that had previously caused us to slow down to a crawl and hold our breaths waiting for a crash every time we turned a tight corner. Bowling along, we were, after we'd got used to it.

We were out quite a while and, on the way back, long after darkness had fallen, we came across a very amenable-looking pub called The Flag and stopped to let the vibrations in our bones die down a little. The pub is run by a tiny little scrap of a man called Jack Gorin. There was a good crowd in there. After a while, Norah got on the piano and we sang, mostly non-religious songs but working some of the religious ones in as well. As usual, it was the comedy songs they liked the most. 'When Father Papered the Parlour You Couldn't See Pa for Paste' and 'Don't Play Marbles with Grandad's Glass Eye, He Needs it to Look for a Job'. We usually find that if you do one of them, followed by a sentimental one like 'That Old Irish Mother of Mine' or 'Alice Blue Gown', followed by a wartime one, 'Tipperary', or 'Sister Susie's Sewing Shirts For Soldiers', they're usually more than ready for 'The Old Rugged Cross' or 'What a Friend We Have in Jesus'.

Jack Gorin was pleased as punch that we had put on such a rattling good entertainment and asked if we could come back another time. We said we would be delighted, and Norah asked if he knew of some sort of hall – a village hall or some such – where we could hold regular meetings of the mission. As you know, borrowing a chapel to do some preaching, like we did with the Methodists, is all well and good but the oversight of the resident minister can be oppressive. Jack Gorin took us through the back of the pub and showed us there was a row of good solid brick stables out there as well as a huge old barn, unused. He said he used to run dances in there at one time and St Michael's, a neighbouring church, had used it for jumble sales and the like when their own church hall lost its roof but now it went unused for the most part, especially at this time of year because if you served drinks in there they would most likely come out as ice lollies. There was a stove at either end, but he said both were temperamental and given to smoking.

It looked just the job for our purposes, and I do have some knowledge of the ways of stoves. Sometimes it is just a question of adjusting the chimney. I remember our dad having trouble with the stove in the rehearsal room at the Pavilion Theatre in Rhyl. He said it was a downdraught that was doing it, so he made a little cowl out of scrap metal to put at the top of the chimney. It worked a treat and I am sure that I could make something very similar for these ones. At the ironmonger's I'd also noticed they'd got oil heaters, 12s 6d for the small and 26s 6d for the large, and I thought I could use some of the money you kindly donated to buy a couple of those and a few cans of Royal Daylight Oil.

Jack Gorin asked if I had any objection to people drinking before, after or during the meeting. I said that I would draw the line at during because it could be a distraction if people were rattling bottles of brown ale through the songs and sermons but that I had no objection before or after. He seemed surprised at this because in his experience religious people, excepting the Catholics, are quite down on drink. I told him my thoughts on the matter. Drink can bring anger and disaster, but for every man I've seen fighting drunk or miserable drunk, I've seen a hundred happy and companionable. It can bring misery; it can bring joy. In that respect it's no different from most other things you come across in this life: marriage, work, knowledge etc. It makes no sense to ban drink while, at the same time, leaving people to court disaster and misery by getting married or studying the works of Schopenhauer.

We had our first meeting in the barn on Wednesday – more of which in a moment. Jessie Dutton came in her car, a bull-nose Morris Cowley driven by her gardener whose name, we have learnt, is Mr Gough.

The following day we went for tea at Jessie's house.

She reminds me of the elderly actresses Dad used to have to look after when they were at the Pavilion Theatre. She talks in the same slow, exaggerated way and everything she speaks of is either a great tragedy or a great delight. There is nothing in between. She seems to have no understanding of normal. Even her grieving, with the bombazine, the drawn curtains, the black ribbon around the photographs and the hushed tones when she speaks of the departed, seems to be part of an act. I am not suggesting that she is not really grieving, only that, perhaps, she does not know how to express emotion like other people and therefore has to fall back on an impersonation.

Norah is sure that she is drunk all the time. I pointed out that she did not have a drink at The Flag even when it was offered to her. Norah said that means nothing. Secret drinkers are the worst. I hope that she is wrong but do fear otherwise.

Perhaps the most significant information from your point of view is that Jessie Dutton will not speak the name of Mary Dutton but refers to her merely as 'The Murderess'. Her conviction that Mary killed Ted is unshakeable. She is also convinced that Mary killed Sid, her late husband. You mentioned that Mary nursed her father-in-law at the end of his life.

Jessie's version of the story is that she 'stole' Sid, then 'worked her way with him' to get him to change his will so that the entire inheritance – which had originally been split between his two sons – would now all go to Ted. Then, before Sid could change his mind, she poisoned him. And then she poisoned Ted so that the inheritance would be hers.

As soon as Ted died, she knew he had been poisoned because of what had happened to Sid, but she was sick and could do nothing but brood and brood and brood, then, on the day of the funeral, when she could stand it no more, she sent her maid Minnie to the police station.

I said that I had read in the newspaper that it was the lady who laid out the body – a Mrs Curtis whom we have not met but will seek out if you think it might be useful – who had alerted the police. She confessed that was an untruth which she had asked Mrs Curtis and the police to maintain. I asked how she could possibly have got the police to collude in such a fabrication and she said, 'People around here do what I tell them.'

Norah wondered why she had found it necessary to conceal the truth. Jessie said that she didn't want anybody to know that she suspected Mary of poisoning Sid as well as Ted. Norah asked why not. Because they'd want to prove it by digging up Sid's body and she doesn't want his bones being disturbed. She wants him left in peace. And it doesn't matter because Mary is going to hang anyway. It doesn't matter whether she hangs for one murder or two so long as she hangs.

I tried to tell her that forgiveness is central to the Christian message and she asked me whether Christ forgave Satan in the wilderness.

She gave us a lovely tea, though. We had three sorts

of sandwich (egg, ham and cheese), a plum cake and some ginger things that weren't quite cakes and weren't quite biscuits.

Our first meeting at the barn was a thumping success. We had not expected a big turnout seeing as it was our first so were pleasantly surprised to find the room more than half full, which, by Norah's calculation, would be forty or fifty people. A six o'clock start time was clearly bang on the button for Collingford; late enough for people to have finished work but still early enough for children to come.

I'd been up on the roof earlier fixing the little cowls to the chimneys and they worked a treat. We had both stoves on the go and the two paraffin heaters, but the stoves were so efficient that after a bit the heaters were deemed surplus to requirements and extinguished. Warm as toast it was and made even warmer by the vigour of the singing. We ran through all the usuals, but the highlight for Norah and I was when I asked, as I usually do, whether anyone had anything particular they wanted to say or to sing to the rest of the congregation and two brothers, both in their fifties or sixties and both from South Wales, stood up and sang 'Myfanwy' in beautiful two-part harmony. I cried my eyes out and I am not ashamed to say so because so did everybody else in that barn. It is a glorious example of how a song does not have to have religious words to do the work of God.

When there is some warmth in the sun, like there has been today, it is very easy to start thinking that winter is over, leave your scarf at home and breathe a little more easily. But it often happens like that in February, doesn't it? Then a week later you have snow and ice all over again. I like to think that this is proof that the Almighty has a sense of humour. I imagine Him delivering the sunshine and warmth and then, when He delivers the snow, peeking through the snow clouds, shouting 'Fooled you' and laughing His blessed head off.

I am ever yours faithfully in the joy of Jesus,
Alan

As well as Alan's report, the post bought a rather snide letter from Dr Russell, the pathologist who had performed the post-mortem on Ted. Edgar had written to him asking whether it was possible to be sure that rat poison was the source of the arsenic rather than, say, sheep dip or weedkiller.

Dr Russell pointed out that if incautious use of sheep dip could have fatal consequences then half the populations of Australia and New Zealand would be dead or dying. Similarly weedkiller – some brands of which do indeed contain arsenic – was used in practically every English garden and on every farm. Yet, strange to relate, gardeners and farmers are not dropping like flies and many of them manage to live long and active lives.

Furthermore, the poison in Ted Dutton's body had been administered in initially small but gradually increasing doses over a period of time, possibly three months or more. Sheep are dipped only once or twice a year.

Most damning of all was the information that sheep dip is a mixture of chemicals, one of which is arsenic. But sixty-five per cent of the mixture is sulphur. Further analysis of Ted Dutton's body had revealed no abnormal quantities of sulphur.

Dr Russell concluded that, although he could not confirm that rat poison *was* the source of the arsenic, he could with great certainty say that it *was not* sheep dip.

Skelton stood by his window, opened it to the February air and shouted in a voice loud enough for the whole of London to hear, 'Oh, bugger.'

CHAPTER SIXTEEN

Skelton's dreams were geometric. That was the only way he could describe them. They never seemed to be about identifiable people or creatures. They were never the sort of dreams you could tell people about. Not the – 'I was at a party, and Miss Bassett who made hats was there and I noticed her feet, which were encased in cake mixture, weren't touching the floor' – sort of dreams.

The closest he'd ever got to describing it – and he'd only ever tried twice – was that they were generalised emotions, worries and anxieties in different arrangements, sometimes making patterns and sometimes warring with each other. The odd thing was that when he woke up, he could nearly always identify at least one of the things that the worries were related to.

More and more, since he'd taken on the Mary Dutton case, it was Elsie Grace. He didn't hear the animal howl in his sleep, but he felt the pain that had provoked it.

After that there was no more sleeping. He looked at the luminous hands of the alarm clock when it was twenty past two and again when it was half past, then looked again every twenty minutes or so until it was ten to four.

He made himself think about cold rice pudding with tinned pineapple.

Mila slept as if anaesthetised. In novels, sleeping women always look vulnerable and innocent. Mila looked cunning, as if she was planning to overthrow something or other; the monarchy, capitalism, organised religion. One day she would run off to some remote land in Africa or South America, lead a revolution against an oppressor, be acclaimed supreme ruler and wear live leopards as shoes, the better to run very fast indeed. And she would forget all about the barrister she left behind in Berkshire.

In *Daphne, or the Seven Temples of Rapture*, one of the filthy books he'd read while preparing the Dryden case, there were two poisonings, one that failed and one that, by chance, turned out to be more successful than intended. In the first, a husband, suspecting that his wife was about to attend an orgy, poisoned her underthings. Her return home, alive and well, supplied all the proof he needed that she had indeed attended an orgy for *she had not bothered to wear her underthings*. In the second, a wife poisons her husband and inadvertently, but satisfyingly, also kills four of his lovers who 'supped at his spring of engenderment'.

If he didn't get up and force himself to think of something else, he'd have a sore spot the following day where he'd been chewing the inside of his cheek.

Mila stirred as he got out of bed.

'Where are you going?'

'Something I need to check in some case notes,' he said.

'You work too hard.'

'I work exactly the right amount.'

CHAPTER SEVENTEEN

Alan had been right about snow coming. It snowed worse than it had since 1895; six feet of it on Dartmoor. Some parts of the country had 30 degrees of frost.

For four days Lambourn was cut off; no post, no milk, no trains or school for the children.

Mrs Bartram struggled heroically over from her cottage every day, boiled snow to make tea when the pipes froze and did clever things with packets and tins to keep them fed. She also loaned Skelton some choice items from her small selection of novels when he ran out of things to read, with the result that he developed an unhealthy taste for the works of Elinor Glyn.

Dorothy, the 'nanny', lived right over on Lambourn Edge

and was even more cut off than they were, so it was up to Skelton and Mila to keep the children clean and entertained.

On the first day of isolation, Skelton had spent most of the morning trying to put a telephone call through to London to make sure the courts had all shut up shop and the cases he was supposed to be working on (a theft and a very dull divorce) had been postponed. After two hours of keeping his temper with operators, he at last managed to get through to some junior official at the Old Bailey at which point the line went dead. Though he shouted at the apparatus and jiggled various parts of it, there was no further communication.

The electricity died, too. This was no surprise. It crept into the house along a fragile wire slung between the neighbouring houses. The lights would flicker when the bread van drove past. Mila dug out candles and oil lamps, and he lit a huge fire in the drawing room, hoping the weather would break for the coalman to get through before they ran out.

He played Ludo with the children, allowed them to dress him up like a Red Indian, helped them cut out the pieces for a toy theatre they'd been given for Christmas and never opened, and stole their plasticine to block the gaps in the window frames. He made snowmen with them, too, in the garden, and cleared a path to the road knowing it was a pointless exercise because the road itself was impassable.

Mila got cabin fever and kicked the furniture. She

164

pretended to remember the nonchalant way they treated much heavier snowfalls and much colder temperatures in Sweden where she had, as a child, visited her grandparents: this despite the fact that – as Skelton very well knew – she'd only ever been there in the summer.

The children and Mrs Bartram kept out of her way, so she turned her irritability mostly on Skelton.

'Why are you wearing two pairs of socks?' she asked.

'To keep my feet warm.'

'You have thick socks. Why don't you wear one pair of thick socks instead of two pairs of thin?'

'Because two thin pairs keep your feet warmer than one thick pair.'

'Don't be ridiculous.'

'I'm not being ridiculous. The trick is to trap air between the skin and the cold, and many layers do that better than a single layer.'

'Who says?'

'Scott of the Antarctic.'

'And what happened to him?'

'Roald Amundsen said the same thing.'

'Who to?'

'And many scientists have concurred.'

'Name them. You see, you say these things with no evidence and still have the presumption to call yourself a lawyer. Why don't you walk around the place in nine shirts?'

'I might do that.'

'And then go and boil your head.'

On the Wednesday, it brightened up a bit and Mila decided to take the children sledding on Pinkney's Hill. There had been no more than a light dusting of snow in the previous year, so the sled had lain unused in the garden shed, rusting. Skelton dug a path to the shed, forced the door open, untangled the sled from the garden hose and had a go at it with oil and sandpaper until the runners looked as if they might run again.

There were no other sledders on the hill.

'We've got the world to ourselves,' Lawrence said.

'This is because the rest of the world consists of sensible people who know better than to come out in weather like this,' his dad replied.

Skelton took the first run with Elizabeth in front. He took it carefully, braking every few yards with his foot to keep the speed down. Elizabeth complained. She wanted to go fast.

Then Elizabeth took the sled back up the hill while Skelton stayed at the bottom 'to catch people if they fall'.

Mila didn't use her feet as a brake. She and Lawrence flew past Skelton, hit the snowdrift at the bottom of the hill and vanished, completely buried. Skelton ran towards them, waiting for the snow to turn red but knowing there's no blood with a broken neck. They emerged before he got to them, laughing and ran back up the hill to do it again.

'I'm not sure Elizabeth would want to go quite so fast,' Skelton shouted after them.

'Oh yes, she would,' Mila shouted back.

In the event, nobody died, but on the way home, as the sun set in a sky of gaudy blues and oranges, Mila wondered whether the reservoir at Lambourn Edge would be frozen hard enough for skating, and Skelton wondered whether the death of a whole family would attract a discount at the undertaker's.

The following day, the march to Lambourn Edge would have challenged Amundsen. When they got there, Skelton vigilantly poked at the ice with a stick, looking for weak spots, then noticed that Mila was already executing figures of eight and neat pirouettes like a dancer on a music box. She took Elizabeth's hands and skated backwards, shouting encouragement.

'Can you show me, Dad?' Lawrence asked.

'No, son. I can't do it myself.'

'Really?'

'When I were a lad,' he said in his best Hunslet, 'we were too poor to have ice.'

Elizabeth was a natural. Within minutes she could skate on her own, and seemed to have mastered the more important skill, when she fell, of falling neatly on her bottom instead of her face. Lawrence, too, when it was his turn, made it look easy enough for Skelton to want a go. He had no skates but remembered making ice slides in the playground at school and reckoned it couldn't be any more difficult than staying upright between the coke heap and the toilets. Not bothering with the skates, he ventured out in his boots. He fell immediately, backwards, skull first, and spend the rest of the morning wondering whether the subsequent dizziness counted as concussion, in which case could the head injury merit a visit to the doctor?

It thawed on the Friday, thankfully without any of the pipes bursting, and by the Saturday it was positively balmy. After lunch, they went for a walk along Brickett's Path to the woods and round down the lanes. Skelton tried to tell the children the names of the trees, but they knew more about it than he did, so he told them about his childhood in Leeds, and they made fun, reciting the stories they'd heard a thousand times before, word for word, along with him.

There was a Lagonda parked near Tommy Northwood's farm. Lawrence was impressed.

Skelton told him about the Daimler they'd had in Birmingham.

'Was it fun to drive?' Lawrence asked, and Skelton had to tell him he hadn't actually driven it himself and knew that, as a result, his son thought less of him.

They were surprised to see that work had already begun on the housing estate Parker-Ellis had been complaining about. Areas had been marked out with string and four men in heavy greatcoats and boots stood around a trestle table looking at plans.

'Has it occurred to you that when they build this housing estate there's a very good chance the village will get a connection to the central electricity thingy?' Skelton said. They were still cut off at home. The central electricity thingy, he'd heard, provided an uninterrupted flow of the stuff in quantities sufficient to light Blackpool.

'And even better,' Skelton said, 'sewers.'

Mila had, since her schooldays, campaigned for adequate housing for the poor, providing ample light, clean air and effective sanitation, never suspecting that one day she'd pine for such things herself.

'What about gas?' she asked.

'Don't ask for the moon.'

They walked down the hill to the little stream that ran through the valley. It was running free now, with just a little ice clinging to the banks. They stopped at a clearing in the woods that the children called, for reasons lost to history, the Radishes. The clearing looked as if, at some time or other, it had been a garden, although the house to which the garden belonged was long gone. There was still a wall, though, some fruit trees and a mass of rhododendrons. Here the children did the Radish Run; from the bridge, up to the crab-apple tree that bent over the stream, jump across to the wall, run along the top of the wall, grab hold of the nearest branch of the oak and swing back to the bridge.

'Are you sure that wall is safe? It's just that frost can wreak havoc with the mortar. If it fell it could crush them.'

'It will only crush them if they are underneath it. They are running along the top of it. They would collapse with it and suffer a broken leg or arm, but they would not be crushed.'

The surveyors or architects or whoever they were came near, walking around the boundaries of the new development and nodded a hello.

'I think I know that man,' Mila said, when they were gone.

'Which one?'

'The tall one with the moustache. He used to be one of my patients during the war. Eliot Dean.'

They climbed a little way up the bank to where they could see.

'He's walking remarkably well,' Mila said.

'Shouldn't he be?'

'He has a prosthetic leg.'

'Has he? You'd never know. He walks better than I do.'

'I think I might go over and say hello.'

'Yes, of course.'

Skelton waited with the children, who he knew would do the Radish Run until the end of days if they were allowed. They had made up a chant to go with the run: 'Raaadish, run, run, run. Raaadish, run, run, run,' which amused them a lot. Then Lawrence started singing, 'Raaadish, bum, bum, bum,' which amused them even more. Skelton probably ought to have stopped him but couldn't be bothered, and anyway it amused him, too.

Mila vanished from view behind the shrubs, then appeared again on the other side of the valley, hurrying across the rutted, frozen earth and calling, 'Mr Dean.'

Dean turned. He seemed alarmed by Mila's approach but perhaps he was merely surprised. Then he looked delighted. He made a few words of explanation to his colleagues and drew Mila aside to speak.

There was an odd intensity about their conversation,

an air not of old acquaintances exchanging small talk but of accomplices communicating vital information. Perhaps it was the weather. The easy poses and expressions of the cocktail party are not so easily adopted when you're trussed up in overcoats on a hillside with a cold wind blowing.

They shook hands and, as they did so, Mila touched Eliot's arm with her left hand, not like a nurse supporting a patient who might still find it difficult to stand, but tenderly. Almost like a lover.

Skelton's sister, Winnie, had, after first meeting Mila, warned him not to marry her.

'The rest of your life you'd be eleventh man in a second reserve team up against Syd Barnes,' she said. Skelton was surprised that Winnie had heard of Syd Barnes, then remembered her new boyfriend was a keen cricketer. Winnie tended to share the passions of her latest beau and got in a temper when you mentioned it. 'I've always been interested in cricket/whippets/rambling/the geology of the Cretaceous Period' – she had a job in the canteen at the Science College for a while and went out with a lot of students.

'You'll be forever looking over your shoulder,' she'd said. 'Mila's lovely but she's attractive, she's posh, she's clever, she's strong-willed, she's witty and she's charming. You're a rasher of nothing with glasses and a limp.'

'I'm very tall,' Skelton had said, in his defence.

'She's nearly matching you on that an' all. What is she? Five foot ten? Five-eleven?'

'She's five foot nine,' Skelton had said.

In truth, Winnie was only voicing his own doubts. He wasn't good enough for Mila. He consoled himself with the thought that this was part and parcel of being in love. Obviously, you think the person you love is better than you. You love them more than you love yourself. That's what proper love is.

That's what he thought anyway. He didn't really have a clue.

In novels, he'd read about beautiful women who toy with the affections of gullible men either for monetary gain or vicious pleasure, just to prove they can. It used to worry him a lot.

He'd had no money in those days. As far as he could make out, Mila did not seem to have the vicious nature of someone who would toy with affections, but a truly vicious person would know how to disguise a thing like that. When they'd first started holding hands and kissing, he was aware that a man of the world might have said, 'No, my affections will not become your playthings,' but he was not a man of the world, he was a man of Leeds Central Library who'd rather have his affections used as playthings than have them ignored.

Fifteen years of marriage had made him feel a little more secure but never entirely. Still he had to console himself. A permanent state of insecurity. That's what proper love is. Isn't it?

She was much more grown up than he was. He'd watched her grow during the war, when she was working with the

172

soldiers. She didn't talk about it much but Skelton, during his brief visits to the hospital, had glimpsed what she lived with every day. Men with no faces, with no limbs, in such pain, physical and mental, that they begged you to put them out of their misery.

It had changed her. By 1916 every trace of her girlishness had gone, and she emerged as an adult. An extraordinary adult. Sometimes Skelton was frightened of her, in much the same way as, when he was a nipper, he was frightened of God. But that was different because he'd never loved God.

Years later, not long after they moved to Lambourn, they went to dinner with neighbours. Among the other guests was a couple, a little older than Skelton and Mila, who had called each other 'Darling' and practically billed and cooed at the table.

Mila never billed and neither did she coo. She was loving, and all was well in the marital bed, but she was never affectionate, not overtly so, anyway. She teased Skelton a lot. She mocked him when he deserved to be mocked. Sometimes she punched his arm and hooted at his antics even when he didn't want to be hooted at. But she was never overtly affectionate.

He had asked her about it once.

'You've spent time with my parents,' she said.

Skelton knew what she meant. Mila's parents teased each other so ingeniously that an outsider could easily take it for hatred.

'Come to that,' Mila said, 'I've never seen your parents go in for displays of affection, either.'

'Ah, but they're from Leeds,' he said.

When she came back down the hill to the bridge, Skelton took her hand. She kept her eyes to the ground. She had a secret.

CHAPTER EIGHTEEN

'I've made a list,' Edgar said.

'Is it numbered?'

'Of course.'

They were in the easy chairs enjoying their morning tea. The weather had improved again. Pipe smoke always looked better when there was a bit of sun in the room and the sight of it was helping Skelton shake off the terrible gloom his dreams had once again left him with.

'I've already crossed off sheep dip and weedkiller.'

'What's number three?'

'They were bracketed together as number one.'

'So, what's number two?'

'Murder by an as-yet-unknown party.'

'Such as whom?'

'We've said a thousand times that Ted Dutton must have had some fierce enemies.'

'None of whom have emerged.' Skelton reached for the pot, poured himself another cup, then noticed the milk was all gone so left it undrunk. 'And anyway, enemies like that bludgeon you to death or come at you with a knife. They don't administer poison over the course of several weeks.'

'They might.'

'How?'

'The pies.'

'Which pies?'

'Mary Dutton said he took meat and potato pies out with him with lots of pepper. Somebody could have sprinkled arsenic on the pies while he wasn't looking.'

'A nameless enemy?'

'Or a love rival.'

'A what?'

'A love rival.'

'You mean Mary was having an affair with another man who killed Ted?'

'Or woman.'

'What?'

'Mary seems to have a very close relationship with Enid Fellows.'

'Oh, for God's sake.'

'Sapphism is a lot more common than you like to believe.'

'Not in the Midlands. What's three?'

Edgar put a star next to number two to indicate that, despite Skelton's doubts, a sapphic pie-poisoner was still a front runner. 'Three: suicide.'

'Same thing. Hanging, shooting, drowning, one big dose of poison, yes. But I can't see us convincing a jury that he killed himself by taking it in dribs and drabs.'

Edgar crossed out *Suicide*. 'Four: the mother did it.'

'Killed her own son?'

'It's a possibility.'

'Why?'

'I haven't thought that through.'

'How, then?'

'Ted Dutton would often vanish who knows where without any explanation to Mary. What if he was going home to Mum? There was bad blood between Mary and Jessie, so he wouldn't want to tell his wife in case she'd make a fuss.'

'I don't see Ted worrying much about his wife making a fuss,' Skelton said.

'If you believe Mary's picture of him. What's Mary's cooking like?'

'Who knows? She was in service.'

'Yes, but as a housemaid, not in the kitchen. So, Mary cooks inedible food, Ted goes home to Mum, perhaps two or three times a week, for some decent grub. Mum poisons his food.'

'You're forgetting his mum has a cook called Minnie.'

'And she says to the cook, "I'll make the gravy, Minnie. I know how he likes it."'

'If she was poisoning the gravy, she'd be dead too,' Skelton said.

'Not if she doesn't like gravy.'

'Everybody likes gravy.'

Again, ignoring Skelton's doubts, Edgar put a star next to *The mother*. 'Five: one of the children did it.'

'Oh dear.'

'What?'

'I'd already thought of that. But I fear that Mary would make a false confession and hang rather than see one of the children take the blame, so it's no use to us.'

Edgar put a squiggly line under 'the children'. 'Six: Billy did it.'

'The brother?'

'He could have poisoned Ted's food when Mum wasn't looking.'

'Why?'

'Brothers kill each other. Cain slew Abel over a mess of potage.'

'Not by poisoning several messes of potage, though. Anyway, Billy's never around. He's off around the country racing his motorcycle on the Wall of Death. Is that the end of your list?'

'No. There is a seventh possibility, but I don't think you'll like it.'

'Go on.'

'Plead guilty.'

Skelton stretched out his leg to ease his bad hip

and nodded to acknowledge that pleading guilty and thinking of some mitigating circumstance other than the husband's cruelty – perhaps find a doctor or two willing to testify to Mary's insanity – would be an option of the last resort.

Edgar put away his list and pulled out another file. 'I think we should talk about *The Matlock and Ripley Textile Bank versus The Imperial Bauxite Trading Company*.'

Skelton would do anything rather than talk about *The Matlock and Ripley Textile Bank versus The Imperial Bauxite Trading Company*.

'William Allen, the solicitor acting for The Imperial Bauxite Trading Company, believes that *Erlanger versus the New Sombrero Phosphate Company, 1878*, might have some bearing—'

Skelton interrupted him. 'I don't suppose you could be right about Enid Fellows, could you?'

'It's a possibility.'

'One of the things the Hannah Dryden case taught me is that there are more things in heaven, earth and boudoirs than are dreamt of in my philosophy. I don't think they could have had sapphism in Leeds when I was growing up, though. If Leeds women had known it was an option, I can't see they'd have bothered with men at all. My mum once said she'd rather have a dog than a husband because dogs don't get ointment on the clock.'

'Did your dad do that a lot?'

'Just the once, but the grudge still simmers.'

'If we could . . .' Edgar gestured to *The Matlock and Ripley Textile Bank versus The Imperial Bauxite Trading Company* file. 'William Allen has suggested that all interested parties should meet to see if the matter can be settled out of court.'

'How tall would you say Mary Dutton is?' Skelton asked.

'I don't know. Small. Barely five feet, I'd have thought.'

'So, she wouldn't have been able to reach the top shelf.'

'In the pantry?'

'She'd have had to get a chair to stand on every time she used it. She'd have had to take a chair from the kitchen into the pantry, take down the poison, sprinkle a bit on his food, put the poison back, then take the chair back. Even if there was, say, an orange box in there, it's a bit ostentatious. And it's not as if she was just sprinkling a bit on the potatoes. If that was the case, she and all the children would have perished with him. It was just the one plate of food. She'd want the poison hidden somewhere more accessible. The back of the knife and fork drawer or in a cornflour packet at the back of a cupboard.'

Edgar closed the file. 'I once knew a man,' he said, 'who could think about two things at the same time.'

CHAPTER NINETEEN

Monday 18th February, 1929

My dear cousin Arthur,

I hope that the snow was a little more forgiving in Lambourn than it has been here in Collingford. We have been subjected to the harshest of conditions, in terms of both the depth and severity of the snow and the freezing temperatures, that I have ever known. I think you had the snow a little earlier than us, but when it came here my goodness it came.

On Wednesday last, we set off for the meeting as per usual, with Bible, accordion and banjo. Rather than going around the lanes to get to The Flag for the

Wednesday meetings, we have been taking a shortcut across the fields.

It had started to snow a bit, but it was not settling and there were still gaps in the clouds, so it looked as if it would be no more than a flurry. I actually remember saying as we left that it was too cold to snow properly.

We were about halfway there when it came on. You should have seen it. Nothing one minute, a full blizzard the next. I have never seen such snow. We could not see our noses in front of our faces. And the worst of it was the way the snow got in our scarves and down our boots so that in no time at all our clothes offered no protection.

We stumbled about. We had no idea in which direction we were heading, probably going around in circles. There were no visible landmarks, you see. Now and then we would come across a hedge or some trees but could not tell which hedge it was or which trees.

After a bit, I decided that any sort of shelter would be better than stumbling around, so we sat down in the lee of a hedge and thought that we would wait the blizzard out. The snow came over us and covered us.

This is how Eskimos stay warm, I told Norah, but she knew I was making it up. Eskimos carve the snow into blocks and make houses with it. The snow must have to be compacted to do that, not freshly fallen.

I told Norah that I had read – in something by Jack London, I think, either *White Fang* or the story *To*

Build A Fire – that freezing to death is not a bad way to die. You are cold, and then you are colder, and then you go warm and sleepy, and then you fall asleep and wake up basking in the smile of Jesus.

Norah was not having any of that sort of talk and began to sing robustly. I joined in with the harmonies. We did not get the instruments out for fear that the cold and the wet might damage them, and besides our fingers were too stiff to play the notes. But we did 'Praise My Soul the King of Heaven' and 'Immortal Invisible God Only Wise' and 'If You Knew Susie' and had just started on 'Yes, We Have No Bananas' when a Border Collie came along and licked my face.

The poor dog looked more frozen than we did and had icicles hanging around its mouth, so we pulled him close and tried to share with him the warmth of our bodies. I would have given the poor thing a biscuit if I had had one for it looked hungry as well as cold. But then we learnt that the dog was not so lost as we had thought it was. In fact, it was not lost at all because a few minutes later, along came its owner, a shepherd looking for his sheep. The shepherd had a beard and for a moment I entertained the notion that this was the Good Shepherd and He had come to lead us safely through the Valley of Death. He said that he had lost his flock, so we joined in the search, keeping close together and shouting so as to be sure to stay within earshot of each other.

The sheep had had the same idea as us and were huddled in the lee of a hedge so close to what had been our own hedge that I was surprised we had not heard them bleating. Sheep are cleverer than people think. Not as clever as pigs but a good bit brighter than cows. The dog managed to get the sheep moving, although one of them seemed to be sick or lame, so the shepherd carried it on his shoulders. I had never seen anybody do this before, except in one of the pictures of Jesus the Good Shepherd in the book we sometimes use for Sunday school. If you remember, it was just how little Wilf Dutton said his poor departed dad sometimes carried sheep. I asked the shepherd whether the beast was heavy, and he said it was, thus dispelling once again the 'gentle Jesus meek and mild' impression that some people have. He trained as a carpenter, lifting heavy planks. He would have had a muscular build.

The shepherd now told us that he was himself completely lost in the blizzard but that we were not to worry because we could trust in the dog to lead us to safety. So, we left the dog to it and followed behind the sheep. The shepherd said his name was Simon and the dog was called Breck. After twenty minutes (and long, cold minutes they were) we came to the shepherd's barn. We did not see it until we practically had our noses pushed against it, such was the lack of visibility. We helped Simon get the sheep into the barn. He found that the one he had been carrying was not lame at all but had just got its legs tangled up with thorns, so he laid the beast down, gently untangled the thorns, then rubbed it with some straw to warm it up. He said it would be fine. Norah and I copied him and rubbed some of the other sheep as well, and he thanked us for that and invited us into his house.

His wife was a lady so thin that, as the lads in Rhyl would have said, 'If she swallowed an orange pip, the neighbours would have started talking.' Her name was Annie. She made a pot of tea and cut big slices of bread for us to toast at the fire and then spread with butter and honey. There was cheese too and some slices of turnip. I had never had toasted turnip before. It turns wonderfully sweet in the flames.

Simon and Annie said we could stay there until the weather cleared and, in the event, we were there all night. We sang for our supper, of course we did.

When our fingers had sufficiently thawed, Norah got the accordion out and I the banjo and we did some Christmas carols, because they seemed appropriate on such a snowy night, and then 'K-K-K-Katy' and 'Why Am I Always the Bridesmaid Never the Blushing Bride'. 'Yes, We Have No Bananas' was new to them. They laughed a great deal. The lamp ran out of oil, so by the light of the fire's embers we sang 'Only a Bird in a Gilded Cage' and 'After the Shadows' before deciding that the mood had got too sombre and brightening things up with '"Aba-daba daba-daba, daba-daba, dab," said the Monkey to the Chimp.'

We all fell asleep by the fire in our clothes and stayed there, too, because anywhere else was punishingly cold.

The snow had stopped falling by morning and lay deep. Annie gave us a good breakfast of bread, bacon and tea and we went out with Simon to look over the sheep in the barn. They all seemed nice as ninepence, even the one that had got tangled in the thorns. We fed them with hay and also – I had never seen this done before – with holly leaves cut from the highest part of the holly hedge, where the prickles are the least. Then Simon took us outside and pointed out our way back to Collingford.

Now, here is something that will perhaps be of interest to you. At one point he said we should go over a stile and cross 'Sid Dutton's forty', by which I assume he meant 'forty acres' over to Steps Green (or Steppes Green – I haven't been able to find the name on a map). I asked, as casually as I could, whether the land had belonged to some relative of the late Ted Dutton. There was no harm in doing this. The talk of Ted and Mary Dutton is all around Collingford, so it was only natural that I should show an interest. Simon told me that it had indeed been owned by Ted Dutton's father. Sid had bought it just after the war, but never farmed it himself. He rented it out to a local man. I did not want to enquire any further for fear of showing too much interest in Sid Dutton thereby arousing suspicion.

Anyway, the route he showed us brought us round to the back of Jessie Dutton's house, so we called in to find out how she was faring in the terrible cold.

Minnie the maid told us that she did not think Mrs Dutton was well enough to receive visitors but that she would ask. She did this in a certain tone of voice and with a certain look which was her way of saying – or so Norah thought – that 'not well enough' meant 'very drunk indeed'. Anyway, she came back and said we should go in.

The drawing room was more airless than ever, with the thick curtains drawn and a huge fire in the grate. Mrs Dutton was lying on a day bed, swathed in blankets. She made a great show of being ill but this time even I could smell the drink.

She wanted me to come close, so I did. She took my hand and said, 'You are at my right hand,' and 'I have set the Lord always before me, because He is at my right hand and I shall not be moved,' which was a paraphrase of Psalm 16. She clutched my hand very tightly and said, 'Thou wilt not leave my soul in hell; neither wilt thou suffer thine Holy One to see corruption. Thou wilt show me the path of life: in thy presence is fullness of joy; at thy right hand there are pleasures for evermore.'

She was, frankly, raving. She told me her glorious, golden boy had been to see her. I knew who she meant right off. There are three photographs of Billy Dutton on her sideboard. He has fair hair and – not that I'm much of a judge – seems very handsome. I asked whether Billy came frequently, or had he heard she was ill and rushed to her bedside? But she began to weep. She seemed disturbed by Billy's visit. She told me that the firstborn is set above the other children, but Isaac loved Joseph above his brothers even though Joseph was the youngest. I took from this that she is disturbed either because she loved Billy more than Ted or Ted more than Billy – either way she finds the inequality of her affections somehow disturbing. She wept. I patted her hand and after a while she subsided into a drunken sleep, poor woman.

Norah and I pray for a lifeline that we can throw to this troubled woman, so that we can haul her back to the peace of the Lord.

The trek home took it out of us, for it was still cold and the snow and ice were deceptive, so both of us took a tumble. The Rover Sunbeam was half snowed in and inside everything was covered in ice. I got the little stove going, but it was a while before there was any warmth in it at all, and, even then, you did not feel it until you were practically sitting on the thing. Outside it began to snow again. We put on all our clothes and sang lustily but still we froze. The ice that covered everything melted. The bedding was damp, and we did not have a hope of drying it. It vexed us to say it, but it was clear there would be no sense in staying there the night. The damp bedding would most likely have frozen around us. So, when the snow looked as if it had given over a bit, we took ourselves off to The Flag. We had the sense to go round by the roads rather than the shortcut over the fields but it was still a mighty trek.

When we got there, Jack Gorin had got a beautiful big fire going and the place was warm as anything. And Jack's wife had made a batch of bread, and they had cheese and ham and pickles.

Now, I think I may have mentioned this but outside the pub, out at the back, as well as the barn where we hold our meetings, Jack has a number of good brick stables all well roofed and bone dry, but freezing cold, of course. With Jack's permission we put the paraffin oil heaters from the barn in there and got them going, then we stuffed the gaps in the door and windows with straw to keep the worst of the draughts out. Jack loaned us a few blankets and so on and we camped there for the night. The heaters give off a funny smell, but it is worth it for the warmth.

The plan now is that, when it thaws a bit, we'll drive the Rover Sunbeam over to Jack Gorin's yard and live half in the van, half in the stable and hold our meetings in the barn as before. It is such a convenient arrangement I cannot think why we did not think of it before, apart from the fear of asking too much of Jack. Some people say they are friends of Jesus but do not act like they are. Jack is the other, better sort who acts like a friend of Jesus without claiming to be one. One good deed is worth a thousand pious words.

I am ever yours faithfully in the joy of Jesus,
Alan

Edgar came in with notes on *Erlanger versus the New Sombrero Phosphate Company (1878)* and other cases that might have some bearing on *The Matlock and Ripley Textile Bank versus The Imperial Bauxite Trading Company*. Skelton handed Alan's letter to Edgar and pretended to look through the New Sombrero notes while he read it.

'What does a police inspector earn, Edgar?' Skelton asked when Edgar had finished.

'A police inspector?'

'£200 a year? £500?'

'Sid Dutton, do you mean?'

'Yes, what do you think he would have earned?'

'I've really no idea.'

'Enough so that his widow could afford to keep a sizeable house, a car and three servants? Enough to buy forty acres of land?'

'I wouldn't have thought so.'

'Is forty acres a large garden or a small farm?'

'We had a dispute over fifty acres a couple of years ago,

if you remember. Gentleman by the name of Romney. He seemed to think fifty acres was a lot, so forty acres would be a lot minus twenty per cent.'

'Quite a lot, then.'

'Exactly.'

'Would a police inspector earn enough money to buy quite a lot of land?'

'As I say, I've no idea.'

'Have we heard from Mr Critchlow?'

'We had a letter from his daughter this morning.'

'Rose.'

'A pleasure to read; she really does have the most beautiful handwriting. She says her father's gradually improving but still not quite tickety-boo.'

'Let's see what she can dig up about Sid Dutton's forty.'

CHAPTER TWENTY

'Some girls like to do Scouting but Scouting for girls is not the same as for boys,' Agnes Baden-Powell, Founder and Vice-President of the Girl Guides had written. 'The chief difference in the training of the two courses of instruction is that Scouting for boys makes for MANLINESS, but the training for Guides makes for WOMANLINESS, and enables girls the better to help in the battle for life.'

Rose's father had had reservations about the Girl Guides. For a start, there was the title of the handbook: *How Girls Can Help to Build Up the Empire.* He had never read Bukharin's *Imperialism and the World Economy* or Lenin's *Imperialism, the Highest Stage of Capitalism,* but he knew that every right-thinking person should be suspicious of the very word 'empire' with its connotations of jingoism, unless, as somebody in the *Daily Herald* had once argued, it could become a vehicle for bringing the blessing of socialism to people of many lands.

Rose thought he was being silly. Guiding embraced all sorts of tastes, beliefs, nationalities and races. She had worked hard to get her Clerk's badge, with its strict handwriting requirements, and her Pathfinder badge, but had no interest in Boatswaining or Floristry. Other girls she knew had no interest in Pathfinding but were accomplished Florists or Boatswains. The movement could accommodate all tastes, temperaments and beliefs. Some Guides were Church of England, others, Methodists. Overseas, there were even Hindu Guides.

And some girls were keen on empire, others on socialism. In Russia, she assumed, they probably had communist guides and in Italy, fascists. Round the campfire all such distinctions were quickly forgotten. A message that had been hammered home in meeting after meeting was that Boy Scouts and Girl Guides of all ages should be 'Little Friends of All The World' prepared for daily acts of kindness, understanding and heroism.

Comrades all! Then let us forward
Strong in body, heart, and mind;
Guides are we, our true endeavour
Friends in all the world to find

'Girls need not wait for war to break out to show what heroines they can be. We have many everyday heroines whose example might be followed with advantage,' Miss Baden Powell had said.

Rose could think of nothing better than to be an everyday heroine whose example might be followed with advantage. The letter that Mr Skelton had sent to her father, saying he was taking the case and commending her own 'efficiency and enthusiasm for the task in hand' had made her blush and her father weep with pride. This was her chance then to prove her everyday heroism.

The task was not to slay a dragon or cross a mountain range. Her task was to get to the District Land Registry and seek out documents relating to the purchase of a parcel of land, approximately forty acres in area, just outside Collingford in a place called Steppes or Steps Green and known locally as 'Sid Dutton's forty'.

Shakespeare or Jesus or Kipling once said, 'They also serve who only stand and wait.' Well, she was not standing and waiting. She was rattling down the Coventry Road on a No. 15 tram and there was no stopping her.

She would save Mary Dutton.

CHAPTER TWENTY-ONE

They were staying at the Grand again for another of the Birmingham cases.

The *Hinckley Clarion*, a weekly newspaper, had published a story suggesting that A. F. C. Kidsen, the Warwickshire slow bowler, had indecently exposed himself to a group of elderly women at a white elephant sale. The story also alleged that, as he did so, Kidsen had shouted, 'If it's a white elephant you're after, ladies, feast your eyes on this.'

Kidsen sued for libel. The *Clarion* apologised, maintaining that the indecent exposure story had somehow been muddled with an entirely different story about Kidsen's hat-trick against Glamorgan. A mere apology did not cut the mustard, said Kidsen. Only substantial damages could properly redeem his reputation.

Skelton had been briefed by Edgar's old pal William Allen to appear for Kidsen.

Edgar assured his chief that he need not be over-conscientious in his preparation. The *Clarion*'s case was weak, and they knew it. As soon as they heard that a man of Skelton's stature and fame was on the case, they would settle. Edgar put money on it, betting Allen £5 that his chief wouldn't even have to show up at court. He won, too, and on the proceeds hosted a champagne dinner at a little restaurant in the Bull Ring that Allen had recommended, known for its jolly atmosphere and wholesome portions.

It was gone midnight and pouring with rain when Skelton and Edgar, bloated with beef, burgundy and brandy got back to the Grand.

In the foyer an embarrassed porter told him that there was a young lady waiting to see them.

Rose Critchlow sat huddled. She'd prepared for the weather with mackintosh and sou'wester but still she was soaked. She looked so forlorn that Skelton's first thought was that her father must have died. But if that was the case what was she doing here?

'Miss Critchlow, whatever's the matter?'

'Oh, Mr Skelton, I can't tell you how good it is to see you.'

Behind the reception desk a snooty under-manager was eyeing them suspiciously. Decent male guests did not entertain lady visitors after midnight. He was aware who Mr Skelton and Mr Hobbes were, but rules are rules.

'I put a trunk call through to you in London and it took nearly all day and then, when it got through, they said you were here in Birmingham. And the tram wasn't running because the rain had got in the works, so I got on my bike only something went wrong with the chain and I fixed it, but it just went again, and then the same thing another time. So, I left the bike behind a shed in Small Heath and I walked the rest of the way. And then, of course, like an idiot – you wouldn't believe I've got my Pathfinder's badge – I realised that I hadn't asked the man in London where you were staying, so I've been going round all the hotels, asking.'

'What is it?'

'It's Dad.'

'Oh, the poor man.'

Rose looked confused. 'No, he's not dead. I've discovered he's done something ever so wrong and he might have to go to prison.' Rose was shivering.

'We need to get you dry,' Edgar said and went to tell the snooty under-manager that Rose was the daughter of a friend. She was in some distress and he would be grateful if a towel, tea and toast could be arranged. He also asked whether there might be somewhere private where they could talk. The under-manager gave instructions to the porter and showed Skelton and Rose into the coffee lounge, which had a glass door big enough for the manager to be sure that nothing untoward was taking place.

The porter brought the towel.

'I got the deeds of the land at Steppes Green,' Rose said, 'purchased by Sidney Dutton on 21st August 1919 for £585 2s 5d including duties and sundries. And the thing is the solicitors overseeing the purchase of Steppes Green were Critchlow and Benedict.' Rose was forcing herself not to cry.

'I don't quite see what the problem is,' Skelton said.

The porter came in with the refreshments. He looked at Rose sympathetically and at Skelton as if he was the kind of brute who made young women cry. Skelton motioned him to put down the tray and he left.

Edgar buttered a slice of toast and offered it to Rose. She was taking deep breaths. 'A very great step to success is to be able to stand disappointments,' she said. '"Smile a little, sing a little, as you go along, not alone when things are pleasant, but when things go wrong."'

'Did Agnes Baden-Powell say that?' Skelton asked.

'Yes.'

'I thought she might have done.'

'Will Dad go to prison?'

'What for?'

'For taking the Mary Dutton case. Conflict of interest.'

'You're suggesting that because he did a little conveyancing for a client ten years ago, he should disqualify himself from defending the client's son's alleged murderer. I don't think . . .'

'Surely from the point of view of ethics . . .'

'Ah, but I think we have to consider the overriding

198

principle, stressed by my tutor at Cambridge, that most ethical deliberations come under the category of *multum stercorum*.'

'We could either do Latin or music and I was having flute lessons. Dad said solicitors only have to know a few key phrases.'

'It means it's not a matter that would worry the law.'

'You're sure?'

'Absolutely certain.'

'So, Dad won't go to prison?'

'No.'

'Well, that's some relief, anyway. But the other thing is the £600.'

'Which £600?'

'The £585 2s 5d it cost to buy the land in the first place. You asked me to find out how much a police inspector earns. It struck me that Sid Dutton was only a police sergeant in 1919. He would have been earning something between £2 13s and £2 17s a week. With overtime and so on that could perhaps be made up to, say, £150 a year. How does a police sergeant keeping a wife and two growing lads on £150 a year save up enough to buy a piece of land worth £585 2s 5d?'

'An inheritance, perhaps.'

'I thought of that. There's a boy I was at school with works at Births, Marriages and Deaths. He looked through the records for Duttons and Whitehouses – that's Jessie Dutton's maiden name – going back three or four generations while I did the census records back to 1881. Sidney Dutton comes from brass finishers and metal turners; Jessica Whitehouse is all farm labourers. There never was an inheritance. And they didn't have football pools in 1919.'

'We've heard well-substantiated rumours that Sid Dutton was not an honest policeman,' Edgar said.

'All the same. £600?' Rose said. 'Even if he was taking bribes, it's Collingford. I doubt if there's £600 for criminals to steal in Collingford, never mind use for bribes.'

She was right. Where would even a corrupt police sergeant in Collingford get his hands on £600 in 1919? Edgar knew no end of bent coppers in London and even they'd be hard pushed to lay their hands on that amount.

'If the money was obtained by criminal means would that make Dad an accessory?' Rose asked.

'When conveyancing a property it is not the business of a solicitor to question the source of the funds.' Skelton said this with all the authority he could muster even though he had no idea what he was talking about.

'So, Dad won't go to prison for that, either?'

'Of course not. Have you spoken to your father about this?'

'No. I didn't want to upset him.'

'Quite right.'

'I looked through some of the old files at the office and as far as I can make out, ten years ago it was mostly Mr Benedict who dealt with agricultural. Dad did houses and businesses.'

'So, you could find no paperwork relating to the purchase of the land at your father's office?'

'After Mr Benedict died, Dad shoved most of his papers into the big chest.'

'The big chest?'

'It's in the cupboard under the stairs.'

'Could we have a look inside the big chest?'

'It's locked.'

'But your dad would have a key.'

'Somewhere . . .'

'Could you get it?'

'I could try.'

'Sugar?'

CHAPTER TWENTY-TWO

They put Rose in a taxi and sent her home to Yardley. The following morning a porter interrupted Skelton's breakfast to tell him he had a telephone call. It was Rose. She had her father's keys and had found which one opened the cupboard under the stairs, but none of them came close to fitting the big chest. What should she do?

They were not in court until the afternoon and had planned a morning visit to Mary's children at Enid Fellows' house in Collingford, but a detour to Yardley would not put them far behind. 'Pop open the chest, quick look what's in there, on to Collingford, back in time for a late lunch.'

Rose needed a lot of persuading. Her conscience was troubled. Skelton explained that what they were planning was not burglary. Rose had been left in charge of the office. She needed to access some documents that were in a locked box to which the key was mislaid. Mr Hobbes was a trained locksmith who would be able to open the lock without damage. Edgar told her that locksmithing was a trade he had learnt before becoming a clerk. This was substantially true. He'd been apprenticed to Tyser Knapp, who was eventually nicked for the Melton House job and died twelve years later in Pentonville.

Edgar did not travel with the tools of the locksmith's trade so had to improvise. He borrowed Skelton's pipe-smoker's knife with tamper, reamer and spike. A search of the main office turned up a useful-looking letter opener. With the proper tools he could have sprung a simple mortice in less than a minute. With the pipe-reamer and letter opener it took longer.

'Everything all right?' The postman, very light on his feet, had come upstairs to find Edgar on his knees fiddling with the lock. Rose was out of sight, watching from inside the office.

Skelton and Edgar turned, both with the 'bang to rights' expressions of felons caught in the act. The postman, frightened, backed a couple of paces down the stairs.

'I was just . . .' he said.

Rose came out of the office.

'Oh, hello, Bert. This is Mr Skelton, the barrister from London, and his clerk, Mr Hobbes. They're helping us with the Mary Dutton case.'

The postman, still suspicious, came back up the stairs.

'We mislaid a key and Mr Hobbes is a trained locksmith,' Rose said.

Edgar, looking piratical with the letter opener clenched between his teeth, nodded.

'You left the front door open and I've got this, wouldn't fit in the letterbox.' The postman gave Rose a parcel and a pile of letters.

'Thanks, Bert. Can you shut the door behind you on your way out?' The postman left and Edgar sprang the lock.

'You will be able to lock it again afterwards, won't you?' Rose asked.

Edgar smiled reassuringly. He was a pro. The question did not need asking.

Rose was ashamed of the haphazard way the papers had been stored. There was no order to them at all. Some were creased, others showed signs of mould.

'I was only fourteen when Mr Benedict died,' she said. 'I expect Dad was upset and worried about the future so you can't really blame him for being sloppy.'

Skelton divided the papers into three rough piles, and they began to search for anything connected with the land at Steppes Green or the Dutton family in general.

Edgar scored first with a copy of a will, dated 24th September 1925, in which Sid Dutton left the Steppes Green forty acres in equal shares between Ted and Billy and the remainder of his estate to Jessie. This, presumably, was the will replaced by the deathbed will that Jessie reckoned Mary had finagled Sid to sign.

'What's the Jubilee Fund?' Rose asked. She was holding up a thick envelope. Neither Skelton nor Edgar knew. She tore open the envelope and began to read.

'Sid Dutton was a trustee of the Jubilee Fund.' Rose handed a sheet of paper to Skelton.

'5th May 1918.'

'What's that?' Edgar asked.

'The date of trust.'

They looked through the contents of the envelope and pieced together the story.

Lord Kinver, whose estates covered a huge expanse of land between Collingford and Hinckley, had served with Colonel Scott and, this gave Rose a frisson of excitement, Baden-Powell in West Africa during the Ashanti Wars. A man of conscience, he was shocked by what he saw. In 1897, the year of Queen Victoria's Diamond Jubilee, he established a school and a leper hospital in Kumasi and set up the Jubilee Fund with assets of £40,000 for the upkeep of both. In his will, he made Sid Dutton sole trustee of the fund. Lord Kinver died in April 1918. Sid Dutton bought his forty acres in August 1919.

'Let me get this right,' Rose said. 'Sid Dutton stole money from lepers.'

'I don't think that would be an unreasonable assumption to make, do you, Edgar?'

'Not at all.'

'I think the question we need to ask is why did Lord Kinver

appoint a lowly police sergeant to administer the trust?'

'People would do that? Steal from lepers?' Rose said.

The look on Rose's face reminded Skelton of how he'd felt the first time he had opened the Maw of Hell and shone his torch into the cesspit at the bottom of his garden.

CHAPTER TWENTY-THREE

The children ran into the garden as soon as Doris, watching from an upstairs window, said she could see a big car coming up the Hinckley Road. They were already in their best clothes with their faces washed. They'd all done each other with the nit comb the night before, so nothing was visibly jumping.

Mrs Fellows had shown them the letter. The postmark said London. It was type-written and bore an illegible signature in blue-black ink. She had written back saying yes, it would be convenient for them to visit at their convenience. Then they'd written back with the date and time. And as if seeing a lawyer from London who'd had his picture in the paper wasn't exciting enough already, that morning a man had come to the door with a telegram saying they might be a bit late.

Edgar stepped down from the car, saw the children and stepped back in again.

'You should understand,' he said, 'that I have reservations about children.'

'You've spoken very fondly of your nieces and nephews.'

'It's like dogs. You can be very fond of a dog you know personally, but not dogs in general. Or not strange dogs that you've never met.'

'I'm sure these children don't bite.'

'Sometimes they can be very boisterous.'

Skelton looked out of the window at the children, lined up by the front door.

'These ones look very orderly.'

'Now they do. But they all have the potential to be boisterous.'

'If they get boisterous, I'll have a word with Mrs Fellows.'

Edgar got out and stood by the car waiting for his chief. When Skelton unfolded himself, it seemed to the children proof that lawyers from London are of a different species. Tall like giants and thin like saplings.

Skelton smiled and said hello, and shook hands with Mrs Fellows. He asked which one of the children was which. Doris had to coax the younger ones, who were too shy, and when they would not be coaxed, she had to answer for them. Susan curtsied. Jean, the youngest, she said, was asleep in her cot. Edgar stood back trying to avoid eye contact.

Mrs Fellows had put the kettle on as soon as Doris had called out, so by the time they'd sat down in the parlour, the tea was brewing.

The children sat and stared at Edgar. It was disconcerting. He gave them a nervous smile.

Eventually Jimmy said, in little more than a whisper, 'Is that your car?'

'Pardon?' Edgar said.

'Is that your car?'

Edgar still couldn't make out what the boy was saying – it was the accent as much as the volume – and looked to Skelton for help.

'No, it's not ours,' Skelton said. 'We've hired it.'

'Have you hurt your leg?'

'No.'

'I saw you limping.'

'I was born with a bad leg.'

'I've got some rag if you wanted to tie it up.'

'No, that's all right, but it's very kind of you to offer.' This opened the floodgates.

What is London like? Could I have a ride in the car? What are those gloves made of? Have you ever been up in an aeroplane?

Mrs Fellows fussed with the tea things. She straightened the children's hair, noticed marks on their clothes and rubbed at them with a licked finger. She was, as Alan had said, a woman who was incapable of sitting still.

Jimmy, pointing at Edgar, turned to Skelton and asked, 'Why has he got mud on his face?'

Edgar had had his head out of the window all the way from Birmingham. The road had been flooded for some of the way, and he'd been splashed. He asked to be excused and went into the kitchen to wash his face and comb his hair.

Skelton, with raised eyebrows, asked Mrs Fellows if she'd mind coming outside with him to show him 'the disposition of the house'. Mrs Fellows understood this to mean he wanted a word without the children hearing, so told them to stay where they were and to behave and took Skelton into the back garden.

'Have you been to see Mary?' he asked.

'I went last week.'

'And how did she seem?'

Before answering, Mrs Fellows picked a sprig of rosemary, rubbed it between her fingers and smelled them. 'Older and thinner,' she said.

'Is she eating?'

'I don't think she is, no. Not properly. I took her some things – some cakes I'd made and a bit of bread and boiled ham – but she just looked at them and nearly left them behind when they took her away. I had to remind her. She misses the children a lot. She dotes on 'em. Have you got kids?'

'Two.'

'Do you dote on yours?'

'Is it wrong to dote?'

Mrs Fellows smiled. 'I never had any, so I wouldn't know.'

'Is Mary actually ill, do you think?'

'I don't know.'

'I'll see if I can arrange for a doctor to see her.'

'I'll take her a drop of nerve tonic when I go and see her again. Bit of a pick-me-up.'

Skelton thought there might be tears in her eyes, but, before he could look properly, she knelt down and fussed with the dead leaves under the hedge, pulling them into a pile.

'And how are the children faring?' Skelton asked.

'They miss her, course they do, but they're kids, you know. They get used to things ever so quick. Few tears now and then. Sometimes at bedtime. But Doris is the mum.'

'It's a lot of responsibility for a girl of eleven.'

'It isn't so much for a bossy madam like her, though. She loves it.'

'It must be hard on you, too, looking after the six of them.'

'Keeps me busy.'

'And are you all right for money?'

'I get my widow's pension from the war. Wal – my late husband – had a carpenter's yard in Barnes Cross. Reg runs it now. He used to work with Wal. I don't have much to do with it, but it gives me a wage.'

She carried the pile of dead leaves over to a bonfire heap waiting to be lit and tucked them under the twigs so they wouldn't blow away.

Skelton took out his wallet. 'The chaps in the . . . er . . . office had a whip-round for the children and wanted you to have this.' He was, of course, lying, but it was less embarrassing for both of them to pretend. He gave her seven pound notes, because five or ten seemed too neat and seven might be the amount a collection would have raised.

'Thank you very much.'

She folded the money and tucked it into a pocket in her pinny. Then she looked at her feet, shod serviceably, and said, 'Er . . .'

'What is it?'

'She didn't do it.'

'I'm sure she didn't, and I promise to do my very best to convince a jury that she didn't.'

Back inside, they found Edgar standing in the middle of the room surrounded by children, trying and failing to look dignified, like the stag at bay in the Landseer painting. *Do you wear socks? Have you seen the King? Have you got a dog? Have you got a cat? Have you got a wife?*

'Oh, I nearly forgot,' Skelton said. 'Is it all right if they have a few sweets, Mrs Fellows?' Enid smiled and nodded. From both side pockets of his suit jacket Skelton took bags of them.

They had stocked up at Vimto Vera's before leaving Yardley.

Doris tried to stop them clamouring. Mrs Fellows told them not to have too many or she'd have them all coming down with bellyache. Then Jean woke up and started crying, so Mrs Fellows had to go and see to her.

'Are there any ju-ju's?' Wilf asked.

'I'm not sure what ju-ju's are,' Skelton said.

'They're like fruit jellies,' Edgar said.

'Like wine gums?' Skelton asked.

'They're nothing like wine gums,' Edgar said.

'You said they were like fruit jellies.'

'They are like fruit jellies. But fruit jellies are nothing like wine gums.'

'Yes, they are.'

'Fruit jellies are much more sugary. And they're made from fruit. Wine gums are made from wine.'

'They're not.'

'Of course they are.'

'They wouldn't sell wine to children.'

'Not real wine. They just taste like wine. Fruit jellies taste like fruit.'

'When Uncle Billy comes, he always brings ju-ju's,' Wilf said.

'Would you mind not interrupting when the grown-ups are talking?' Edgar asked.

Skelton turned his chair towards Wilf and gave him his full attention.

'Does Uncle Billy come to see you very often?' he asked.

'He comes all the time and brings loads of ju-ju's.'

'Not just ju-ju's,' Susan said. 'He brings sherbet dabs and liquorice bootlaces and everything.'

'When was the last time he came?'

'He hasn't been since Mum went. Before that he used to come a lot.'

'To your house at Farrier's Cross?'

'Sometimes there, but most of the time he'd come here when we were with Mum seeing Mrs Fellows.'

'Did he just bring sweets for you, or did he bring them for your Mum and Dad as well?'

'He brought boxes of chocolates for Mum and Everton Mints for Dad.'

'Have you still got those Everton Mints you found in the jacket?' Edgar asked when they were back in the car.

'I think so. In London. I put them in a drawer.'

'Should we send them for analysis?'

'They did me no harm.'

'You might have been lucky and picked the only one in the packet that wasn't poisoned.'

CHAPTER TWENTY-FOUR

Wednesday 27th February, 1929

My dear cousin Arthur,
We have settled nicely into the stable. It is our first home without wheels for a very long time. We have the van parked alongside but use it only for cooking because it is where we have our stove and pots etc. It's also nice, if you will excuse a moment of shameful vulgarity, to have proper facilities. We have so grown used to using holes in the ground that Jack Gorin's ladies' and gents', primitive though they might seem by your London standards, are to us the very height of luxury.

I think the snow lasted longer up here than it did down your way and the thaw brought with it floods. We were all right being on a bit of a hill, but in some places the houses had two feet of water in them. Nobody came to any real harm, but some were fairly stranded in the upstairs of their houses and those who did not have upstairs, like those in the cottages in Collingford Lower Town, had to move out completely. Everyone rallied round. It is marvellous to see how quickly the true spirit of Christ's message comes to the fore at times of crisis like this. Neighbours opened their doors to neighbours, and Norah and I pitched in bringing essential supplies to old folks. If you are in touch with Mary Dutton, please tell her that her children are safe. Enid Fellows' house is on the higher ground and so was unaffected by the flooding.

We went up Summers Hill to make sure all was well there but received no answer when we rang the bell or even when we hammered on the door. We went round the back, but there was nobody there, and nobody answered when we hammered on the back door either.

You know how you get that feeling that something is not right here?

The back door hadn't been locked, so we crept in calling 'Hello' and 'Is anybody home?' so as to announce our presence and not startle anyone into thinking we were burglars.

Jessie Dutton was in the front parlour, lying on the divan with her head lolling, out cold with nobody in attendance. Norah tried to rouse her by slapping her hands while I looked around for some smelling salts. One of those boxes that people have was on the floor next to her. You know the ones. They call them home medicine chests or travelling medicine chests. This one had full bottles of iodine and camphorated oil and empty ones of tincture of opium and sulphate of morphine and something labelled 'Soothing Syrup.' But there was a bottle of smelling salts, too. They revived her a little. Her eyes fluttered open and she looked first at Norah and then at me with an expression of intense hatred, told us to go away – but not using those words – and lapsed back into a half-sleep.

I asked Norah if she knew the telephone number for the doctor. This woke Jessie again. In no uncertain terms she told us not to send for a doctor. Norah asked her what happened to the maid.

'I sacked her,' Jessie said.

'Is there nobody else here?'

'I sacked them all. They wouldn't get my rum.'

That was it, then. The servants had cut off her drink supply, so she had polished off the tincture of opium, the sulphate of morphine and the Soothing Syrup.

'I'll make her some custard,' Norah said.

'Is that good in cases like this?' I asked her.

'I can make it quick and get it down her,' and

added, 'Bird's', just in case I suspected her of planning to mess with eggs and cornflour.

While Norah was making the custard, I tried to arrange Jessie's pillows so that she would be more comfortable. She was trying to speak to me. It is possible that she thought she was conducting a perfectly normal conversation, but the words did not make any sense. I wondered if she'd had a stroke. A stroke can take you like that. We used to know an old man in Colchester who had a stroke. You could have wonderful nonsense conversations with him.

'Are you grandly observant in the hands?' he would ask.

And if you said, 'A lot nicer than yesterday, anyway,' he would perhaps say, 'And on the speed cross measure. Spattering the beef. Spattering the beef.' He died in a state of blissful idiocy.

If Jessie had had a stroke, then of course we would have to call a doctor whether she liked it or not. It did seem more likely, though, just from the way we found her, that she was mad from the bottles in the medicine chest.

The odd word here and there led me to believe that she was telling me about her childhood and by the way she was talking about it I do not think it was a happy time. I will not even try to record what she was saying word for word, but the impression was – and I could be very wrong indeed – that her mother told her she was evil because she allowed boys to look at her 'and they wanted to roll up and down and I knew she was a pool of begrudging and peeve'.

Norah came back with the custard and by sheer force of will got Jessie to eat some of it. There was tea, too. Hot, sweet tea is the cure for most things and seemed to have a remarkable effect on Jessie's morphinomania, if that is what it was. It certainly brought a bit of colour back into her cheeks.

We spoke for about an hour, none of it very coherent, but here are some of the impressions I got. Again, they could all be wrong.

1) She never loved Ted. She couldn't love him. All the love had been taken from her.

2) She never loved her husband. For much the same reason.

3) She either loved or didn't love her father.

4) Her father was a farm labourer who used to do a bit of scrap metal on the side.

5) She talked more of her 'glorious, golden boy', who, as I said, is most likely Billy, but we are now also wondering whether it might be Sid. Did Sid have fair hair, do you know? In most of the photographs that we have seen, he is wearing a hat. Anyway, either Billy or Sid went to see Ted and told him something that he shouldn't have told him as a result of which she got angry with Billy or Sid and told him she never wanted to see him again. If it was Sid, then perhaps this is why

he went to live with Mary and Ted at the end of his life. If it was Billy, then all I can say is that she is now very frightened of him. Do you know of any reason why she would fear Billy? Has Billy even been to Collingford since his brother died? We certainly have not seen him. The difficulty was that she gave no indication of whether any of this happened three months ago or twenty years. And when I questioned her further, she did not seem to know what I was talking about.

6) She has been to Hull. Or hell. Or a hill somewhere. She lives up Summers Hill, of course, so she may have been talking about that. At one point she may have said 'Camp Hill'. There is a place in Birmingham called Camp Hill. Something might have happened there.

7) The Lord God is merciful and gracious, long-suffering and abundant in goodness and truth. He keeps mercy for thousands, forgives iniquity and transgression and sin.

She went to sleep for about ten minutes.

Outside the birds made a huge racket and there seemed far more of them than usual; pigeons and sparrows mostly but there was a robin quite near singing its heart out. It is, I am sure, too early for skylarks, but I could have sworn there was one out there somewhere, miles away probably, carolling the clouds.

Jessie woke and said she wanted to be taken to the toilet. Norah did the honours. At four o'clock the maid came in. She had been all the way to the other side of town to get a bottle of Buckfast Tonic Wine which she hoped would be better for Jessie than the rum. I asked her whether Jessie had sacked her. She said that Jessie did that at least three times a week. It was best, she said, to take no notice, just like it was best to take no notice of anything else that Jessie ever said or did. She said the gardener and the cook were both in Lower Town helping people who'd been flooded out. We asked whether Billy had been to see his mother. She said he hadn't as far as she knew but that doesn't mean anything. He has his own latchkey and there have been many times in the past when he's come in late at night, stopping off on one of his long trips across the country just to get a bed for the night, then leaving first thing, and she's known nothing about it until she comes to make up the beds in the morning.

By the time we left, she had Jessie sitting up and drinking the tonic wine.

Yesterday, after we had made our visits, Norah said she was fed up of darning my socks (darning is a skill I never managed to acquire – something to do with pulling the stitches too tight) and had heard of a general store in Barrastone Hill, a little village to the south of Collingford, that sold good woollen socks for half the price you'd get them anywhere else. I said we'd have to pack the Rover Sunbeam up to drive there and she said it was no distance at all if

221

we walked along the canal towpath. It was a lovely walk. Many boats are moored in the canal, some apparently occupied – although we saw no sign of the inhabitants – others abandoned.

We got the socks. Grey. Sixpence a pair. Hard wearing by the look of them. Then we had to walk back along the towpath. It was getting dark.

I have no idea if canal towpaths everywhere are the same, but this particular length of the Birmingham–Leicester is a terrible place. The darkness and abundant arches and the boats themselves, inhabited and abandoned, give licence to awful concupiscence. Behind the filthy windows of the boats one sees satanic shadows of men with women and men with men. Some have not even the shame to hide in the shadows but lie in full view, their clothing asunder, sometimes alone and smiling as if inviting all comers. There is spewing drunkenness here, too (it was no more than half past five in the afternoon), and huddles of children too frightened even to cry. Norah wanted to stop and speak to the children, but I had seen men in the shadows waiting to take the skin off us and hurried her on. And, indeed, as we turned up the alleyway that leads from the canal to the road, one such rogue appeared, brandished a knife and demanded our money, our coats and our shoes with very great menace. He was drunk, so not hard to pass by at a run, but he threw a length of rusty iron at us and it caught poor Norah on the back of her heel, leaving a nasty and very painful graze which bled quite a lot.

I had thought up until now that Collingford was a healthy place. I now know that Norah and I have barely scratched the surface. There is murder here.

The psalmist who walked through the shadow of the valley of death and feared no evil was made of sterner stuff than I.

I am ever yours faithfully in the joy of Jesus,

Alan

CHAPTER TWENTY-FIVE

Lily Langtry died, Sonja Henie triumphed at the World Figure Skating Championships, the stock market wobbled, St Valentine's Day was marked by one lot of gangsters gunning down another lot of gangsters in Chicago, there was trouble in Ireland, two people were killed in an East London warehouse fire, a train was derailed in Lancashire, a banquet was held for horses who were veterans of the war at which carrots, apples, bread and sugar was served to eighty horses and six donkeys, but still the papers never tired of Mary Dutton. Even when there was no news about her, which was most of the time, they kept the story alive by seeking out other women who had been cruelly treated by their husbands or by pillorying men who defended the right of husbands to whip recalcitrant wives. The phrase 'locked in a Dutton-style marriage' came into use. A bruise on a woman's face would prompt questions, 'He hasn't done a Dutton on you, has he?' In pubs strong ale became 'a pint of Dutton'. The Labour Party pledged, if they won the general election, to introduce 'Mary Dutton's Law', which would make it easier for women to divorce cruel husbands. One newspaper proprietor calculated that his circulation went up by five or ten per cent every time he put *that* picture – the Lillian Gish one of Mary – on his front page. Thankfully, the appetite for Skelton had abated a little, but still, once every couple of days, they'd find some excuse for showing him looking gawky.

The crowd of women outside the Winson Green prison was four times the size it had been the last time Skelton had visited, but then the weather was a good bit warmer than it was before. The two ringleaders spotted the Daimler first. By the time the car had pulled up, the women were all clustered around it. Skelton was made to pose for more photographs.

In the prison meeting room, the table had been moved a few feet and the wobbly tile had been taken away, leaving a brown gap, like a missing tooth. The noise of the prison was different too. In the distance he could hear laughter, snatches of song and clattering as if the inmates were preparing for a party.

'When I spoke to you before, you said that you hardly ever saw Billy.'

Mary didn't say anything. She seemed to have aged a good five years in the month since Skelton had last seen her.

'He used to come and see you quite a lot, didn't he?' Skelton said.

'I didn't think it was important.'

'He brought you chocolates. He brought sweets for the children.'

'I thought . . . I was worried if I mentioned it people might jump to the wrong conclusion. I thought people would think I was having it off with Billy. I wasn't, though. Such a thing never crossed my mind.'

'Was Billy sweet on you?'

'I don't know. I never wanted to think that way.'

'He brought you chocolates.'

'He knows I like chocolates. I think he felt sorry for me. Cos of Ted. I think he felt sorry for me because he knew what I had to put up with.'

'Did you tell Ted about his visits?'

'No.'

'Why not?'

'Because Ted was always jealous. He'd have thought straight away that I was having it off with Billy.'

'Surely he would have been less likely to think that anything untoward was happening if Billy had come while he was at home. A family visit.'

'You didn't know Ted. He didn't like anybody coming to visit,' Mary said.

'So, Billy would only visit when Ted wasn't there.'

'When Ted was off at market or something. Because he knew there'd be trouble otherwise.'

'Billy didn't get on with Ted?'

'Hated the sight of each other.'

'Yet Billy used to bring sweets for Ted, too.'

'How do you know all this? I don't want you speaking to the children. I don't want them brought into all this.'

'Please try to remember, Mrs Dutton, that my sole aim is to secure your release from this place and your safe return to the children. If the children can be . . .'

'I don't want you talking to the children. It's not right for them to have to know about all this.'

'I'll bear that in mind.'

'I don't want you talking to the children.'

'Could we . . . ?' Skelton gave her a second to compose herself. 'Did Ted get the sweets that Billy brought for him?'

'Course he did.'

'And did you tell him they'd come from Billy?'

'I used to say I'd got them with some coppers I saved up.'

'And he never suspected?'

'Didn't give it a second thought. Didn't care where they came from as long as they was Everton Mints.'

Edgar had remained silent throughout, taking notes in his little book with his fountain pen. He looked up when his chief stopped speaking. Skelton indicated that he wanted something from the file that sat at Edgar's left elbow. Edgar knew immediately what he was talking about, opened the file and passed over the summary he'd prepared of Sid Dutton's involvement with the Jubilee Fund.

Skelton studied it for a moment. 'When Sid Dutton died,' he said, 'Ted inherited some land.'

'What land?'

'He inherited the forty acres at Steppes Green.'

'Steppes Green?'

'Yes.'

'I don't know where that is.'

'Did you ever hear talk of the Jubilee Fund?'

'Is that to do with Manston Road Elementary?'

'No, it's to do with a school and a hospital in Africa. You never heard anything about it, or Sid's involvement with the fund?'

'Sid? I don't know,' Mary said. 'Is there some trouble about this?'

'Would you say that Sid Dutton was an honest policeman?'

Mary looked at Edgar taking notes and then back to Skelton. 'No.'

'In what way was he dishonest?'

'I don't know.'

'So why did you say he was dishonest?'

'Everybody knows. Collie police are on the take. Bent as an orphan's bones, the lot of them.'

'Can you think of a specific instance?'

'What?'

'What kind of fiddles were they up to?'

'I don't know what they did; I don't think anybody does. Just knows they did it.'

Skelton wrinkled his nose. He would have liked a smoke, but there were times when a formal approach can produce better results than his customary informality and this was one of them. His pipe would make him seem too pally.

'After Sid died, you didn't notice Ted spending more?' he said. 'He didn't buy a tractor or a lorry or more sheep?'

'He always borrowed a lorry to take the sheep to market. Never had one of his own.'

'If Ted got some money, what would he do with it?'

'When he come back from market, if he'd sold some sheep, he used to put the money in a box with a lock on it. Kept it in the cupboard in the front room.'

'And where is the box now?'

'Down the police station, I should imagine,' Mary said. 'Enid told me, when she went round to get some stuff for the kids not long after they put me in here, the house had all been cleared out. And when she asked, the copper said it had all been taken away for evidence.'

'Do you think they stole it?'

'Shouldn't wonder.'

'The police seem very certain that you are guilty.'

'I expect that's because Jessie told them I was.'

'Do they do everything Jessie tells them to?'

'Pretty much.'

'And why is that, do you think?'

'Loyalty. She's Sid's widow.'

'No other reason?'

'They're all on the take and she's in on it.'

'You can prove this?'

'Course I can't.'

Skelton stood and paced. The move brought a note of the courtroom to the occasion. He was, to some extent testing Mary's ability to stand up to cross-questioning, but, more urgently, he wanted to know.

'Did Billy kill Ted?' he said.

'What?'

'Did Billy kill Ted?'

'Why would he want to?'

'You said they hated each other.'

'Not that much.'

'Because he's in love with you, then. And he's jealous because Ted got the land from Sid and possibly a great deal more that you don't seem to know about, and he didn't get anything. And he thought that if his brother was out of the way, he could marry you and inherit the lot.'

'Where did you get this from?'

'Are you in love with Billy?'

'Don't be daft.'

'If none of this had happened, if the funeral had not been stopped and there had been no post-mortem, and if Billy had proposed marriage, would you have considered it?'

Mary put her hands to her face. Skelton could not tell whether she was hiding her smiles, her blushes, her shame or her incredulity. Whichever it was, he knew she was going to perform magnificently in court.

She straightened her hair, sat up and, speaking slowly, said, 'I'm trying to think what my honest answer is. And my honest answer is that the children would need a father and Billy was always kind to 'em.'

'Do you think he killed Ted?'

'If he was in love with me, he'd own up to it, wouldn't he? He wouldn't want me to be in prison.'

CHAPTER TWENTY-SIX

Mila was out when Skelton got home. This was not unusual. She belonged to a discussion group that met in Maidenhead and often invited guest speakers to their Thursday meetings – philosophers, economists, scientists, psychologists. Most of them were Bolshevists of one sort or another but it seemed to Skelton that, since the war, all intellectuals had to be. Academics weren't allowed in the Senior Common Room unless they had something nice to say about the workers.

He found Mrs Bartram in the kitchen shrouded in steam.

'Did Mrs Skelton say she'd be home for dinner, or will she be dining in Maidenhead?'

'No, she's not gone to Maidenhead. She just popped out for a walk.'

'Oh, not been gone long, then?'

'Well, I wouldn't say that. She went out just after lunch.'
It was nearly seven and dark out.

Skelton drank his sherry alone.

Mila came in at about twenty past seven, looking slightly flushed.

Skelton didn't like to ask where she'd been for fear of betraying suspicious or untrusting thoughts, but she told him anyway.

'I needed new stockings and they didn't have the kind I liked at Manning's, and when I came out the bus was just there, so I went into Slough. And just outside Suters I ran into Eliot Dean, the architect, you remember?'

'Yes, of course.'

'And we got chatting and he suggested we had tea at the Crown, and the next thing I knew it was past five, and you know how unreliable the buses can be.'

Was she relating the events of her day in that slightly breathless way because she had hurried, eager to be home, or was the breathlessness caused by something else? Was her explanation a roundabout way of apologising? Was she excusing herself? Was she adding a little too much detail? Was she lying?

Skelton chided himself. The habit of cross-questioning witnesses, of doubting everything they said, had become so ingrained that he mistrusted even his wife.

Respectable married women did not, he knew, have tea with unmarried men in provincial hotels, but Mila had never been respectable in any conventional sense. Had her libertarian views now stretched to encompass adultery?

'Did you get the stockings?'

Mila reached into her handbag and produced them, perhaps a little too triumphantly; as if he had challenged her to produce evidence to support her story and she, with a defiant flourish, had done so.

He gave her a glass of sherry and they talked of snowdrops.

The following morning, as he was waiting for his train, he saw, through the railings, Parker-Ellis getting out of his car. Skelton moved swiftly down the platform to hide among the second-class passengers. Too late. Parker-Ellis saw him and joined him.

'The first class is usually up at that end, isn't it?' he said.

'Sometimes it's a short train and it's more towards this way,' Skelton lied. 'How's your wife?'

Just that morning, Mila had told him that the postman had told her that Mrs Parker-Ellis had some problem with her eyes and might even need an operation to save her sight.

'What?' Parker-Ellis said.

'How are her eyes?'

Parker-Ellis looked at his briefcase. In the perfect world his secretary would have prepared some notes on his wife's eyes so that he could answer questions like this with more confidence.

'I hope she's feeling a little better,' Skelton said.

'Oh, yes. She can see quite a lot of things quite well.'

'Good.'

'Listen, I was having a word with Jix the other day and he's getting very, very concerned about these rioters.'

'Jix', Skelton knew, was Sir William Joynson-Hicks, the Home Secretary, scourge of nightclubs, D. H. Lawrence, *The Well of Loneliness* and Marie Stopes.

'The rioters?' Skelton asked.

'The Mary Dutton women. Have you seen this morning's *Telegraph*?'

'I don't think I have, no.'

'Seven thousand of them in Parliament Square yesterday.'

'Rioting?'

'Thankfully, the police did not shirk their duty, otherwise God knows how it could have ended. The thing is, far too many of these women are over the age of twenty-one.'

'How many would be the right number?'

'What?'

'You said far too many.'

Parker-Ellis looked at Skelton's boots to check for signs of insanity, he'd been told on good authority that the mad can't tie their laces, and said, 'What?'

'It doesn't matter.'

Another moment while Parker-Ellis wondered whether he was being made the victim of some sort of ruse or jape, then, carrying on regardless, 'So, they'll be voting in this election. You do realise that if this Mary woman hangs it will reflect very badly on the government.'

'I didn't realise Conservative voters were so against capital punishment.'

'No. They like it. Well, they don't like it. Nobody likes it. But they deem it necessary. As do we all. But these five million new voters – these women – whether or not they approve of capital punishment in general, they are most certainly opposed to this specific example of capital punishment. Certain newspapers, I'm afraid, have irresponsibly whipped up a lot of female hysteria about this Mary Dutton woman.'

'I'm not sure why you're telling me this.'

'Because the last thing any of us want, I'm sure you'll agree, is a Labour government.'

Skelton looked up at the platform clock.

'The train's late,' he said. 'There have been a lot of cancellations lately.'

'I expect that'll be blamed on us, too. Look, all I'm asking is that you do what you can to sort this thing out as quickly as you can. Get the woman set free.'

'As counsel for the defence that is an exact description of my job.'

'Good. As long as we have an understanding.'

They hadn't, of course, but, all the same, Parker-Ellis looked pleased with himself. He had boasted to Joynson-Hicks that he knew Skelton personally. Joynson-Hicks had asked him to have a word. Oil the wheels. Whatever was necessary. Parker-Ellis could report back that they had reached an understanding. Joynson-Hicks would say, 'Good man, I knew I could rely on you.' And Parker-Ellis would feel like a schoolboy given a pat on the head for remembering the date of the Treaty of Westphalia.

Skelton thanked God he had nothing to do with politics.

'By the way,' Parker-Ellis said, 'I see they've started work on the houses just below you. And actually, they might not be as bad as we'd feared.'

'How so?'

'Well, you know who the architect chappie is, don't you?'

'Eliot Dean.'

'Oh, you do know.'

'Is he a particularly gifted architect?'

'He won a VC at Neuve-Chapelle with the Lancers. Lost a leg. Remarkable story. You should try and get him to tell it sometime, although he never would. Modest to a fault. I was too old for that show, of course, although I saw a bit of action at Bloemfontein. You?'

'Unfit for service, I'm afraid. I was born with a dicky hip.'

Parker-Ellis looked down at Skelton's hip, then looked away, not wanting to betray his feelings, which were, Skelton was sure, similar to those he might harbour against a traitor who'd made a pile of money selling mustard gas to the Germans.

'Well, anyway, he's a marvellous chap,' Parker-Ellis said.

'So, you're not as worried about the houses?'

'I'm sure a chap like that would never do anything unseemly.'

'My wife actually knows him quite well. Just yesterday, she had tea with him at the Crown in Slough.'

Had Parker-Ellis been wearing a monocle, it would have fallen from his eye. He twitched. His contempt for Skelton had doubled, tripled. What kind of snivelling, conchie coward would allow a man – even a VC – to take tea with his wife at a provincial hotel without reaching for the nearest horsewhip to correct the wife's error, and a pistol to teach the man a thing or two?

'She said the ginger cake was very nice,' Skelton went on. 'Extra spicy.'

The train came. They couldn't find two seats in the same compartment and missed each other at Paddington.

CHAPTER TWENTY-SEVEN

After a second meeting in Birmingham with representatives of The Imperial Bauxite Trading Company, Skelton and Edgar emerged into Bennett's Hill, drunk with boredom. The rain which had been torrential when they'd arrived had almost stopped.

Keeling was there with the Daimler.

'Warwick, is it, gentlemen?'

'We have an appointment at the Judge's House in Northgate at three.'

'Be there by two, I'd have thought. Half past at the latest.'

The route from Birmingham to Warwick took them along a mile or so of well-tarmacked, arrow-straight, completely empty road. Skelton picked up the speaking tube.

'This looks the ideal spot.'

Keeling guessed what he meant. 'I'd be more than happy to oblige, Mr Skelton,' he said, 'but I'm afraid I'd get in trouble with Mr Patterson.'

'Mr Patterson would never need know.'

'I couldn't tell a lie to him. He's the godfather of my children. I'm sorry, sir.'

'No harm done. I just thought I'd ask.' Skelton sat back in his seat. 'Perfect stretch of road for a little run,' he said, but Edgar, with his head out of the window, couldn't hear.

It was market day in Warwick. Keeling parked in a side street, and Edgar went off to see if he could find some nostrum for biliousness at a chemist. Skelton mooched through the crowds looking for somewhere that might offer a late lunch.

The rain here had been as bad as in Birmingham. Rivers were running in both gutters, carrying the detritus of the market – rotten fruit and veg, bits of bread.

At the bottom of the road, a small crowd had gathered around a ragged boy of perhaps six or seven, who had his foot stuck in a drain cover.

It took Skelton a moment or two to understand the nature of the problem. The drain was blocked. A deep puddle had formed – a soup of the market scraps. The boy had no doubt been playing in the puddle and, unable to see the submerged drain, somehow caught his foot in it. He was clearly in pain but bearing it manfully, whimpering rather than howling. Two burly men were trying to help, with their hands underneath the water, wiggling the foot. This hurt the boy more.

A young woman smoking a cigarette stuck her face out at Skelton.

'I seen your picture in the paper,' she said, and turned to her friend. 'I seen his picture in the paper.' She turned back. 'I seen your picture in the paper.'

'Er . . . yes, you probably did,' Skelton said.

'Are you the doctor who cut up all those people and put them in suitcases?'

'No. Thankfully he's in prison waiting for his appeal to be heard.'

'It's something like that, though, innit?'

'It's wossname, Gallerad,' the friend said.

'Oh, it is, isn't it? That's you, isn't it? Sir Gallerad. You're Sir Gallerad.'

The two burly men gave a tug and the boy shrieked.

'What exactly is going on here?' Skelton asked.

'He was fishing for scraps, I think,' the woman said.

'To eat?'

'What else?'

Skelton looked at the cabbage leaves and lumps of bread sodden with the filthy water.

'Can you twist while I pull?' one of the men said to the other.

'No, it hurts too much,' the boy said.

'It's the only way to get it out.'

Skelton looked closer. On the visible foot, the boy was wearing a laced boot, probably a couple of sizes too small. Presumably he had the same on the other foot.

'Wouldn't it be easier,' he said, 'to get the foot free if the boot was off?'

He had the men's attention straight away. He had the attention of the entire street. His voice was loud, he was the tallest person for miles around and he wore the uniform of a professional gentleman – black overcoat, black homburg, rolled umbrella. Even the boy stopped howling.

'I think if you were to remove the drain cover, then remove the boy's shoe . . .'

'No, it's his foot that's stuck,' one of the men said.

By the time he'd explained, he could have it done. Skelton took off his overcoat and suit jacket and passed them to the young woman. He rolled up his shirtsleeves and waded into the water. Drain covers could be removed, he'd seen it done by a man with a hooked implement. He did not have a hooked implement, but he did have an umbrella, the handle of which slotted neatly into the grid of the drain next to the boy's foot. Before pulling he considered the possibility that removing the drain cover could ease the blockage causing the water to be sucked into the drain with enough force to pull the boy with it. It seemed unlikely, but all the same he grasped the boy's arm with one hand before pulling on the umbrella with the other. The cover came away surprisingly easily. Helped by the two men he lifted the cover and the boy clear of the puddle then, while the men held the boy high, removed the boot. With the shoe off, the foot slid easily from the grating. The boy, without a word of thanks, grabbed the boot and, one shoe on and one shoe off, hobbled up a side street and vanished.

Skelton gingerly pulled his handkerchief from his pocket and wiped his hands. The young woman helped him on with his coat.

His shoes squelched. His suit trousers were ruined.

'Do you think there might be anywhere I could dry off?' he asked.

The young woman said. 'Milner's is your best bet.'

'Milner's?'

'Just on the corner, up there.'

Skelton could see the shop. A tailors.

'They'll do you a sponge and press.'

Skelton squelched up Market Street. On the way he met Edgar.

'What . . . ?'

'A boy had his foot stuck in a drain.'

'And . . . ?'

'There's a cafe two doors up from the Green Dragon does sausage roll and peas for 5d. Pot of tea 4d. I'll meet you in there in twenty minutes.'

'And you . . . ?'

'Sponge and press,' Skelton said and squelched away.

'Oh dear, oh dear, oh dear, what happened to you?' Milner said as he entered the shop.

'Yes, I wonder if you could help?'

'I bet you do. Sit there and get your shoes and socks off while I get you a towel. It's all the way up to your knees. What happened, did you forget your bathing drawers?'

Skelton did as he was bidden and explained about the boy with his foot stuck.

Milner took him into the fitting room, sorted him out a pair of flannel trousers and told him to take his wet ones off so that he could have a proper look.

'I'm afraid I might spoil the flannels,' Skelton said.

'They're only second-hand anyway, all ripped at the back if you look. I was going to try and mend 'em and sell 'em but I don't really think it'll be worth it. The rag man'll have 'em. Only, the thing is, I'm never going to get all that mud off just sponging it and, if I press it, that's going to press the residual filth right into the fibres of the fabric and then it'll be spoilt for good. Much better to wait until the mud's properly dried, then you can brush it off.'

'I have a rather important meeting to attend.'

'I'll see what I can do.' Milner picked up the shoes and socks and held them at arm's length, 'These aren't going to be properly dry till tomorrow, neither. Jem! Come here!' A lad of about sixteen with sticky-out ears emerged from a back room into the shop. 'The gentleman is going to need new shoes and socks.' He turned to Skelton. 'What size are you? Ten?'

'Sometimes an eleven. It depends on the width.'

'You can spare a pound, can't you?'

'Yes, of course.' Skelton took out his notecase.

244

'Take the gentleman's pound, get up John Rowe's, ask him for a pair of black Oxfords, like these, size eleven, nothing fancy, and don't pay more than 15s 11d. And get a decent pair of black socks while you're there. And don't talk to any girls on the way.' The boy left.

'He's no harm,' Milner said. 'Now, I've got a pinstripe here I made for a gentleman about your size a couple of months ago. I thought I was going to have to completely remake it much smaller and then you pop along, and I think, *Hello*. It's fate. I could let you have that for . . . shall we say, four guineas? Do you want to pop in there and try it on?'

Skelton did so. The trousers were halfway up his calves and the left-hand lapel ballooned outwards.

'Lovely fit,' Milner said.

'The trousers are too short, aren't they?'

'Or to put it another way, your braces are too tight. Slacken 'em off a bit and they'll fit a treat.'

'And this sort of . . .'

'Yeah, Mr Eversley had one shoulder a good bit higher than the other. I could probably fix that with a bit of padding.'

'Mr Eversley was the man the suit was made for?'

'Lovely man.'

'Why didn't he collect the suit?'

'Unfortunately, he died. Couple of weeks ago. He never enjoyed robust health. Needs a bit of a tuck there and it'll be nice as ninepence. Slip the flannels back on and I'll get it sorted for you.'

The wall of the little changing room was hung with photographs of gentlemen wearing elegant suits, presumably tailored by Milner. One of them, showed an anxious elderly gentleman in full morning suit with topper. It was labelled 'Lord Kinver'. Skelton took the photograph from the wall and brought it out to Milner.

'You knew Lord Kinver?'

'I dressed him for years. Didn't he wear his clothes beautifully? Marvellous man. I went up to Kinver House several times, for fittings and so on. Practically one of the family. Died, what, ten years ago?'

'Did he leave an heir?'

'No. Awful story: he married late to a younger woman, took her to Italy for the honeymoon, she came back with some terrible foreign disease and died six weeks later. He had a new funeral suit and two black lounge suits, and they lasted him out, give or take a few alterations. He went a bit batty towards the end, of course.'

'In what way?'

'Persecution mania. Locked himself away convinced that he was under attack.'

'Who did he think was attacking him?'

'The anarchists. He thought the country was crawling with anarchists who were plotting to assassinate him.'

'Had he done anything in particular to offend the anarchists?'

'Not that I'm aware of.'

Jem came back. The shoes were not top quality but seemed to fit and would certainly do.

'Mr Rowe says you're the bloke out the paper,' Jem said.

'Which bloke?' Milner said.

'He said Gallerad.'

Milner squinted his eyes to look at Skelton.

'Oh, I knew I recognised you. Only I know so many people round here and I couldn't put a name to the face. You're doing the Mary Dutton thing, course you are. Oh, well. Now. There's the thing. Mary Dutton's father-in-law, Sid Dutton, he was very well in with His Lordship as well.'

'Kinver?'

'Very well in. His Lordship thought the world of him.'

'Why was that?'

'The persecution mania. Well, I say that, I mean everybody liked Sid Dutton but with His Lordship it was mostly the persecution mania. Sid looked after him, you see. His Lordship thought Sid Dutton was the only thing between him and the anarchists. Sid couldn't do too much for him. He called Sid his 'trusted champion and saviour and his strong right arm'. He had two coppers on twenty-four-hour watch at Kinver House and had all these electric bells and tripwires put in.'

'He's here about the woman killed her husband in Collingford,' Jem said.

'I know. That's what we're talking about, Jem.'

'I've seen Billy.'

'Her brother-in-law?' Skelton said.

'On his bike. Down Wroxton. And he's always in the Green 'Un.'

'The Green 'Un?'

'It's a book.'

'A book?'

From inside his jacket, Jem took a dog-eared magazine called *Motor Cycling*. On the cover was a dramatic engraving of a motorcyclist spraying earth as he took a tight corner.

'A mate of mine buys it and then, when he's done, he gives it another mate of mine and then, when he's done, he gives it me.'

'Nothing about motorbikes Jem doesn't know.' Milner was sewing with cross-eyed concentration. This pleased Skelton. His mother went cross-eyed when she sewed. 'I've told him if he paid half the attention to his cutting as he does to his bikes, he'd be running Savile Row by the time he's thirty.'

'He's making his own bikes now,' Jem said.

'Billy?'

'At Northampton Motor Cycles. They do engines as a rule but Billy's doing a full bike with 'em and they reckon it'll be the best in the world. If it ever happens.'

'Is there a problem?'

'A mate of mine knows a bloke who works at NMC, says the whole place is going bust.'

'Could I borrow this?' Skelton said, holding up the magazine.

'If you like. I got a big pile of 'em in the back here. I got the Blue 'Un and all.'

'The Blue 'Un?'

'Different sort of book.'

'About motorcycles?'

'Ar.'

'That's marvellous.'

'He beat Albert Stainton in Newcastle.'

'Billy?'

'Ar. I'm gonna get a motorbike soon. I got four pound seven and nine saved.'

'Go and get the camera, Jem. We should have a photograph of Mr Skelton to hang on the wall.'

Milner gave him the jacket back and Skelton tried it on. He had padded the shoulder extensively so that the left-hand lapel no longer ballooned. Skelton looked in the mirror and saw a beautifully dressed hunchback. For the time being, he decided, hunchback would be better than mud-spattered.

While Milner neatly wrapped his muddy suit and wet shoes with layers of brown paper and string, Skelton wrote a cheque for five pounds. When Jem came back with the camera, he tipped him a ten-shilling note.

'There's film in the camera,' Jem said.

Milner looked up at the hunched back and down to the exposed socks.

'Perhaps another time, when Mr Skelton's not so busy,' Milner said, and hurried to help Skelton on with his overcoat, struggling to make it fit. The shoes squeaked.

By the time Skelton reached the cafe, the squeaky shoes were already hurting. He pulled the socks tighter in the hope it might help.

'New shoes?' Edgar asked.

'Very painful new shoes.'

'Given you the hump, I see.'

Skelton nodded an acknowledgement of the joke but neither managed to raise a smile.

They ate sausage rolls and peas.

Edgar took out his pocket watch.

'We'd better forgo the pot of tea,' he said. 'It's only a short walk to the judge's house, but we wouldn't want to be late.'

'Actually, there's no need for you to come, Edgar. Do you think there might be somewhere you could find a telephone?'

'I know people at Lyall and Groves on Swan Street.' Edgar seemed to know every solicitor in the country. 'I sure I could phone from there.'

'See if you can get hold of young Rose at Critchlow and Benedict's. I've a couple of little jobs I'd like her to do.'

'Oh, she'll like that.'

CHAPTER TWENTY-EIGHT

Mr Justice Kirkland was in a snug next to the dining room at the Judge's House, sunk deep into an armchair with what might have been his third or fourth post-lunch brandy at his elbow.

Kirkland had a reputation for being 'a character', 'one of a kind', 'a wit'. Thirty or forty years earlier, before elevation to the bench, he'd been drawn by Spy for *Vanity Fair* in full flow with one eyebrow raised and a half-smile – the expression that people with a reputation for wit often adopt to indicate that they just gave an example of it and expect all those present to laugh.

People told anecdotes about Kirkland's legendary wit in after-dinner speeches and that sort of thing. Skelton had never thought there was much to them. Most people in The Pack Horse on Briggate could be funnier on a wet Sunday morning when there'd just been a death in the family.

One of the anecdotes was about a contested legacy. The legacy included several beehives. The nub of the joke, although Skelton couldn't remember the details, was a pun between 'be' and 'bee'. Another concerned a plaintiff by the name of Jabett. In his summing-up, Kirkland had said, 'Jabett by name and Jabett by nature, for he attacked my client with a jab with the left and a jab with the right.' At the City Palace of Varieties, they threw sharpened pennies at comics who told jokes like that, but he'd seen top lawyers helpless with laughter. Perhaps, he thought, he was missing something.

'I don't think we've met, have we?' Kirkland said, making an effort to stand to shake hands.

Skelton motioned him to stay where he was.

'No, I haven't had that pleasure.'

'Sit down, sit down, sit down. You're at 8 Foxton Row with Clarendon-Gow,' Kirkland said. 'Fine chap. I used to know his father.'

'I didn't realise Mr Clarendon-Gow's father was a man of law,' Skelton said.

'He wasn't. He was a roué. He took me to some disgusting places when were up at Oxford.'

Skelton judged the degree of laughter that would be appropriate and then increased the amount by about fifteen per cent.

'I wanted to have a word with you about this Dutton case. I don't usually do the Midlands, but I've drawn the short straw, I'm afraid. Poisoned chalice for me, in, perhaps, both the figurative and the literal sense.' He snorted a laugh, and Skelton realised, a little too late, that this was an example of the famous 'wit'. He managed a 'ha', tried to extend it to a 'ha, ha', but found he couldn't.

'Pinfield was supposed to be up for it,' Kirkland continued, 'but a horse fell on him, did you hear about that?'

'No.'

'Serves him right, silly bugger, for riding at his age. Do you ride?'

'No, sir.'

'Of course, I was forgetting. You're the slum boy, aren't you? Or is that some nonsense the papers made up?'

'I am from Leeds, sir.'

'Well, so's Harry Lascelles, but he's still got Adam fireplaces and an army of liveried footmen, hasn't he?'

It took a moment for Skelton to remember that 'Harry Lascelles' was the Earl of Harewood.

'I've nothing against slum boys coming into the business,' Kirkland commented. 'Same as women. I can't see what good they'll do but they could hardly make it worse, could they?'

Kirkland laughed so much that he had to wipe his eyes, then stopped, suddenly. Something had caught his attention.

'I never realised you had a . . . thing . . .' Kirkland was flapping a hand at the padded shoulder.

'Ah, yes. I was born with a limp too.'

'Is that why you squeaked when you came into the room?'

Skelton looked down at the new shoes.

'Crookback and a squeaky leg,' Kirkland said. 'My grandfather would have kept you locked in an attic like poor mad Uncle James.'

Hard to know whether to laugh or not. Kirkland didn't. Perhaps he had feelings for Uncle James.

'So, have you got anything?'

'In what way?'

'A defence.'

'Er . . .'

'No, I thought not. Tell you what, though. I was having dinner with Stanley the other night and he's terribly worried about it all, you know.' Stanley Baldwin, Prime Minister.

'Is he?'

'Of course. All these bloody women rioting on the streets. He believes – he's probably talking rot – he believes that if the Dutton woman—'

'Mary.'

'—if she goes down it puts us straight into the hands of the Bolshevists. Do you think it's rot?'

'I don't really think it's my place to—'

'Mealy mouths never catch the worm. Come on, lad. Pull yourself together.'

'Yes, sir, I do think he may be overstating the case.'

'All the same. He might know something we don't know, so anything we can do to keep the reds at bay. What I'm saying is . . . I've lost it . . . what was I saying?'

'Anything we can do to keep the reds at bay.'

'Yes, what I'm saying is if you can cobble together some way of . . . you know . . . as long as it looks. You know. I'm sure we all want what's best for everybody. But the woman mustn't hang. Not before an election anyway.'

'Actually, I wanted to speak to you about a different, although very much related, matter.'

'Go on.'

'It has come to my notice that the local police have not been pursuing their enquiries with quite the vigour one might expect in a case like this.'

'That's the . . . bloody . . . watch committee's business.'

'Yes, of course, but I may have evidence of serious corruption in the local force in which members of the watch committee could be implicated.'

'Few back-handers, bit of how's-your-father?'

'A sum of £40,000 has been mentioned.'

'Good God. You're sure?'

'I have written evidence.'

'Who's the MP?'

'Crawford, J. E. B. Crawford.'

'The cabinet chappie?'

'Secretary of State for Colonial Trade.'

'Have you presented your evidence to him?'

'He's in Bermuda, negotiating a trade deal with the Americans.'

'He's got a woman out there, hasn't he?'

'I'm afraid I don't know.'

'So I've heard. Wife of the assistant governor. Audrey something or other.'

'So, his ability to intervene in this matter—'

'Which matter?'

'The alleged police corruption in Collingford.'

'Stick it all in a letter, I'll have a read and if I think it's worth it, I'll pass in on to Jix, you know, Joynson-Hicks, the Home Secretary. But I can't see how it'll help save this woman's neck,' Kirkland said.

'I'd have thought it could be of great significance.'

'Jix sets up an enquiry. By the time that reaches any sort of conclusion, three or four years have sailed by. Stanley wants this business done and dusted before the election. What else have you got?'

'Some suspicion has been cast on the deceased's brother.'

'Billy Dutton, the motorcycle man?'

'You know him?'

'My grandson's a fiend for that sort of thing. Wants to fly an aeroplane to Australia. Silly bugger. Barely made it to Guildford last time.'

'There is a growing body of evidence—'

'No, no, no. We can't hang the motorcycle man before an election. Not in this day and age. Be like hanging Jack Hobbs.' Surrey cricketer, the greatest batsman in the history of the game.

'Tell you what. Here's a plan. Jix thought it up so I'm not

256

taking any credit. You change your plea to guilty, she gets sentenced, then, eve of the election, he grants her a reprieve and wins the vote of five million happy flappers. Suit you? Shout for the man.'

'I . . .'

'My glass is empty. Shout for the man. His name's Boyce or Doyce or Dice or Bike. Just shout "man". I can't speak above a whisper my throat's so dry.' Kirkland was speaking loud enough to be heard in Coventry.

Skelton shouted, 'Boyce', and the man, whether his name was Boyce or not, appeared at the door so promptly he must have been standing just beyond waiting for his summons.

Kirkland pointed at his glass. Boyce bowed, produced a tiny silver tray, took the glass, put it on the tiny silver tray, took the glass to the sideboard, poured a generous measure, returned the glass to the little table at Kirkland's elbow, vanished the tray as expertly as he'd made it appear, bowed again and left. Skelton wanted to applaud.

'So,' Kirkland said, 'plead guilty, Jix reprieves.'

'Er . . . ethical considerations are beginning to be a concern.'

'So they should, so they should. Shot to bloody pieces. But, you know, Stanley has bigger fish to fry and – like the war – we all have to, you know, for the greater good. What d'you say? Good plan?'

'It is an excellent plan.'

'You're not going to do it, though, are you?'

'I still have great hopes of achieving similar ends by different means.'

'Up to you, of course. But if you actually want to save the woman's neck, I'd say pleading guilty was your best bet.'

'I'll certainly give the matter a great deal of thought.'

CHAPTER TWENTY-NINE

Rose's letters, written in her flawless copperplate, were beautiful to look at but read like military reports.

She had received Mr Skelton's instructions relayed in a telephone call from Mr Hobbes on the afternoon of Thursday, 7th March. At 9 a.m. on the Friday she had walked to the Swan public house in Yardley where she had caught a Midland Red bus that took her, after one change, to the Emscote terminus in Warwick from where a twenty-minute walk brought her to Church Street.

And so on . . .

She had been to Milner's the tailors to look at Jem's motorcycle magazines. Did Jem blush when he saw her? Did he hover over her while she browsed? Did he stand in a corner tongue-tied and terrified? Or did he invent some chore and walk out into the brisk wind, cursing himself for his cowardice?

Or did they strike up an immediate rapport and arrange to meet again? Would Rose take him rambling with a mixed group of Ranger Guides and Rover Scouts who would sing hearty songs as they identified deer spoor, traces of ancient barrows and oxbow lakes?

Rose's letter gave no hint. Just . . .

As requested, I gained access to copies of both *The Motor Cycle* and *Motor Cycling* from Jem Hinton and studied them in order to establish the dates etc. of the race meetings attended or possibly attended by William 'Billy' Dutton.

She had listed the meetings by date, marking them with asterisks to indicate the likelihood he was in attendance; one for possible, two for definite.

As you can see, for instance, from 10th to 15th September he was in Harrogate for the International Six Day Trials, after which he must have ridden to Berwick-Upon-Tweed for the Annual Rough Riders Run, then all the way down to Falmouth (a distance in excess of 500 miles) for the Solo Rodeo, and on and on.

Rose made it clear that within this busy schedule, there were opportunities for him to have called in at Collingford a few days before Ted's death, when he might have delivered the final, fatal dose. And on two occasions more recently when he might have visited and – if Alan had it right – terrorised his mother.

Rose had also turned up and carefully copied out an article from *Motor Cycle News* about the fate of NMC.

The company had, as Jem had indicated, been a successful manufacturer of motorcycle engines. Billy Dutton had been brought into the firm in 1925, since when he had been working closely with the engineers on a motorcycle of revolutionary design. But there had been setbacks. Prototypes had been disappointing and the firm, which had borrowed heavily to retool, was facing bankruptcy.

'He is in money trouble,' Skelton said, as he and Edgar drank their morning tea at 8 Foxton Row. 'His father left a big house and an unspecified amount of money to his mother and forty acres to his brother, and possibly nothing to him. He therefore poisons his brother – possibly with gifts of Everton Mints . . .'

'Is "Everton Mints" too silly to be plausible?'

'It would depend on how it was presented to the jury. I think it might be all right as long as one avoided using the actual words. "Confectionery" might work better.'

'Go on, he poisons his brother with confectionery.'

'He poisons his brother with confectionery with the intention of subsequently marrying his brother's widow thereby securing the inheritance. When, in an unexpected turn of events, the widow is arrested for the murder he hoped would never be detected, he sees the inheritance slipping away to the children and therefore begins to pester his mother –

who might possibly have, or have access to, what remains of the £40,000 that Sid stole from the Jubilee Fund.'

'So why doesn't she give it to him?'

'As I said, perhaps she hasn't got it.'

'She's keeps a big house. Servants. Sid would have left her well-provided.'

'Has the analysis of the Everton Mints turned up anything?'

'I haven't heard back yet. I'll telephone this afternoon.' Edgar looked at his pocket watch. 'And you're in court in twenty-seven minutes.'

'Am I?'

Skelton gathered up his wig box and other accoutrements while Edgar sorted out the papers.

'Old Bailey. *Rex versus George Bainbridge*, a shoe repairer, *and Sergeant Gordon Madeley*, a quartermaster serving with the Middlesex Regiment,' Edgar said. 'The cobbler and quartermaster have been putting in bills to a total value of £12 18s 6d for boots that were never repaired and are charged with theft and conspiracy to defraud the Secretary of State for War. You are defending. You bring the court's attention to a score of other, entirely unrelated, discrepancies in the adjutant's record-keeping, a list of which you have in your hand – the other hand – blame the whole thing on shoddy administration, they go home to their cobbling and quartermastering, and with any luck you'll be back here by lunch.'

CHAPTER THIRTY

Skelton was in fact back well before lunch and found Edgar and a couple of the lads in the hallway at 8 Foxton Row remonstrating with Billy Dutton. He guessed it was Billy Dutton, anyway. It couldn't really have been anyone else.

In his fur-lined coat, fur-lined boots, huge gauntlets and flying helmet with yellow-tinted goggles pushed back, Billy had the swagger of a Hungarian cavalry officer and seemed to occupy far more space than physics should allow. Edgar seemed fussed, if not downright terrified. The lads, on the other hand, seemed admiring.

Skelton lurked for a moment. His prime suspect in a murder case – an intrepid motorcyclist who had once half-killed a man over a game of shove ha'penny – was standing in the hallway of his place of work. Had he come to do mischief? Was there a concealed weapon about his person?

'What's the fastest you've ever been?' one of the lads asked.

'Not now, Mitch,' Edgar said. He turned to Billy. 'There are certain protocols and procedures attached to witnesses speaking to barristers,' he said, in a voice somewhere in the piccolo register.

Skelton decided the nettle must be grasped. He cleared his throat, forced his face into his friendliest smile and advanced with outstretched hand.

'Mr Dutton, isn't it? I'm Arthur Skelton and I see you've met my clerk, Mr Hobbes.'

'It's very nice to meet you, Mr Skelton.'

Billy's voice rumbled like snow sliding off a roof.

'And what can I do for you?'

'Well . . . I just thought we might have a word.'

'Of course—'

'I really don't think—' Edgar said.

'I've been hearing things here and hearing things there,' Billy said, 'and I've had a bloke been to see me from the Director of summat or other telling me I was going to be called as a prosecution witness and I mustn't do this and I'm not to say that, and I'm pissed off to the eyeballs with the lot of it. And so I thought the best thing would be if you and me could sit down and get all this business properly sorted out, without all the malarkey.'

'I think the "malarkey" you're talking about is the tradition of English justice which has served—' Edgar said.

Skelton interrupted, 'Perhaps it would be best if Mr Dutton and I did have a quick word, Edgar.' He turned back to Billy. 'Let's go up to my rooms, shall we? Tea?'

'Be lovely.'

Skelton nodded to one of the lads and led the way upstairs. Edgar followed anxiously.

'I think I saw you the other day in Collie,' Billy said. 'In the back of a Daimler Double-Six. Lovely car. Is it yours?'

'No, it's hired, just by the day.'

'I wouldn't mind a go at driving a car like that. I had a go in a three litre Bentley a couple of years ago. Up by Manchester. On a track. I got her up to 70 mile an hour. What's the Daimler do?'

'I wouldn't know,' Skelton said. 'The driver takes it very carefully, especially around the country lanes.'

'Oh, you'd have to. That Bentley was bloody heavy on the steering, I'd imagine the Daimler's the same.'

'Certainly, it would be compared to my Wolseley.'

'Oh, you got a Wolseley. Which one?'

'The 12-32 saloon.'

Skelton thought he detected a slight smirk.

'Oh, they're nice, them,' Billy said. 'How much did you pay for it, if you don't mind me asking?'

'I think it was £425.'

'Oh, you should have said, I could have got you one sixty or seventy quid cheaper than that. Brand new. Off a bloke I know at the factory. He'd have looked it over for you and all, make sure you weren't getting a duff 'un.'

'I'll bear that in mind next time. Take a seat.'

Billy did so. He looked around Skelton's room and sniffed. Skelton had always liked the smell of his room – coal, leather, tobacco, books and ink. They sat in the easy chairs. Edgar stood by the window, ready, perhaps, to fling it open and call for help if the need arose.

'Now, what can I do for you, Mr Dutton?' Skelton asked.

'I just want to get a few things straight. Cos – some of the things I've been reading in the paper – they've all got the wrong end of the stick. And then, I know there's rumours going round about me and our Ted that are just plain wrong. People are saying it's like I'm the bad 'un and I ain't the bad 'un. All I'm doing is the same as you're doing.'

'And what might that be?'

'Getting at the truth of things. What you should be doing anyway, only the way you read it in the papers it's like it's a football match. Villa versus The Albion, *Rex versus Dutton*, and you're centre forward for the away team. It shouldn't be like that, though, should it? I mean, I'm not on anybody's side. If we find out that Mary didn't do it, I'll be happy as Larry.'

'Of course.'

'Only this bloke come and see me and it's like he's coaching me to win, and I don't want to win, do I? Not for the sake of winning. That's just nasty. I want what's right.'

'The way in which a criminal trial is—'

'And I thought it'd be a lot easier if you and me have a chat, put our cards on the table and work out the best way forwards, never mind about *Rex versus Dutton*, just to get it all straight.'

'Good.'

The tea came. Edgar left his post by the window to pour, then took his cup and saucer back to the window and sipped. Billy helped himself to three lumps of sugar, tasted, added a fourth and vigorously stirred.

'First off,' he said, 'I want you to know, I don't think Mary could have done it even though our Ted might have provoked her. I mean, I felt really sorry for her. Lovely woman like that marrying our Ted. I mean, don't get me wrong, Ted could be the nicest bloke you could wish to meet. But only now and then. Other times he'd just lash out. See that?' He showed them a scar on his forehead. 'And I've got two busted ribs as play me up in the cold and a big scar down my leg where he had a go at me with a rake. People think I did it on my bike, but I've never had a nasty spill on my bike, ever. It was all our Ted when we was kids. Only Mum could never be bothered with us . . . Dad was Dad.'

'What do you mean by that?'

'I think everybody in Collie knows about my dad, but nobody ever says nothing cos, even though he's been dead three years now, he's still got the police, the magistrates, the council, the watch committee and the bowls team all tied up.'

'By tied up . . .'

'Back-handers. He knew where the bodies were buried. And my mum still does. I couldn't stand the sight of none of them by the time I was fourteen. I got a job with a big garage in Northampton mending cars and bikes. The gaffer let me have a room in his house. I haven't been home much since. Weddings, christenings, funerals and Christmas, and I've had a bellyful.'

'But you knew how Ted was treating Mary?'

'I'd heard.'

'From Mary?'

'No, she'd never have said a thing,' Billy said, 'but people up town had told me things.'

'Did your mother and father know about the way Ted treated Mary?'

'I don't think my mum would have cared. She hated Mary from the start. I mean Mum was Queen and here comes another woman in the family. She wasn't having that, was she?'

'So I believe. And what about your father?'

'No, my dad never said nothing, so I think Ted must have behaved himself when my dad was living there.'

'This was when your father became ill?'

'Yeah, Mum couldn't look after him no more. D'you mind if I take this off?'

Billy had removed his gauntlets, helmet and goggles but was still wearing the fur-lined coat.

'Of course,' Skelton said.

It took a while. There were buckles involved.

'You were saying your mother couldn't look after your father when he fell ill,' Skelton said. 'Was she ill herself?'

'She makes like she's an invalid but half the time she's just pissed,' Billy said. 'I've seen the empty bottles. Bloody rum. Can you imagine? I mean gin wouldn't be so bad, but rum? Anyway, she couldn't look after Dad, so Mary said she'd have him. Six, seven months until he died. Fed him and washed him and dressed him and took him to the lav and helped him to the po when he couldn't get to the lav any more.'

'There was, I believe a will,' Skelton said.

'The will, yes,' Billy said. 'Right at the end. He signed it a couple of days before he passed away. And he'd left all the land to Ted.'

'The forty acres.'

'Left the lot to Ted. Well, I won't say I wasn't a bit peeved cos the rent off that land's bostin' never mind what it'd be worth if you was to sell it but, you know, easy come easy go. I'm doing all right with my bike, thank you very much.'

'You're sure about that?'

'What d'you mean?'

'I believe you have a stake in NMC, Northampton Motor Cycles.'

'Yeah, I said, I been having to do with 'em since I was fourteen and Mr Bryson the gaffer put me on the letterhead four or five years ago to . . . Oh, I get what you're talking about. Yeah, Mr Bryson's lost a lot of money on this bike I'm supposed be making with him, but that's his money not mine. I'm hardly anything to do with the bike, to be honest. I mean, I know my way around an engine, but I couldn't invent a bike. Wouldn't know where to start. But they thought if they put my name on it, you know, they'd sell a few more.

Only Mr Bryson had no idea really how much it was all going to cost, and it all got out of control and the bank started getting shirty about all the money he was borrowing. But it's all right now, cos he's got Bill Morris interested.'

'Of Morris Motors?'

'That's the one. He's done a deal with Bill Morris and last time I saw Mr Bryson he was buying lathes in Coventry, twenty at a time, so he's all right, isn't he?'

'So, you're not personally in any difficulty with money?'

'Me? Year before last, I went to Italy, France, Austria and Germany, exhibition riding in something they called a Speed Circus. You know how much they pay for that sort of thing?'

'I've no idea.'

'Let's just say I'm all right for money.'

'So, the will didn't bother you?'

'Like I said, I was pissed off, but not so much as I made a fuss. And to be honest if I'd asked Ted to give us half the land anyway, I'm pretty sure he would have done.'

'But you didn't ask.'

'He had a wife and six kids.'

'Please feel free to smoke, Mr Dutton,' Skelton said and looked around for the cigarette box he kept for visitors. 'Edgar, where is the . . . ?'

Edgar sprang into action and found the cigarette box, but Billy was already unwrapping a cigar. He trimmed the end, then lit it, in a way no connoisseur would condone, with a cigarette lighter of foreign design which he snapped into life by sparking it on the side of his boot.

'As well as the house and the land, was money mentioned in the will?' Skelton asked.

'I think Mum got most of the money, didn't she?'

'How much money was there?'

'I don't know. A lot, I think.'

'Do you know anything about the Jubilee Fund?'

Billy sighed. 'I've heard. I never asked. Didn't want to know. Like I said, everybody's on the take around there. Police, town council, I've seen kids in school diddling other kids out of conkers. I'm not saying I didn't get my share sometimes. You know, I had a bike and ten times as many soldiers as any of the other kids at school. And me and Ted did terrible things other kids would have gone to Reform School for, but we'd just get a belting off Dad and everything else'd get sorted out. Ten quid here, a fiver there.'

'Was it your mother who told the police to stop the funeral?'

'Oh, you've found out about that an' all, have you? Yeah, Mum thought Mary must have poisoned Ted cos she was convinced she'd poisoned Dad. Only, she's never wanted people to know she thinks Dad was poisoned in case they decide to dig him up and check. She doesn't want his bones disturbing. So she asked 'em to say it was Mrs Curtis, the woman who laid him out, who spotted Ted had been poisoned.'

'She asked who to say?'

'The Collie police. She told 'em to say this Mrs Curtis saw something on his hands or something and Mrs Curtis was fine to go along with that that cos she'll do anything Mum says. Mum had it in her head that Mary got Dad to change his will so her and Ted would get the forty acres. Then she reckons Mary killed Dad before he had chance to change his mind. She went on and on about it. I told her – he was dying six or seven months. The doctor said he was dying. But she wouldn't have it. She thought it was suspicious that all the time he was ill they said he had something wrong with his chest and then, when he died, they put on the death certificate that he died with something wrong with his stomach. And I told her he had something wrong with his chest *and* something wrong with his stomach and in the end it could have gone either way, but it was the stomach that saw him off. But Mum wouldn't stop going on about it. "There was nothing wrong with his belly till she poisoned him." And I told her not to be so daft and she was only saying that cos she'd never liked Mary in the first place.'

'Have you been to see your mother since Ted died?'

'I went once after to make sure she was all right.'

'And was she?'

'She's always all right once she's got half a bottle of rum inside her.'

'And you haven't seen her since?'

'No.'

'She says you have. She suggests that you told your brother something that you should not have told him and she said she didn't want to see you ever again.'

Billy looked mystified.

'But then, later,' Skelton went on, 'she became worried that you would do something that might cause harm to somebody.'

272

'Where d'you get all this from?'

'One hears things.'

'She says I told Ted something I wasn't supposed to have told him? What am I supposed to have told him?'

'She calls you her "glorious, golden boy".'

'First I've heard of it. The thing you have to remember is, it's best not take any notice of anything Mum says, ever. She got it into her head once that the Red Indians from Buffalo Bill's circus were coming to kill her. And another time she had a secret cat called Bernice. We had a cat. It was called Tiddles. Bastard little ratter. But she said this other cat used to come and sit on her lap and purr, and it had a bow round its neck. She sounds mad when you say it, but it's just the rum really.'

'If Mary didn't kill your brother,' Skelton said, 'where did the poison come from?'

'He'd had rows at one time or another with practically everybody in Collie. They bear grudges, you know. Have you been to see her in the prison?'

'Yes.'

'How is she?'

'She misses the children.'

Billy poured himself another cup of tea, added milk and sugar, stirred and threw it back in one gulp.

'London tea's never the same,' he said. 'I think it's the water.'

He placed the cup and saucer on a side table with elaborate care.

'I don't know what to do,' he said. 'They're my nieces

and nephews and I've always, you know, brought 'em presents and that.'

'You brought them sweets.'

'Yeah. Whenever I come to Collie I'd load up with sweets for 'em.'

'And chocolates for Mary.'

'Yeah. She likes chocolates.'

'And Everton Mints for Ted.'

'Half-hundredweight every time cos otherwise I knew he'd nick the kids' sweets. Have you been to see them at all?'

'Mrs Fellows is looking after them very well.'

'I'll send her some money. Would that be all right, d'you think? If I sent her some money for the kids. I don't know what to do. Do you think it'd be all right if I went to see her?'

'Mary?'

'Yes.'

'That would be up to you and, of course, Mary.'

'Right.'

'Mr Dutton, are you sweet on Mary?'

'Could have been. When he first brought her down I thought, *Blimey our Ted's done all right for himself*. And before you start thinking me and Mary was having a bit on the side and killed Ted so we could go off together, you're wrong. I've got a girl in Northampton.'

Billy looked at his wristwatch. It looked complicated and expensive. 'Anyway, I've got to go and see a bloke,' Billy said. 'If you write to NMC in Northampton, they'll always know how to get hold of me.'

Edgar and Skelton walked him downstairs. As they were shaking hands, he said, 'All I want is, I want to know what the right thing to do is. Whether Mary did it or whether she didn't . . . personally, I'd rather she gets off even if she did do it, for the kids' sake. The thing is, my mum's got a grudge against Mary, but I ain't. I just want to see what's right and that's my only stake in it.'

When he'd gone Skelton said, 'He seemed like a nice chap.'

'Unless he was lying,' Edgar said.

'About what?'

'About everything.'

'He does it awfully well, though. And I'd imagine there'd be strings of witnesses and mounds of evidence to support every single assertion. Did you phone about the Everton Mints?'

'They said they'd have the results this afternoon.'

'If they're poisoned, we'll know he's lying about everything.'

'And if they're not?'

They weren't.

'No trace of arsenic.'

'Could you pass me a cigarette, please?' Skelton said.

'You don't smoke cigarettes.'

'The pipe seems so fiddly. What do we do?' Skelton asked.

'Plead guilty. And hope the Home Secretary keeps his word and reprieves her.'

'And if she ever gets out of prison the children will all be in their forties or fifties.'

'It is our only hope of saving her from the scaffold.'

'No. We can find something else.'

'Find what?'

Skelton lit the cigarette. He'd forgotten how pointless they tasted to a pipe-smoker.

'We'll know when we find it.'

CHAPTER THIRTY-ONE

By half past three in the morning he'd decided to emigrate. That would be the best. He'd go to California. There would be some way that an English barrister could qualify as an American attorney without having to start all over again. Some exams he'd have to take.

Being careful not to wake Mila, he found his dressing gown and slippers, went into the study and took down the atlas of the world. Not Los Angeles nor San Francisco. A smaller town. Fresno or Bakersfield. Or somewhere nearer the coast. Monterey or Santa Barbara. San Luis Obispo. He would become San Luis Obispo's most respected attorney. He'd read things in books. He'd seen films and pictures in magazines. He'd have a white clapboard office, like a shop, with a window and a venetian blind. It would say, painted on the window, 'Arthur Skelton, Attorney-at-Law'.

He wasn't sure if they hanged people in California. He knew in some parts of America they used the electric chair or the gas chamber. Anyway, there wouldn't be any capital offences in San Luis Obispo. It's the opposite of Chicago. A sleepy town. Sometimes the town drunk would be arraigned for public indecency. Sometimes the town show-off would be arrested for driving his Stutz Bearcat Coupe down Main Street without due care and attention. He would say 'Objection, Your Honour' and the judge would bang his gavel. 'Thirty days.'

It would be a long way for the children to come and visit, but cripes what an adventure.

Their new dad might be a one-legged VC and famous architect but their old dad was an attorney-at-law in California who drove them to his beach house in his yellow Packard Twin 6 Roadster and took them fishing in his sixty-foot sailboat and cooked the catch on a fire right there on the beach. They would wash the fish down with sodas and malted milk, and they'd say, 'We don't ever want to go home.' And he would be magnanimous and tell them that it was best they did go home because their mother loved them very much and so did their new stepfather, and they were kind, good people. And anyway, what about all their friends at school? They could come again next year. And, perhaps, when they were grown up, Lawrence could study law at Harvard or Princeton and join him.

Arthur Skelton and Son, Attorneys-at-Law. And Elizabeth could do the same if they had women attorneys. Otherwise she could be one of those tanned, open-faced American women who win at tennis and run things.

Meanwhile, Mary Dutton's kids would grow up without a father and with their mother in prison, if she was lucky and Jix kept his word.

Why did he have to be a bloody lawyer? Why did he have to be such a bloody bighead who thought he was better than his father or his brothers and sisters? He should have gone to work with his dad at Trevis and Nash. His dad would have given him tips. *Make sure you've got your cap on before you go in the pressure rooms in case there's any drips from the corrosives.* He'd have been proud.

But it would be all right. His mum and dad could come and visit too, in California. And his brothers and sisters and their families. They could all come and visit. *You could come and live here if you like, you and Mum. In the sunshine. Fresh orange juice for breakfast. You can't get Senior Service or proper tea, but we can have them sent over, like I do my Balkan Sobranie. Do you remember that time the buses had stopped and you walked home from work and your face was so froze by the time you got in you couldn't speak and then your throat went bad and you had quinsies? That'll never happen here.*

Saving Mary from the gallows would be difficult enough even with an uncorrupted police force and a capable solicitor on his side. But he didn't have either. He had two religious manic cousins and a Girl Guide.

And it wasn't just Mary and the future of her six kids, was it? From the way they were talking it looked like it was up to him to decide who'd win the general bloody election.

And there was another thought. Surely, in Mila's eyes, the man who was even partly responsible for returning a Labour government to Westminster would be twice the hero as a man who had his leg blown off at Neuve-Chapelle in what Mila had often described as a tragically pointless, bourgeois war.

Saturday dragged, mostly because he was half-dead from lack of sleep. Mila took her archery class, Lawrence his piano, Elizabeth her ballet. They had fish for lunch. In the afternoon he drove into Slough for new shoes to replace the ones he'd ruined rescuing the puddle-boy, but couldn't find any to fit and decided he'd have to have them made. In the evening, while Dorothy and Mila were putting the children to bed, he lit up his pipe and switched the wireless on. Miraculously, the wind was in the right direction or something and he actually managed to get a decent signal. Norah Blaney was singing a song called, 'Masculine Women, Feminine Men, which is the rooster, which is the hen?' – a brave choice, Skelton thought, given Miss Blaney's much-publicised friendship with Radclyffe Hall and her lesbian coterie. Perhaps Edgar was right. There was a lot more sapphism about than Skelton imagined. Perhaps he should not have dismissed Edgar's suggestion that Enid Fellows was the jealous lover quite so readily.

Norah Blaney finished her spot and some other singer started on, 'There's nothing left for me, of times that used to be, they're just a memory among my souvenirs,' which seemed too apt a description of the state of Skelton's marriage to be bearable. He switched off the radio and sat in silence, looking at the fire.

After a while, Mila came back.

'Did the children have their baths tonight?' he asked.

'Yes.'

'I don't suppose there'd be enough hot water for me to have one yet, then?'

There was a back boiler to the stove in the kitchen which took an age to heat up.

'Eliot told me that the new houses will have electric water heaters in the bathrooms,' she said.

CHAPTER THIRTY-TWO

On the Monday morning, Skelton got to 8 Foxton Row when the cleaners were still sweeping the stairs. Some of the lads were in, but Edgar wouldn't be in until half past eight or quarter to nine at the earliest.

He told one of the lads to bring tea and make up his fire. At his desk, he got his pipe going and started composing a letter to Mr Justice Kirkland, laying out his complaints against the Collingford police, the watch committee and the local council.

In his final paragraph he turned to the matter of Mary Dutton, said that, with great regret, he would do his utmost to persuade her to change her plea from not guilty to guilty, adding – with a hint at the 'arrangement' they'd agreed – that he 'hoped that judgement and the Home Secretary would take into account the full circumstances of the case before confirming sentence'.

The lad came with the tea and the coal scuttle.

Skelton made a fair copy of the letter and put it in an envelope.

Then he drafted letters to Norman Bearcroft, to Rose Critchlow, to Enid Fellows, to Billy Dutton, to Alan and Norah, informing them of his intention to plead guilty. He didn't write to Mary. He'd travel up to Birmingham either that night or the following day and speak to her in person.

Just after nine, Edgar came in with the morning post.

'The lads said you were in.'

'I've just written to Kirkland. You were right. We'll plead guilty and trust that Jix saves her to win the election.'

Edgar sat down heavily. 'It is the right thing to do,' he said. 'There's nothing else.'

'I'll brace myself for the onslaught of cabbages.'

They both pretended to laugh. While Edgar looked through the morning post, Skelton squared his blotter and brought the calendar, the inkstand and the telephone into line.

'Are you all right, old chap?' Edgar asked.

'Of course.'

'I'll organise some more tea.' Edgar left. Skelton spotted a letter from Alan and opened it.

Friday 15th March, 1929

My dear cousin Arthur,

I hope this finds you in sparkling good health and happiness and your loved ones equally blessed.

We went to Boots the Chemist yesterday. Norah has been getting her headaches again and the aspirin does not seem to work. She remembered when she was a child and she had headaches our mother used to give her something called Dr William's Pink Pills for Pale People and we wondered whether they still sold them. The lady in the shop asked whether she had the St Vitus' Dance. Norah said she just had a bit of a headache. The lady said she didn't think Dr William's Pink Pills were much use for headaches. People mostly take them for tropical problems and St Vitus' Dance. I asked whether they were effective and the lady said she didn't think they were. She suggested a mustard plaster on the back of the neck, for a headache, or drinking one drop from a tube of smelling salts dissolved in water. Norah said she'd try both.

On the way out we ran into Minnie, Jessie Dutton's maid, who was investing in a new hot-water bottle. We got chatting. Our conversation ranged over various subjects, but we managed quite naturally to steer her to talk again about Billy and Ted, just as you had asked us to. We can report that, as far as she knows, Billy has not visited his mother for several weeks and Ted, when he was alive, very seldom visited and when he did it was always on necessary business of one sort or another. He never stopped for a meal and did not usually even have a cup of tea. I imagine that this is not what you wanted to hear.

Otherwise there is very little to report. We had our meeting as usual and the crowd gets bigger every time. This week we ran out of chairs and so we cleared a lot of the chairs out so that people could sit on the floor. You can get more in that way and the younger ones don't mind.

Do you remember Simon and Annie, the shepherd and his wife who were so kind to us in the terrible snow? They have been coming to the meetings and making a lusty contribution to the singing. I have a mind to ask Annie to do a solo for, although her voice might not pass muster in operatic circles as a conventional soprano, what she lacks in timbre and absolute accuracy of pitch, she certainly makes up for in enthusiasm.

Jessie Dutton was there as well, brought in the car by her gardener/chauffeur and looking, mercifully, a good bit better than the last time we saw her. Possibly she was sober, but it's hard to tell with inveterate drunkards because often they need a certain amount of drink inside them just to look ordinary. She greeted Mary Dutton's children, who come to all the meetings now, with a pained smile, making it clear that she was too infirm to have to do with them. The children seemed quite content with this state of affairs. Jessie was very standoffish with Mrs Fellows, though. And Mrs Fellows with her.

Afterwards, as I was saying goodbye to people, Annie said she was a little bit aggrieved because Jessie Dutton had been standoffish with her as well. And I asked her, 'Do you know Jessie, then?'

She said they'd been at school together. This surprised me because Annie looks at least ten years younger than Jessie and I said as much. Annie pretended to go coy and accused me of being a smooth-tongued old flatterer. I did my best to assure her that I was not that sort of person at all and I must admit I was a little bit put out by her suggesting I was, particularly in front of the other celebrants. So, she apologised.

I asked whether she'd known Jessie well at school and she said she hadn't. They were in the same class, but Jessie was always off with some boy or other and when she was no more than fifteen might even have taken a trip or two to Daisy Grove. I asked what she meant by 'Daisy Grove' and she said that was for her to know and for me to find out. I assume it means the same thing as 'the primrose path of dalliance' that Shakespeare talks about in *Hamlet*.'

'No, it doesn't,' Skelton said.
'What?'

'Read this. From there.'

While Edgar was reading, Skelton took the letters he'd written to Kirkland, Norman Bearcroft, Rose Critchlow, Enid Fellows, Billy Dutton, and Alan and Norah, tore them into tiny pieces and threw them on the fire. Then he filled and lit his pipe, trying to stay calm.

Edgar finished reading. 'What about it?'

Skelton began a slow and wonderful dance around the room, waving his pipe in the air to make patterns with the smoke.

'Billy isn't her "glorious, golden boy", Edgar. There's another son. A third son, not Billy, not Ted, a third son who possibly – probably – certainly – is our poisoner.'

CHAPTER THIRTY-THREE

Daisy Groves was the baby farmer that Elsie Grace, the poor seventeen-year-old who was hanged for killing her child, was supposed to have visited. At the time Skelton had seen it as something of a triumph to be able to point out that Elsie could not have sought the services of Daisy Groves because Daisy herself had been hanged for infanticide in 1919, several years before Elsie had fallen pregnant.

According to Annie, the shepherd's wife, when Jessie Dutton was fifteen or so, which Skelton reckoned would have been somewhere between '90 and '95, she took a trip to Daisy Groves.

Was this to dispose of her 'glorious, golden boy'? And did that child, miraculously, survive, grow into adulthood, haunt her, blackmail her perhaps? And then, when his stepbrother inherited, did he turn his attentions there? And when, perhaps, Ted stood against him, did he, out of jealousy or rage, find ways of administering . . . ? Skelton stumbled. It was always at this point that conjecture came up short. How to administer the poison in small but increasing doses over a period of time?

'The pies,' Edgar said.

Skelton was grateful. 'The pies.'

'With lots of pepper.'

'Of course.'

Skelton saw a pained expression on Edgar's face. 'I'm clutching at straws, aren't I?' he said.

'Tiny, fragile wisps of it.'

'All the same, we might be able to work it up into something credible.'

'We *could* put a pig in an aeroplane,' Edgar said.

At 8 Foxton Row Skelton had his notes from the Elsie Grace trial brought up and read through them. They brought back bad memories. There was a photograph and note in another hand, not his own, that said her end came in the execution shed at Holloway on 15th June 1923. He'd never seen the execution shed at Holloway or anywhere else. Was it really like a shed? Would the sun shine through the cracks in the boards? He should have made a lot more of the lies about Daisy Groves. He had picked so many holes in the prosecution's case but he could have gone further. He hadn't because he thought he had it in the bag. He was so confident – puffed-up with vanity. He could have saved her.

While he read, Edgar composed a long telegram to Rose.

'What date was Daisy Groves sentenced?'

Skelton turned back a couple of pages in the notes. '24th November 1919.'

'What was Jessie Dutton's maiden name?'

'Whitehouse.'

'If an unmarried woman parked a baby at a baby-farm, would she use her real name?'

'Probably not.'

'How's Rose supposed to find him without a name?'

'She's a Girl Guide. They're trained for such things. When's the next meeting with the Bauxite people?'

'Wednesday.'

'Birmingham again?'

Edgar nodded.

'Breakfast on the train?'

'I'll make sure it has a restaurant car.'

'Remind me to ask where they get their sausages.'

'I'll be sure to do that.'

Keeling had the Daimler waiting at New Street.

'Where to?' he asked.

'How far is it to Smethwick?'

Edgar, who was tying a piece of string tightly around his head, said, 'I thought we were going to Yardley to see Rose this morning.'

'I thought I'd like to see Daisy Grove's baby-farm house.'

'Why? There'll be nothing there to see. And we've got to be back in Bennett's Hill by lunchtime.'

'What are you doing?'

'Chap I know – used to be a purser on the *Mauretania* – said a string tied tightly just above the ears is a prophylactic against sea-sickness. I thought I'd give it a try. I'm putting in ear plugs as well, so I won't be able to hear you.'

'Smethwick's right the other side of Birmingham to Yardley,' Keeling said.

And Edgar replied, 'Pardon?'

The string didn't work. They'd barely been ten minutes on the road before Edgar had his head out of the window again.

They arrived at the baby-farm house in Smethwick, but, as Edgar had predicted, there was nothing to see. On the corner of the street, Skelton spotted a chemist and said he needed a new toothbrush. The one he'd brought with him had a celluloid handle which was too slippy. He preferred bone.

While he was gone, Edgar removed the string and examined himself in his little metal mirror. It had left a deep groove across his forehead and partially paralysed his eyebrows. It had also made the edges of his hair stick out like a frill. His pocket comb made no difference.

It had acquired a permanent kink.

Skelton returned and was saying something. He removed the earplugs.

'I'm sorry, I couldn't hear. I had the earplugs in.'

'I said, when it first started it was actually quite a respectable private orphanage, but later Daisy Groves took to drink, grew slapdash and the poor mites started dying. The local police were shockingly complacent about it and seemed to be of the opinion that a few dead bastards didn't make much difference one way or the other. So, a group of local residents made an official complaint to the chief inspector and he came down hard. Had the place closed down, the surviving babies taken away to properly registered orphanages and Daisy Groves arrested. In the early days, though, Nellie said, they kept proper registers.'

'Who's Nellie?'

'Lady in the chemist shop. She's seventy-eight next birthday and hasn't had a day's sickness in her life, a blessing she attributes to her regular intake of something called Parker's Tonic. Nellie's granddaughter was Birmingham Carnival Queen in 1925 and now she's engaged to a man who lives in Solihull and works for the Wesleyan General Insurance. Oh, and a celluloid toothbrush is actually better than a bone one because a bone one can absorb microbes and bacilli.'

'And a celluloid one can't?'

'It's an impermeable surface.'

'I'll bear that in mind.'

From his pocket Skelton took a sachet of brown powder.

'Try some of this.'

'What is it?'

'Ginger root extract. Nellie's grandson used to get sick on buses and it worked wonders. She's got eight grandsons and seven granddaughters. It would have been eight of each but one of the girls was taken by the scarlet fever.'

'I'll need some water.'

Skelton gave him a bottle. 'Vichy water,' he said. 'Marvellous for rheumatism, Nellie says.'

'I don't get rheumatism.'

'Drink that and you never will.'

Lunch with three gentlemen from the Imperial Bauxite Trading Company was exciting only inasmuch as the auditors working on the case had just discovered that the Matlock and Ripley Textile Bank quite possibly owed them a great deal more money than they had previously imagined. A figure of £760,000 was mentioned. Skelton tried to be gracious but celebrating a possible gain of three-quarters of a million pounds with men who already had far more money than they needed did not feel like the sort of thing he should be doing with his life.

They didn't need to go to Yardley. Rose came to them. While Skelton had been celebrating with the Bauxite people, Edgar had been back to the Grand and found a telephone message from Rose saying she would meet them there after lunch. They found her in the coffee lounge in her little knitted hat and oilskin coat looking delightfully incongruous among the furs and feathers.

She told them she had been to see her friend at Births, Marriages and Deaths and he had sorted her out a pile of likely birth certificates issued in Smethwick between 1890 and '95, all with a blank where the father's name would be. She'd copied out the details. None of them mentioned the name Dutton nor Jessie's maiden name, Whitehouse.

'Would they even have registered the birth?' Edgar wondered.

'Let's see if the police can help,' Skelton said.

Newton Street police station, five minutes up the road, was a slum that was supposed to have been replaced thirty years earlier. The police themselves, once Skelton had introduced himself to the desk sergeant, could not have been more helpful.

'Here, Bernie, come here. See who this is? It's the bloke on the Mary Dutton case.'

Constables and sergeants assembled and in general behaved much like the ladies of the Defence League had. If anything, they were a little more simpering.

Sergeant Duggan took them down to an entanglement of cellars where the records were kept and, after a half-hour search located a sizeable box labelled 'Daisy Groves', with various dates and numbers, carried it upstairs for them and left them in a room that might at some point in history have been used for purposes of torture.

They opened the box. The court records and case notes were damaged by damp but still readable. Other than those, the box contained bags and envelopes filled with evidence taken from the house in Smethwick and, perhaps most usefully, the registers, two thick ledgers that traced the progress of Daisy Groves' lapse into drunkenness; the early entries, neat, spidery and complete; the later ones scrawled and blotched and unfinished. Sergeant Duggan said he'd fetch them some tea and left them to rummage.

In the early days at least, the registers told them, Daisy had taken about fifty babies a year, from newborns to toddlers, and kept them until they could be found foster parents or places in other institutions. The mothers would pay a lump sum for the baby's keep, although some mothers, who could not pay, were taken on as wet nurses.

Rose went through the entries, methodically comparing details to those she had taken from the birth certificates. Edgar studied the court records and case notes. Skelton sorted through the evidence in the envelopes and bags.

The bags were packed with scraps of fabric, bits of coloured string, coins, lockets, little medals and other trinkets. Skelton had seen their like at the old workhouse in Leeds. They were foundling tokens. Mothers, who could not bear to be parted from their newborns, would leave something so that perhaps, one day, mother and baby might know each other and be reunited.

The fabric scraps, patterned, would be torn diagonally. Mother would keep one half and baby the other in the hope that they would soon once again be brought together. Their existence in the envelopes was proof that they never were.

There were poems and inscriptions, 'Though I know I must, it is not just', 'You smiled and must have felt so grand, to hold my finger in your hand' and 'Know me'.

Skelton thought about Lawrence and Elizabeth and knew he could never go to California.

'Something?' Edgar asked.

'Foundling tokens.' Skelton showed him a tiny heart beautifully fashioned from fabric and human hair.

'"The world's more full of weeping than you can understand."'

'Bible?'

'W. B. Yeats. Irish poet.'

Skelton poured out the contents of another envelope.

He found a piece of bone with tiny writing on it. If he held his spectacles an inch or two from his face they worked like a magnifying glass. The letters, in purple, made most likely with laundry ink, said, 'My glorious, golden boy'.

On the other side of the bone, he read, 'J. W., Sammy Bell.'

'Rose, have you found a Sammy Bell?'

'No.'

'Look for one.'

Rose remembered something from the first clutch of birth certificates she'd dug out. 'Bell was Jessie Dutton's mother's maiden name.'

'If the children found foster parents, would that be recorded somewhere? Or if they went to a proper orphanage? Would there be records somewhere of admissions to orphanages or . . . workhouses?'

'Yes. All those things,' Rose said.

'Do you know where to find them?'

'Of course.'

'Sammy Bell, Sam Bell, Samuel Bell, Samuel Whitehouse, Samuel Whitehouse-Bell. Samuel Bell-Whitehouse. Here's a pound. Take cabs if you need.'

'I'm faster on my bicycle.'

Sergeant Duggan came in with the tea to find them putting their coats on.

'Found everything you needed?'

'Yes, thank you, Sergeant, very successful.'

'Don't bother putting the stuff away. A lot of it needs re-bagging anyway if the damp's got to it.'

'Waxed paper boxes can help,' Edgar said. 'We use them sometimes for storing papers in the cellar.'

'You can get them, can you?'

'Yes, I'll send you the name of the manufacturer.'

'I'd be very much obliged for that. Now, is there anything else I can help you with?'

'Is there a decent toyshop in town?' Skelton asked.

'A toyshop? Depends what sort of thing you're after.'

'My lad, Lawrence, has been collecting model ships.'

'For on a pond or just for having?'

'No, he's got a little yacht for the pond; it's the metal ones.'

'The Bassett-Lowke ones?'

'That's right.'

'Oh, they're very good. Very accurate. Our nipper's got two of them.'

'Which ones?'

'He's got a light cruiser and a torpedo boat, but the one he wants is—'

'—the Super-Dreadnought. It's the one they all want.'

'I tell you, you're not going to get one in town. I've seen 'em at a shop called Haskins, bottom of the Alum Rock Road down towards the Pelham.'

'Thank you. I'll call in.'

'Our kid's not getting one.'

'No?'

'I told him, he ain't getting nothing until he does his lessons at school and starts smartening himself up. Run's around like a blinkin' scruff.'

'Oh, I know. I've seen our Lawrence with the arse hanging out of his trousers. Been sliding down the gravel.'

'I said to our nipper, I said, "I'm a police sergeant, I've got a position to maintain. I can't have my kids running round like they just come out of Riley Street."'

'What's Riley Street?'

CHAPTER THIRTY-FOUR

Riley Street, in Aston, was a special school for children who'd been rejected by the better-quality orphanages because they were too unruly, or because they suffered from idiocy or from some chronic or disabling disease. They were given beef once a week, beatings twice daily and taught simple skills according to their abilities, carpentry for some, speaking clearly for others. Many of Daisy Groves' waifs, in the early days at least, had ended up there.

Sammy Bell, Rose discovered, had been admitted to Riley Street in 1901, at the age of seven, and remained there until he was twelve when he was taken on, possibly as an apprentice, by Messrs Needham and Stokes, manufacturers of buckets.

Mr Needham had died some years earlier, but Mr Stokes, now well into his seventies but still running the business, remembered Sammy well, and with good reason. Sammy had been a willing worker when he had first arrived, if a little simple-minded. But as time went by, his behaviour became erratic. He fell in love with one of the girls who did the books and, when she spurned his advances, he took off his clothes and tried to throw himself in the acid vat they used for pickling the steel. He was restrained. Police were called and he was sent to Middleton House, a lunatic asylum in Perry Barr.

Rose phoned the asylum and was told that it was for men only. For reasons of safety, women were not allowed in even to look at the records.

'More tickets for Birmingham, Edgar. And order up the Daimler.'

'For when?'

'Tomorrow.'

'You can't, you're in court.'

'There's nothing interesting or important, though.' Skelton looked at the diary. 'You could cancel that meeting and that one, and Briardale or Pratt could deal with all that and that.'

Briardale was still doing his pupillage but ready for a challenge; Pratt was a new boy who'd be glad of the work.

'I couldn't possibly spare the time for another trip to Birmingham,' Edgar said.

'And you've got tickets for *Journey's End* at the Savoy.'

'It's had terrific reviews.'

* * *

'Perhaps, since Mr Hobbes isn't here, it would be a good opportunity for me to take a turn behind the wheel.'

'I'd like to oblige, sir, I really would. But I'm not sure the brakes are all they should be.'

The asylum looked much like similar institutions Skelton had seen at Colney Hatch in London and at Virginia Water: a huge building set back from the road behind a high wall. The central clock tower was flanked by two wings, each of which looked like a good ten-minute walk from one end to the other, five stories high and pierced, like a prison, with hundreds of identical windows, some of which were barred.

Skelton had to sign in at a gothic fairy-tale gatehouse with arched windows and carved gables. A commissionaire, or perhaps guard, in a blue uniform wrote his name in a ledger, dipping his pen in the inkwell frequently and each time examining the nib to be sure it would not blot. Skelton told him he had an appointment with Mr Kirkby, the hospital almoner. The commissionaire checked in another ledger, running his finger down a list and turning to another page before finding evidence that there was some truth in Skelton's claim and he was not, after all, a dangerous lunatic lying to gain entrance. Skelton wondered why dangerous lunatics would want to get into the place, but then again, he supposed, irrational behaviour would be a hallmark. With the same cautious fear of blots, the commissionaire filled in a permit that, he said, Skelton must keep about his person at all times and show only to members of staff.

'How will I tell the difference between staff and patients?'

Skelton had meant this as a joke, but the commissionaire earnestly warned him to be on the lookout for patients impersonating staff and advised him, if he was in any doubt, to demand to see the permit which members of staff are required to carry with them at all times.

'Mr Kirkby will be waiting for you in B74,' the man said. 'Gregory will show you the way.' And he called, 'Gregory,' then whispered to Skelton, 'Gregory is, by the way, a patient, but he has been with us a very long time.'

'A trustee,' Skelton said, but the commissionaire was unfamiliar with the expression. 'It's a prison term.'

'This isn't a prison, it's a hospital.'

Gregory was a cheerful-looking, elderly man.

'If you'd like to follow me, sir.'

A side door led into a bedraggled garden.

'Seems nice,' Skelton said for the sake of saying something.

'Bit of a wasteland at this time of year,' Gregory said. He was officer class, clipped and formal. 'But in the summer, there's usually a good show of geraniums, marigolds, lupins. No roses of course because people scratch themselves on the thorns and it can cause terrible upsets, but, you know, pansies, snapdragons. We did sweet peas one year, but there was trouble with the sticks. I always think we should have more in the way of shrubs and bushes, but they say that would be missing the point. The garden is here for looking at, but more importantly it's here to give people something to do. Shrubs look after themselves. Annuals make work for idle hands.'

Skelton wanted to ask why Gregory was here. What exactly was wrong with him? But he wasn't sure whether it would be deemed impolite.

They passed through a pair of elaborately carved oak doors beneath the clock tower and into a hallway the size of a cathedral with tiled floor and walls. Here, at a counter – the sort you'd find in a bank – another commissionaire asked to see Skelton's pass.

Gregory led the way down a long corridor, up a flight of stairs and down another long corridor. They encountered no patients but could hear them everywhere, shrieking and screaming, their cries made all the more unnatural by the endless echoing scale of the place, which made the sounds swirl like voices in a dream or on a defective wireless set. At an exhibition of Dutch masters some years earlier, Skelton had seen Jan van Eyck's *Last Judgement*. This was what the painting would have sounded like.

'Don't wander off,' Gregory said. The corridor ended with a barred gate beyond which another, gloomier corridor stretched. 'And never go down there.'

To their right was a baize-covered door with red and green lights over it, like his headmaster's office at the grammar school. Gregory knocked. The red light turned to green. The door had padded, studded leather on the inside, like a sofa. Beyond it were more corridors but here the asylum sounds melted away and they were in a different world. Skelton glimpsed a largish room where men – presumably patients – worked at sewing machines, some attending to their work with rather more concentration than one might expect, but others chatting amicably. Even the air was different here, warmer, almost muggy.

A patient walked past, pushing, with a melancholy sense of purpose, a cart filled with sheets and blankets.

Gregory said a cheerful 'Hello' but received no reply. 'Laundry's downstairs,' he told Skelton. 'You would not believe the amount of washing they get through. And the cleaning. There's a general idea that if they keep us busy, we'll get better. It doesn't work, but it's as good as anything, I suppose.'

They turned into another corridor, this one of offices. Gregory knocked at a door and entered. Kirkby was seated behind a desk the size and heft of which suggested that it had been chosen as much for purposes of defence as it had been for efficiency – certainly it was big enough to put Kirkby out of the immediate reach of, say, a homicidal patient with a notion to rip his throat out.

They exchanged greetings. Skelton kept his pipe in his pocket. You could tell by the smell – Manila and well-brushed rugs – that Kirkby was not a smoker.

'Mr Bell's file doesn't make very happy reading, I'm afraid,' Kirkby said. 'I didn't know him personally. He was here before my time. Admitted on 22nd September 1910. He'd been arrested for causing a disturbance in Rackhams the drapers, threatening members of staff and shouting at customers. He was examined by doctors who declared him to be a lunatic and brought here. From the look of subsequent reports, he suffered from what these days we would call a manic-depressive disorder. Much of the time he was perfectly lucid. Then he would lapse into near catatonia, would not eat and seemed scarcely to have the energy to open his eyes. At other times his head would be filled with wild notions, a conviction, for instance, that we are all gods and the only thing preventing us from performing miracles was a lack of self-belief. It's not uncommon. These episodes often ended in violence and he would have to be restrained.'

'Is there a photograph?'

Kirkby passed it over the front page of the file, which had a photograph attached. The family resemblance was there. The face was handsome, dashing almost. Cover the mouth and it could have been Billy.

'I see from these notes that Mr Bell was discharged from the hospital in 1916. Would this suggest that his condition was improved?'

'I'm afraid not. During the war, Middleton House was pressed into service as a military hospital and many of the poor inmates turned out into the streets.'

'Might he have joined up?'

'I doubt it, given his medical history.'

'Is it known what became of him?'

'I'm afraid not.'

Gregory collected Skelton from Kirkby's office and took him back to the entrance hall where he was required, once again, to show his pass. Gregory didn't speak until they were back in the garden.

'Sammy Bell,' he said. 'You were talking about Sammy Bell. I know you were because I listen at doors.'

Gregory announced this as an accomplishment like 'I play the piano' rather than a confession.

'Did you know Sammy Bell?' Skelton asked.

'When they kicked us out in the war, they gave us the address of a lodging house in Nechells. We went there together, Sammy and I, and a chap called Dennis Monk. Then after the war, I had to come back here because I stole a tram, but Sammy and Dennis stayed in Nechells.'

'You stole a tram?'

'Yes. Huge fun. You should try it.'

'Might Sammy still be at this lodging house?'

'Possibly.'

'Do you have the address?'

'Number 15, the Quinnel.'

'The what?'

'The Quinnel.'

'Could you spell that?'

'With a Q.'

'Is that Quinnel Road or Quinnel Street?'

'Just the Quinnel.'

'In Nechells?'

'Yes.'

'Thank you very much, Gregory, you've been very helpful.'

'Pleasure to be of service and give my best to your family, sir.'

* * *

Skelton gave Keeling the address, still wondering whether Gregory was pronouncing it right, not just the 'Quinnel' part. Should 'Nechells' be '*Knee*-chulls', which is how Gregory was saying it, or something more French-sounding, 'Ne-*shells.*' Keeling laughed and assured him it was Knee-chulls.

'Horrible place. You know there's some places you wouldn't want to go in the night-time? Nechells you wouldn't want to go in the daytime, neither.'

Keeling had never heard of the Quinnel but said they'd get directions when they got there if they saw anybody they thought might not kill them as soon as look at them.

They drove through Aston and a smog closed in, acrid as all Birmingham fogs seemed to be. This one was green. If Skelton had served in the trenches, it would have had him reaching for a gas helmet.

They passed endless rows of gasometers, looming out of the fog like ocean liners threatening to smash the blackened back-to-back houses in their way. Some of the houses didn't have windows. Rags had been stuffed into the gaps, or they'd been covered with newspaper. They had passed from the world of work and manners into an alien world of base survival. At one place a crowd of cats was fighting over a length of intestine. Skelton worried about burial customs.

Keeling saw a corner shop and stopped to ask directions.

'He says it's up here under a bridge on the right. But he was holding his left hand up when he said it was on the right so it could be either way.'

They found it after two passes, not so much a road under a bridge as a cobbled alleyway between two houses that were joined above. The sign – much older than any of the other road signs you saw about the place – definitely said 'The Quinnel'.

'Can't get the car up there,' Keeling said.

Skelton got out and tried to see where the alley might lead, but the fog was dense. He went back to the car.

'When you mentioned the danger of coming here, to what extent were you exaggerating for dramatic effect?'

'Is this bloke you want to see a suspect in your murder case?'

'I'm afraid he is.'

'D'you not think we should get the police in?'

'That would seem the sensible thing to do, given the circumstances, but the trouble is he's most likely a man of unstable mental condition.'

'Isn't that all the more reason to bring in the police?'

'But I can't help feeling they might be a bit heavy-handed about it all.'

'Round here, heavy-handed's got to be for the best, hasn't it?'

'I'm sure you're right.'

'But if they get heavy-handed,' Keeling said, 'he'll clam up and then you won't get nothing out of him and, if you don't get nothing out of him, it ups the chances of Mary Dutton getting hung, is that it?'

'That's exactly it.'

'Right. If you put it like that, then.'

Keeling got out of the car and, from the toolbox, took the starter handle and handed it to Skelton. For his own use he selected a spanner the size of a felling axe. Skelton practised with the starter handle and discovered it was a terrible weapon, unbalanced and the corners got in the way.

The alley was as dark as it gets and ran for much longer than seemed feasible, but eventually brought them to a cul-de-sac. At the end he could make out two factory chimneys which were, by the looks of them, responsible for most of the green fog. The road itself was unpaved and flanked on either side by rows of houses. Some of the house had actually fallen down and the bricks piled up to make shanties with roofs of corrugated iron and tarpaulin.

Gregory had told them number 15. Few of the houses were numbered, but they found a 19 and guessed that two doors back from there would be about right. It was the biggest house in the street, three stories, upright and approximately intact apart from one of the top floor windows which had fallen out.

Skelton knocked on the door, twice, without answer. From across the road two dogs of uncertain but bulldog-related breed ran at them, snarling. Keeling stood ready to smash them with his spanner, but they were brought up short by chains.

'I bet you could break every bone in their bodies and the teeth'd still work,' Keeling said.

Another knock, heavier now with the end of the starter handle, brought the face of a man to the window next to the door.

'What do you want?'

The window hadn't been opened, and Skelton was nervous of shouting too loudly in case he attracted the attention of neighbours who would see him as meat.

'We're looking for Mr Samuel Bell.'

'Eh?'

'We're looking for Samuel Bell.'

'Eh?'

'Are you Samuel Bell?'

'Who are you, then?'

'My name is Arthur Skelton. I am a barrister. And this is Mr Keeling, who drives motor cars for a living.'

'What kind of motor cars?'

'A Daimler,' Keeling said.

'It's red,' Skelton said.

That seemed to do the trick. The face vanished and a moment later the man opened the door.

'Come in.'

The difference between 'in' and 'out' was theoretical. The temperature stayed the same and the floor felt and looked as if it was made of unpaved earth like the street outside.

The dogs snarled. From a shelf by the door, the man took a short length of lead pipe and threw it at them. His aim was good. One of the dogs whimpered.

'Mr Samuel Bell?' Skelton asked.

'No, I'm Dennis.'

He led the way into a room at the back of the house where there was a chair, a table and a bed, all covered in cans and newspapers, and made a gesture that might have been a hopeless invitation to sit, an apology for the state of the room or the prelude to a dance in the Grecian style. The room stank.

Skelton took out his pipe and Keeling his cigarettes. He offered one to Dennis.

'Can I take one for later an' all?'

'Take three. Take five. Take the whole packet. I've got more in the car.'

'Thank you very much, you're ever so kind.' Dennis looked at the cigarettes with great sadness.

'Here. Have the matches, too,' Keeling said.

Dennis smiled and lit a cigarette, smoking it in an elaborate demonstration of pleasure and gratitude.

'Is Sammy Bell in?' Skelton asked.

'No. Are you from the park?'

'No.'

'Are you from Mrs Bally-tune.'

'I don't know who Mrs Bally-tune is.'

'She's the lady from the park.'

'We're not from Mrs Bally-tune,' Skelton said. 'We're looking for Sammy Bell. I'm a lawyer working on a case that Sammy might be able to . . .'

'He's dead.'

'Sammy?'

'Yes.' Dennis's face folded back on itself.

'When did he die?'

'The lady over the road saw him and she sent her boy to fetch Mr Dewhurst. That's when I came. After Mr Dewhurst had come. And Mr Dewhurst said we'd have to send for the police. But nobody wanted to send for the police. I didn't want to send for the police. But Mr Dewhurst said we'd all get in trouble if we didn't send for the police. And nobody wanted to send for the police. But Mr Dewhurst said we had to. So, the tip man fetched the police and they brought a van and took Sammy away.'

'When was this?'

'We worked at the park. Me and Sammy worked at the park. We planted the floral clock and did the putting green and picked up the rubbish people left, but we weren't to do the bowling green because that was Mr Jeffrey who knows about grass. And Sammy pinched some rope from the shed and he brought it home and he tied one end to his bed – bed like this – and he pushed his bed against the window – the upstairs window – and he tied the other end round his neck and he jumped out the window. And Mrs Ingram over the road saw him and she sent her boy for Mr Dewhurst because Mr Dewhurst has got a ladder. And that was when I come and I saw Sammy hanging down the side of the house with the rope and one of his shoes had fallen off. I've got it here if you know anybody'd want it. He got it from the whatsit shop on Great Lister Street. The what-d'you-call-it?'

'Shoe shop?'

'No, not that one. The other one.'

'Have you eaten anything today, Dennis?' Keeling said.

'I had some jam.'

'That's good. When was that?'

'Breakfast.'

'And you're not going to work today?'

'Mrs Bally-tune said she'd say when I should go in again.'

'Have you had anything to drink, a cup of tea or something?'

'I have cold tea out of a billy. Here.' From beneath the newspapers, he took a soldier's billycan and shook it to hear the tea gurgle. 'I don't like it hot.'

'Do you know why Sammy might have done this?' Skelton asked.

'Done what?'

'With the rope.'

'There's loads of it in the shed. Mr Jeffrey uses it when he plants new grass seed. He knocks stakes in the ground with his mallet and then he ties rope round the stakes so that people won't walk on the grass seed. There's loads of it in the shed. By the sacks with the bulbs in. He killed his brother's dog.'

'Who did? Sammy?'

'He didn't know he had a brother and then he found he *did* have a brother and the first thing he bloody goes and does is kill his brother's dog.'

'Was his brother's name Ted?'

'Do you know him?'

'Did he also see his mother?'

'His brother had chickens and sheep as well as the dog.'

'How did he find out he had a brother?'

'He had a cat as well. Mrs Ingrams has got two dogs. I

313

said you should give him one of Mrs Ingrams' dogs. He got a letter.'

'A letter?'

'He got a letter from his mother. Not here. At the park. At the park a letter come from his mother and he went to see her.'

'When was this?'

'He had to get a 55 to the Fox and Goose and a Midland Red out to Collingford. Have you ever been to Collingford?'

'Yes, I have.'

'Is it nice?'

'It's very nice.'

'I'd like to go there one day.'

'I'm sure you will.'

'I can bend my hand all the way back.' He demonstrated. He could make his fingers bend backwards far enough to touch his wrist.

'How often did Sammy see his mother?'

'He used to have money.'

'Did his mother give him money?'

'He used to have money that his mother give him, and shirts and trousers. He said he was the fancy man about town. He told Mrs Bally-tune about the money and Mrs Bally-tune said we should get a better house and sent us to one by the park on the Washwood Heath Road. The front garden had climbing roses and delphiniums and lupins and pansies. Only they wouldn't have us. And Sammy said we could go and live with his mother. And he asked his mother and his mother said we couldn't do that; she didn't want us to. And he found out he had a brother. He said we could go and live with his brother. So, he went to see his brother and his brother said he didn't know who he was, and Sammy told him who he was, and his brother got very angry, so Sammy killed his dog.'

'How did Sammy kill the dog?'

'In the summer when it's nice, not like now, we put big boots on and get in the pool. It only comes up to here and the big boots come all the way up to here. And they give us big rakes. And we walk in the water raking up all the weeds and the muck and putting it in buckets. And the ducks go mad.'

'What was Ted's dog's name?' Keeling said.

'Gyp. Ted got angry. He hit Sammy and pushed him over because he was angry. So later, when Ted wasn't there, Sammy got a spade and he bashed the dog on the head with the spade. He told me.'

'He killed Gyp because his brother had got angry and pushed him over?'

'He bashed Gyp on the head with the spade and Gyp died.'

'Did Sammy go and see Ted or his mother again?' Skelton said.

'He got the spade from a shed. You can get all sorts of things in sheds. You can get a spade in any shed anywhere in the world you care to mention. And when he'd killed the dog his mother said she didn't want to see him any more.'

'So, Sammy never saw his mother after he'd killed Gyp?'

'I already told you that.'

'Tell me again.'

'His mother said she didn't want him to go and see his brother, and, when he did go and see his brother, she said she didn't want to see him any more.'

'Did he ever go and see his brother again?'

'How many times do I have to tell you his mother said he *mustn't*?'

'So, he didn't go?'

'Mrs Bally-tune said it was no good getting to the Fox and Goose at eleven o'clock because the Midland Red only goes at eight o'clock and three o'clock and eight o'clock in the night.'

'Did Sammy kill Ted?'

'No, he killed *Gyp*. You need your ears cleaning out.'

'And after he killed Gyp, he never went back to see Ted again?'

'He said if he never had to go on a Midland Red again it'd be too soon.'

'So, after he killed Gyp, he never went to Collingford again.'

'For crying out loud! Listen, will you?'

'Bugger.'

'Sorry, sir?' Keeling said.

'I said bugger.'

'That's what I thought you said.'

They were using the speaking tube that linked passenger to chauffeur.

'It would have been so neat, wouldn't it?'

'If he'd done it?' Keeling said.

'Exactly.'

'Save everybody a lot of bother because he's already hanged himself.'

'Heartless but true.'

'And you're sure Sammy didn't do it?'

'The poison was administered in increasing doses over the course of a couple of months. Sammy would have had to have made several visits. Just one visit doesn't work.'

'Unless Dennis is lying.'

'Do you think Dennis is lying?'

'I don't think Dennis would have the faintest idea how to go about lying.'

'And who's Mrs Bally-tune?' Skelton said.

'Irish woman?'

'Ballytoon? Is that a name?'

'Not one I've ever heard.'

'Nor me.'

'She could, of course, be a complete figment of his imagination.'

'That does worry me.'

CHAPTER THIRTY-FIVE

Monday 25th March, 1929

My dear cousin Arthur,

Last night's meeting was without any shadow of a doubt the best I have ever known. The two brothers from South Wales were brought out once again to sing 'Myfanwy'. Then Annie sang, 'When You and I Were Young, Maggie', I am sure you know it – '*And now we are agèd and grey, Maggie /And the trials of life nearly done /Let us sing of the days that are gone, Maggie / When you and I were young,*' – except that when she sang it she changed the name 'Maggie' in a most effective way to 'Simon', which is, of course, the name of her own husband. The woman sings like a waterfall and I don't mean the tinkling kind, I mean the great rushing torrents of Niagara or Victoria. When she hit the high notes ancient dust and dead beetles fell from the rafters. The effectiveness of her rendition was further enhanced when, as she approached the final verse, the oil ran out in one of the lamps, which darkened the rest of the room but seemed to wrap her in a cloak of light and of love. After my sermon, in which the joke that goes, 'A teacher asks a naughty boy "What kind of skins makes the best shoes?" and the boy replies, "I don't know, but banana skins make the best slippers,"' went down very well, Norah and I did 'The Old Rugged Cross' and 'What a Friend We Have in Jesus', then sent them all home with 'When Father Papered the Parlour You Couldn't See Pa for Paste', which has become such a great favourite that you hear children singing it in the street and in their playgrounds. Mary Dutton's children, sitting in their usual place in the front row with Mrs Fellows, were standing up (all except the baby, course) clapping their hands and dancing. I can't tell you what pleasure it gives me to bring a little joy to those poor mites.

We were both astonished and saddened to hear your news about poor Sammy Bell. You asked whether we thought it right to tell Jessie about Sammy's death and, after a great deal of thought and consideration – and not a little disagreement between Norah and myself – yesterday we decided it would be wrong.

Let me tell you our thinking on this matter. First of all, if we were to tell her, it would immediately raise the question of how we came by this information and this would require either that we betray our connection with you or that we tell a lie.

The latter of these alternatives is easily dealt with. Sometimes in order to do our work we have to resort to half-truths and concealment, but a downright lie would fly in the face of the ninth commandment.

The former is a little more complicated. We do not spy on people. We speak to people – often people who are in trouble of one sort or another – in the hope of bringing them comfort and spiritual guidance. Our footsteps sometimes are led by you because you can let us know where we might find people in need of such comfort and guidance. We report to you because, as well as spiritual guidance, people are often in need of practical and legal guidance which we cannot offer, but you can. Yet one can easily see how this arrangement could be confused with spying. It is a distinction which – like I'm sure many legal distinctions are – is defined by motive more than by actions: what we do may look like spying, but the reasons we do it make it nothing like.

If we were to reveal our links with you, Jessie Dutton would most certainly accuse us of spying on her, and immediately any bridges of trust that we have built would lie shattered and ruined. What comfort and guidance we have been able to offer her would be ground to ash and there would even be a danger that she might turn her face against God entirely. We could not risk that.

But it is clear now that the existence of her illegitimate son weighs heavily on her conscience.

Norah suggested that perhaps by skirting around the issue, we might encourage her to tell us the whole story herself. You do not have to subscribe to Roman Catholic dogma to know that confession can be cleansing.

We went to see Jessie yesterday afternoon. She seemed sober and treated us to the usual substantial tea. Norah took charge.

She began with what seemed like small talk. Had Jessie always lived in Collingford? What changes had there been around the town since she was a girl? Where did she go to school?

Jessie is not good at small talk but answered the questions with good enough grace.

Then, 'I suspect you were quite a beauty when you were a girl, weren't you?'

You might have thought that Jessie would have been flattered by this, but instead it made her suspicious. It put her on her guard.

'Who told you that?' she said.

Norah said that she could see it in her eyes and in her cheekbones. Then Norah said, 'Beauty can be a terrible burden.' And this, of course, is just the kind of talk that Jessie likes to hear. 'Burden' is a Bible word. It meant talk of tribulations, and especially of Jessie's tribulations.

'People call it a blessing,' Norah said, 'but Alan and I have known no end of those who have stumbled beneath the punishing yoke of beauty.'

She told Jessie the story of a young girl called Sarah whom we had known in Chelmsford. Sarah was a great beauty with dark hair, piercing blue eyes and skin like bone china. She was just fourteen years old but looked like a woman of twenty-two or twenty-three. At an age when other girls were still thinking about skipping ropes and dolls, she was forced to think about men. It was never her own choice to do so. She saw the way that men looked at her and heard the things they said and saw a light in their eyes that she could never have properly understood. Men, unworthy to be called men, vile beasts, took advantage. She came to us because she was with child and she was certain she would go to hell for her terrible sin. But how can such a child sin? Her beauty was not her fault. It was not in her power to control it. The evil that men do lives after them. In the bellies of women.

Luckily, the girl's parents were kind people and we were able to help them to take pity on her. She was sent away for a while (the parents told neighbours she was a little consumptive and had gone to stay with relatives by the sea). She came back several months later and a month or so after that a baby joined the family. The parents said it was the child of an aunt who had been sadly orphaned. As far as we knew the child grew up believing her mother was her sister – which is not the first time such a delusion has been cherished and I'm sure not the last.

When Norah had finished, Jessie asked to be excused and left the room. I think she went to take drink. The smell of it was on her when she returned. She took a Bible from the cabinet and laid it next to her plate at the table before sitting down.

She spoke even more slowly than usual, and very gravely. She told us that she has no friends in Collingford. Norah tried to assure her that we would be proud to be considered her friends, but she said, 'You come to my house for tea and you talk to me, but I can tell you do it out of duty rather than any enjoyment.'

Norah, rather cleverly I thought, told her that duty and enjoyment are one and the same for us. If we know that what we are doing is God's work, then it brings joy; if it brings joy then we know that it is God's work.

Jessie asked if we could help her find somebody and we said we would try.

She wanted us to swear on the Bible that we would never utter a word of what she was about to tell us as long as we lived.

We did not want to swear.

I said that if what she was about to tell us was connected with finding the person she wanted us to find then there might be certain facts or details that we would have to divulge. And Norah told her that, although we are not Roman Catholics, we respected the Catholic priest's seal of the confessional. Indeed, we saw such confidentiality as sacred to our mission.

This seemed to satisfy her for, without a pause, she said, 'I had a son.' And told us the whole story.

Sid was not Sammy's father. The father was a boy who ran off. Sammy was born in '94. Jessie gave him away. She said that when she gave him up, all the love she had ever had went with him. But her love was tainted with terrible shame which she could never be rid of. Though she tried, she had no love for Sid or for Ted or Billy. And that, of course, made the shame much worse. What kind of woman cannot love her husband and her legitimate sons?

After Sid died, she found Sammy again and wrote to him. He came to see her several times. He was a grown man, but her love had never withered. On the fourth visit he said he wanted to come and live with her as a proper son. She tried hard to think of ways that this might be possible – could he be passed off as a friend or a nephew? But Sammy was 'not all there'. It would only be a matter of time, she knew, before he told someone the truth and exposed her shame. By this time, he had learnt he had brothers and, somehow, found out Ted's address. He said that if Jessie would not take him in, then he would ask Ted if he could live at his house. Jessie begged him not to see Ted. He could not know her shame. Ted could not know that his mother was a 'filthy fornicator'. She could not stand the idea that he would revile and despise his mother and think of her as 'no better than a prostitute'.

As you know, Sammy ignored her and went to see Ted. She was angry and told Sammy she didn't want to see him again, but now she felt that she could cut out her tongue for saying that.

So, she wanted us to find him again – her 'glorious, golden boy'.

There was steel in her when she was done. Almost a defiance. I think it had taken a great deal of courage for her to make this confession.

I tried to tell her that there was no reason to feel shame. The great and merciful God would forgive her. She said that God may indeed forgive her, but Sid never would have done, and Collingford never would. And she certainly could never forgive herself.

We did not tell her that Sammy was dead. Should we have done? Perhaps it would have been kinder if we had, whatever the cost, or perhaps, without knowing, she could live the rest of her life in hope that she would one day find him again. It is a terrible thing to extinguish hope. We chose to lie by concealment and did not tell her.

Instead, I said, 'We will do our best to find him, Mrs Dutton,' knowing that one day she would find him in heaven.

Boldly, Norah asked her whether she thought that Sammy might have killed Ted. This made her angry. She said, 'Mary Cross killed Ted.'

It occurred to me that she, Jessie, might have killed Ted because she could not bear the idea of him knowing her shame, but this is a flight of fancy, and it would certainly have been wrong of me to have accused her to her face.

I took the Bible from beside her, turned to Psalm 27 and began to read.

'The Lord is my light and my salvation; whom shall I fear? The Lord is the strength of my life; of whom shall I be afraid?'

She and Norah joined in because they knew it by heart.

'When the wicked, even mine enemies and my foes, came upon me to eat up my flesh, they stumbled and fell. Though an host should encamp against me, my heart shall not fear: though war should rise against me, in this will I be confident.'

I closed the Book and we all said together, 'One thing have I desired of the Lord, that will I seek after; that I may dwell in the house of the Lord all the days of my life, to behold the beauty of the Lord, and to enquire in his temple. For in the time of trouble he shall hide me in his pavilion: in the secret of his tabernacle shall he hide me; he shall set me up upon a rock.'

I am ever yours faithfully in the joy of Jesus,
Alan

CHAPTER THIRTY-SIX

The Matlock and Ripley Textile Bank versus The Imperial Bauxite Trading Company case never got to court. After weeks of negotiation, there was a hurried pre-trial meeting at Bennett's Hill in Birmingham at which the Matlock and Ripley Textile Bank agreed to give the Bauxite people something or other or vice versa. Skelton never got the details and probably wouldn't have understood them if he had. He'd mugged up on debentures and *Erlanger versus the New Sombrero Phosphate Company* and now everybody seemed to be talking about *bona fides* and *Dafen Tinplate Co Ltd versus Llanelly Steel Co Ltd*. The Bauxite people seemed very pleased, anyway, and, when he brushed off their congratulations saying all the credit lay with William

Allen, they accused him of false modesty and wanted to take him for lunch. He pretended to be mortified that he had to refuse their kind offer but was afraid he had a previous engagement. A barrister's life is a constant juggling act, he said, always rushing from one place to another. And they laughed, scarcely noticing that jugglers, for the most part, stand in one spot and do no rushing at all.

Then he and Edgar had to eat at the Grand, as far from the windows as possible, for fear that one of the Bauxite people might walk past and see them.

Rose had telephoned to say that she had some important matters she wished to discuss so they agreed to meet her for tea at a posh cafe round the corner from the hotel in the Great Western Arcade.

Rose ordered a cream horn and Skelton admired her for that. It takes great courage to eat a cream horn in public. A bad approach means a squirt of cream either in your lap, or, worse, in the face of your companion. He half expected her to dissect it with a spoon, if not a knife and fork, but instead she lifted it whole and in one brief glance calculated the correct angle of attack. Two bites from the big end, both taking in sizeable quantities of cream, and nothing from the thin end until she was sure the interior pressures had been sufficiently relieved to make such a venture spurt free.

'I've been singing your praises to William Allen,' Edgar said. 'If, for any reason, you find you cannot continue your articles with your father, or if you believe that a change of scene might be beneficial, he would be happy to offer you a position.'

Rather than being overwhelmed with gratitude, as Edgar had hoped, Rose asked several subsidiary questions about the terms of employment and whether she would be one of many articled clerks or a select few, all the time taking precise bites from her cream horn.

'Now, who's for more tea?'

She poured. Not a drop was spilt. Not a leaf escaped from strainer to cup.

'You said there was something you wanted to discuss, Miss Critchlow.'

'Yes. Do you mind if I speak frankly, Mr Skelton?'

'Not at all.'

'I mean, very frankly.'

'Please.'

'I read the account of your meeting with Dennis that you sent to your cousin, Alan, and I read his account of how he and his sister, Norah, heard the full story from Jessie Dutton. Thank you for sending them to me.'

'We felt it important that you should see them.'

Rose looked over her shoulder at two elderly women in fur coats at the next table. She leant forward and lowered her voice.

'Men who were denied the affection of their mothers in childhood often become mother-fixated and, in later life, look for a new mother – usually a wife – who is able to give that affection. This means that when they have sexual congress with their wives they are also, in a sense, having sexual congress with their mothers. This triggers the incest taboo, which in turn triggers self-disgust and hatred for the wife, who, the man believes, tempted him to do this terrible thing, and very quickly the whole thing can tip over into confusion, anger and violence.'

'Where did you get all this?' Edgar asked.

'Hilda Bainton.'

'And she is?'

'One of the other Ranger Guides.'

'Do Ranger Guides often talk about this sort of thing.'

'They do if they have an interest in the works of Doctor Freud.'

'And do the Ranger Guides as an organisation encourage an interest in Doctor Freud?'

'Doctor Freud stresses the importance of listening and observation. BP says that listening and observation are skills that all Scouts and Guides should practice.'

'BP?'

'Sir Robert Baden-Powell.'

'I'm afraid,' Edgar said, 'that neither Dr Freud nor "BP" play well in the witness box. Juries – and, for that matter, judges – prefer simple explanations of human behaviour. They have little time for the convolutions of psychoanalysis, and I would imagine they would have a similar lack of patience with campfire yarns.'

Impatience with mumbo-jumbo had made Edgar a good deal more dismissive than Rose deserved. He looked to Skelton to repair the damage.

Skelton mournfully nodded. 'I'm afraid Mr Hobbes is right.'

Rose was undeterred. 'I think he killed himself.'

'Ted?' Edgar said.

'It's the inevitable conclusion. The unresolved neuroses resulting from these complex and contradictory feelings cause the patient to lapse into a deepening melancholia and ultimately suicide.'

Skelton exchanged a glance with Edgar. 'We have already considered suicide,' he said.

'You wouldn't have to mention Freud,' Rose said. 'You'd just say that Sammy came to see Ted, told him the mother he worshipped was a fornicator who'd given birth to a bastard child' – Rose was forgetting to whisper. The two ladies in the fur coats, called for their bill – 'Ted is greatly disturbed by this. Then Sammy kills Ted's dog, which tipped Ted over the edge into the suicidal abyss. And one also must bear in mind that Sammy was a suicide. It runs in families.'

'Suicide?'

'I looked it up. There is evidence to suggest that insanity – which would include suicidal tendencies – is not only passed on from father and mother to son and daughter but also the condition strikes the children at an earlier age than the parents and more severely.'

'Who says this?'

'Sir Edward Needham, Professor of Neuropathology at the University in Edgbaston.'

'And would Sir Edward be prepared to defend these views in a court of law?'

'He'd be glad to.'

'You've asked?'

'Yes. Was that wrong of me?'

'No. Shows great initiative.'

Rose smiled because she thought it showed great initiative, too.

'The difficulty with the suicide defence,' Edgar said, 'is the means. We have already given this matter a good deal of thought. Suicides use the rope, the razor, the pistol or one fatal dose of poison, not dribs and drabs of arsenic over a period of months. I'm not saying there has never been a suicide of this nature, but I am stressing the difficulty of convincing a jury that such a thing might be possible. Sir Rupert Mottram will be leading the prosecution. He is a specialist in the sneering tone that can destroy a less-than-robust defence in a single sigh.'

Rose sat up very straight. She had put a lot of work, a lot of thought and a great deal of research into her theory and did not take kindly to its being so quickly and so patronisingly dismissed. Her lips tightened. Skelton noticed.

'Excellent work, though,' he said. He was, of course, being even more patronising, but having dug his grave thought he might as well lie in it. 'Well done.'

CHAPTER THIRTY-SEVEN

At the assizes in Warwick, Skelton found himself defending a Mr Albert Morrison, indicted for making 'threats to kill' as defined by the Offences Against the Person Act of 1861.

Mr Morrison, a twenty-eight-year-old married man with three children, was a salesman in toilet requisites living in Kidderminster. His travels had taken him to Rugby, where he had met Violet Emhurst, a nineteen-year-old assistant at a chemist's shop. The two had subsequently met infrequently or, according to their own testimony, not at all, but had exchanged letters of a passionate nature. After several weeks they decided to elope. At this point, Miss Emhurst's father discovered a cache of the letters, insisted that she break it off with Mr Morrison forthwith, prevented her leaving the house except for work, nailed her window closed and threatened to 'knock the chap's block off if he dares come near the place'. Morrison had subsequently written to Miss Emhurst, telling her that he had purchased an automatic pistol and twenty rounds of ammunition and intended to shoot any man, including her father, who dared stand in their way. At this point, Miss Emhurst's father took the matter to the police.

Skelton spoke with Violet and Albert before the trial and found them delightful people. Neither were well cast as passionate lovers. Albert had a great moon face and large ears. Violet was a well-rounded ginger-haired woman with prominent teeth.

Albert told him that they'd met in the course of his work as a toilet requisities salesman at the chemist's shop where Violet worked. They got chatting about Love Books, a small selection of which was on sale in the shop. They had a good laugh. Then, with the shop's next order for toilet requisites, Violet included a letter, written in the style of the Love Books and Morrison had replied in like manner. The correspondence went on for a while. Unfortunately, when Violet wrote telling Morrison that her father had discovered the letters and kicked up a stink, Morrison thought it was just the next stage in the 'game' they were playing, so wrote saying he'd bought the gun.

'So, it was just a game, then?' Skelton asked.

'No. Not a game.'

'A joke, then?'

'No.'

'Are you saying you are actually in love with Miss Emhurst.'

'Who wouldn't love a girl like that?'

'So, you were planning to elope with her?'

'I don't know. I might have done when it came to it.'

'Even though you are a married man?'

'I might have left my wife. I might have wanted to do that. I never got the chance to find out.'

'So, it was part game, part joke, part reality and part . . . what, fantasy?'

'It works best if you think it's real.'

'By "best", what exactly do you mean?'

'It's like when you're playing cricket. In the greater scheme of things, it doesn't matter at all whether you score any runs or not, but when you're actually playing it has to matter a lot because otherwise there's no point doing it.'

'So, it is a game?'

'No.'

'Because as soon as you acknowledge it's a game, there's no point doing it.'

'Yes.'

'So, how should we describe it in court?'

'I don't want people to think I was toying with her affections.'

'Were you toying with her affections?'

'Yes. And she was toying with mine. We enjoy toying with each other's affections, but that doesn't mean . . . toy soldiers are toys, right, but . . .'

'The analogies aren't helping. What if we call it a literary exercise?'

'Will they know what that means?'

'Probably not, but it adds a useful note of respectability to the enterprise.'

The interview with Violet ran along similar lines.

'Haven't you ever kidded yourself you're in love with somebody because kidding yourself is better than no love at all?'

Skelton never had, but he was beginning to suspect that Mila had been doing it for years.

The police had done their work well. A search of Morrison's home, car and office had revealed no pistol nor ammunition, and no firearms certificate had been issued without which he could not have purchased a pistol over the counter.

In court, Skelton tried his best to put over the 'literary exercise' tag and when that clearly failed to convince dispensed with it and went instead first with the 'game' and then the 'joke'. Neither of these hit home either. The jury sat stony-faced, failing to see how adulterous elopement or threats to kill could feature in a game or be in any way humorous.

Morrison's wife saved the day. She was a jolly woman who took the stand as a key defence witness. She said she knew all about Violet, had read her letters to him and his letters to her and found them hugely entertaining.

'Did it not concern you that your husband claimed, in the letters, to have fallen in love with this young woman?'

'He falls in love with somebody or something every day. Women, dogs, shirts, gramophone records. He's a very loving man.'

Albert, she said, was a man who liked to make the best out of life. He was adored by his children and was building an aeroplane in the back garden.

'A real aeroplane?'

'With seats for five people, and when he's finished it, he's going to fly us all to Turkey.'

'Why Turkey?'

'Because the children like the delight.'

'Do you think the aeroplane, when it's finished, will fly?'

'One lives in hope.'

The jury were gone for a while but returned with a not guilty verdict.

Mr Justice Kirkland still didn't quite get it. He issued Morrison with a stern warning to keep his sense of humour – or whatever it was – under control in future.

As they were driving back to Birmingham, they encountered a man with a 'Stop' sign who told them that part of a bank up ahead had collapsed, blocking the road. It would be several hours before it could be opened again. Keeling got out a map and planned an alternative route around winding country lanes.

Edgar opened the window wider, swallowed a sachet of ginger extract, washed it down with peppermint cordial and loosened the strings tied tightly around his ankles which weren't doing any good at all.

The roads grew narrow. Keeling began to worry that they might be lost. A particularly tight turn brought him face-to-

338

face with a horse galloping riderless down the middle of the road, coming towards him. He swerved to avoid the horse and put the Daimler in a ditch.

The horse stopped and trotted back to look. Keeling could not gain enough traction on the boggy ground to reverse the car out of the ditch. Even if he had been able to reverse, he would somehow have had to manoeuvre past the horse, which was now standing directly behind the Daimler, apparently enjoying itself.

Skelton, Edgar and Keeling carefully eased themselves out of the car and tiptoed through the mud to safety.

'I'm very, very sorry about this, gentlemen,' Keeling said. 'First spill I've had in ten years of driving.'

The Daimler had come to no real harm but was tipped at something between forty-five and sixty degrees to the horizontal. The front wheels hung over the ditch with only a couple of inches of tyre in contact with solid ground. The back wheels were buried in mud.

'I think I remember seeing a coal yard about a mile back,' Keeling said. 'They might have a lorry that could pull us out.'

'Should I go or Edgar?' Skelton said. 'And you can stay here with the car.'

'No, it's best if I do it. You stop here. There's still some tea left in my flask you'd be very welcome to. I'll be no more than half an hour.'

Keeling marched off and vanished around the corner.

There was nowhere to sit. The car was tipped too far forward to be comfortable. So, they stood next to it. Some crows kicked up a racket. The horse turned to look, then turned back and watched Skelton and Edgar instead.

'Do you know anything about horses?' Edgar asked.

'Nothing at all,' Skelton said.

'I saw a film once in which a man was kicked to death by a horse.'

'I don't think they make a habit of that sort of thing.'

'It has a nasty glint in its eyes.'

'Horses always look like that.'

'I need to go to the lavatory.'

'Hop over the ditch,' Skelton said. 'I'm sure you'll find a gap in the hedge somewhere.'

'The horse might follow me.'

'I'm sure it won't.'

'Perhaps if you could lead it away.'

Skelton sighed and approached the horse. It had no saddle, but it did have some harness – if that's what it's called, he wasn't sure – around its face with a length of leather – possibly reins – hanging down. He tried to take hold of the reins. The horse didn't want him to do that and shook its head. It took a couple of goes to catch hold of them. He pulled. The horse resisted.

Skelton didn't want to pull harder in case the horse grew angry and kicked him to death. The horse shook its head again, and Skelton let go of the reins.

Skelton looked back to Edgar for advice, encouragement or permission to give up.

'Perhaps if you went up the road a little bit and called it.'

'Called it?'

'Like a dog.'

Skelton walked a few paces up the road. 'What should I say?'

'"Here horsey!"'

Skelton was a quite famous barrister in a homburg hat standing in the middle of a country lane near a tipped-up Daimler, a recalcitrant horse and a clerk with a defective bladder. Saying 'Here horsey' could only make matters worse.

'Or call it by its name.'

'I don't know what its name is.'

'Sometimes they're called Dobbin.'

'Here Dobbin' was worse than 'Here horsey'. He wasn't going to say either. It was nearly six o'clock on a cloudy day in early April. Soon it would be dark.

'The horse that won the Grand National last year was called Tipperary Tim,' Edgar said.

From behind the hedge, a voice said, 'His name's Sedgeford.'

Skelton turned and saw a red-faced man peeking through the hawthorn.

'Sedgeford?'

'That's right.'

'Are you sure?'

'He's my horse, i'n' he? I been looking for him.'

'He's there.'

'I can see. He ran off.'

'Do you think you could move him?'

The red-faced man found a gap in the hedge, squeezed through and approached the horse.

'You bastard,' he said.

The horse looked suitably chastened.

'Are you a lord or something?' the red-faced man said.

'A what?'

'A lord or a dignitary.'

'Oh, the car. No.'

'I don't think I've ever seen a motor car as big as that. What's it doing down there?'

'We had an accident.'

'I can see.'

'We came round the corner and Sedgeford was galloping down the middle of the road.'

'He's a bastard like that. Has a look around and goes straight for where he's not wanted. Don't you?'

The man slapped the horse on the rump. It moved a few feet up the road.

'He could pull you out if you like.'

'Our chauffeur went to the coal depot to see if he could find a lorry to pull us out.'

'What at Reg Bodnam's? He ain't got no lorry there. People come with lorries to bring the coal and to take the coal away, but he ain't got no lorry there. I'll get a bit of harness and come back.'

The red-faced man walked up the road a little way and vanished through a gap in the hedge. The horse followed him.

'What did he say?' Edgar asked.

'He said he's gone to get a bit of harness, then he's coming back.'

Edgar slipped through the hedge and relieved himself.

The wind began to blow colder. Skelton moved to the lee of the car and sat on the running board. Edgar joined him when he'd finished. They didn't speak.

The red-faced man returned with the horse, which was dressed as if to pull a cart. The man did things with leather and rings and attached ropes to strategic points of the car.

'You seen the smoke?' he asked and pointed.

A good way off – Skelton had no idea whether it might be a mile or five miles but a good distance anyway – a column of black smoke was rising. The lower part of the column was tinged with orange.

'Where is that?' Skelton asked.

'Somewhere up by Collingford way, I'd have thought.'

'I didn't realise we were so near.'

'No, see that church spire, that's Collingford, so the fire's a bit out to the east, where the canal runs by The Flag.'

'The pub?'

'That way, anyway. Are the brakes off?'

'Just a minute.' Skelton climbed around the car and into the driving seat to make sure.

'They are now,' he said.

The horse pulled. The car came free.

'There you go.'

'You're very kind.'

Edgar gave him five shillings to 'buy something nice for the horse'. Skelton stayed resolutely in the driving seat.

'I think we should go and investigate that fire, Edgar.'

'Keeling will be back in a moment.'

'I think we should get there as soon as possible.'

'But Keeling won't know we've gone.'

'I am very worried about that fire. You could stay here if you like, then you could tell Keeling where I've gone and tell him I'll be back as soon as I can.'

'But you're not insured to drive the—'

The controls weren't that different to his Wolseley. He gave it a little choke and pressed the starter button. The engine practically exploded into life. It took a moment to find the switch for the headlamps, then to locate first gear. He gave it too much acceleration as the clutch came up and the car leapt forward, miraculously without stalling.

'What if you kill yourself and don't come back?' Edgar said. Skelton didn't hear.

The steering was a good bit heavier than his Wolseley, but once he'd worked out how to keep the speed down, it was manageable. The gear changes and clutch were gloriously smooth. He navigated by first heading for the smoke, then, when he came to wider, smoother roads, following the signposts for Collingford. On a straight, wide, empty stretch, he put his foot down and watched the speedometer creep from thirty to forty, braked as he approached the bend, changed down to second, bend to the left, back to the right and up to third as the road straightened again. It was glorious.

He saw the canal and then The Flag. The pub itself seemed fine. The fire was behind. Skelton pulled the car into the side of the road and ran. People with blackened faces and buckets were rushing about.

'Has the fire brigade been called?' he asked.

'They're round the other side. They've had to send to Coventry for extra help.'

'Is anybody hurt?'

'Not as far as I know.'

'Thank God for that.'

Somebody handed him a washing-up bowl.

'Where's the water?'

'Down the canal.'

Skelton ran towards the canal. Alan was coming the other way.

'Arthur, Cousin Arthur, what are you doing here?'

'I saw the smoke. Are you all right?'

'I'm fine.'

'Where's Norah?'

'Just over there. Somebody burnt their hand.'

'How did it start?'

'I don't know. We smelt smoke. Then Mr Gough ran in and told everybody they had to get out.'

'Who's Mr Gough?'

'The gardener who drives Jessie Dutton. We got everybody out. As Norah and I left it went whoosh. Singed my hair, I think.'

Two more fire engines arrived, and the firemen began unwrapping hoses and ushering people away. Skelton's washing-up bowl was redundant, but he held on to it because he didn't know who to give it to.

There were shouts. A crowd was gathering further up the towpath.

A body had been found trapped in the weir beside the lock.

'Jessie Dutton,' Skelton said. He and Edgar were back at the Grand, in the coffee lounge, drinking cocoa laced with brandy. 'She had asked Gough to take her to Alan's meeting. She was apparently very drunk. So, he took her, and, when they got there, he left her to it and popped into The Flag. About fifteen minutes later she came in to find him and said she wanted to go home. He remembered her smelling funny and thought she might have been on the methylated spirits. When they got outside, he could smell burning. Jessie was eager to go, but he ignored her and went to investigate. Six half-gallon paraffin containers – Alan and Norah kept them in one of the old stables – were lying empty on the ground and flames were creeping up the side of the barn.

'Gough spent a few seconds trying to put the flames out – burned his hand quite badly – then realised it was hopeless so ran in, raised the alarm and helped Alan and Norah get everybody out. Mary Dutton's kids were in there apparently. Can you imagine? Gough looked for Jessie and couldn't find her. Then, like I did, he heard the rumpus up by the weir where they'd found her body. Drowned herself.'

'Shame.'

'Exactly. She'd told Alan and Norah her great secret and – this is all conjecture – sober she could stand them knowing, drunk she couldn't. They had to burn. And when that didn't work, she threw herself in the canal.'

'Do you want more cocoa?'

'Just the brandy, I think.'

Through the glass door, Edgar attracted the attention of the night porter and mimed large balloons of brandy. The porter nodded and went off to the bar.

'Did she kill Ted?' Edgar wondered.

'It's tempting, isn't it?'

'He knew her shame, too. And if she was prepared to burn a barn filled with people – including her own grandchildren – to expunge her shame I don't think we have any difficulty at all accepting she'd kill her son.'

'As always, the sticking point is the administration of the poison,' Skelton said. 'Minnie the maid told Alan that Ted never came for a meal at the house and hardly ever stayed long enough to have a cup of tea.'

'The meat pies with lots of pepper?'

'Are you suggesting she somehow walked through the fields to wherever Ted was tending his sheep, said, "Hello, Ted, fancy meeting you here. That looks like a nice pie, could I borrow it a moment?" and then sprinkled while his back was turned?'

The porter brought the brandy.

'You haven't told your side of the story. I am so sorry to have left you stranded.'

'It couldn't have been helped.'

'What happened?'

'I stood there where you'd left me,' Edgar said. The brandy had begun to make the area behind his ears feel a little tight. 'Darkness fell. The sky was thick with cloud. There was no moon and no stars. The world could have come to an end and I would not have known except for the sounds of rustling all around.'

'Rustling?'

'Animals in the ditch and in the hedge.'

'What kind of animals?'

'Wild ones. Large ones.'

'I think the biggest you get in this country is deer.'

'Deer, then. Stags.'

'In the ditch?'

'Exactly. So, I moved to the middle of the road. And then I heard someone, or something, coming.'

'Keeling?'

'I didn't know that, did I?'

'Who else could it have been?'

'Thieves and murderers.'

'I see.'

'So, I didn't know whether to hold my breath and hope they'd pass by—'

'They?'

'He. I didn't know whether to hold my breath and hope he'd pass by without cutting my throat or to call out.'

'What happened?'

'He called out.'

'And you recognised his voice.'

348

'Not at first. It seemed a little ethereal.'

'I didn't know Keeling could sound ethereal.'

'Ghostly.'

Edgar drained his brandy glass.

'Another?' Skelton asked.

'It would make me very drunk,' Edgar said. 'A Virol with milk would be very welcome, though.'

'A what?'

'Virol . . . malt extract, you know . . . mixed into warm milk. I sometimes have it at bedtime.'

'We'll ask the porter when he comes round again, shall we? Go on.'

Edgar looked blank.

'You were being haunted by Keeling.'

'And he asked where you were, so I told him you'd gone off with the Daimler to investigate a fire.'

'Was he cross?'

'Keeling doesn't get cross. I told him we were to wait where we were until you returned. He asked whether I thought you'd be able to find your way back. I said I hadn't thought of that.'

'He was right. I couldn't.'

'So, we started walking. Along the pitch-black country lane.'

'Did you sing?'

'Why would we have done that?'

'To keep your spirits up.'

'No, we didn't sing. We walked – I don't know – five or ten miles, I suppose.'

'Is that an exaggeration?'

'No. It might even have been twenty. And we came to a village and the village had a pub, and even though by this time it was the middle of the night, the pub was open. So, we went into the pub. And we asked at the pub whether we could telephone for a taxi. They didn't have a telephone, but there was a gentleman there who had a motor car, took pity on us and offered very kindly to drive us to a railway station where we could get a train into New Street.'

'And the trains were running, were they?'

'Luckily, yes.'

'In the middle of the night?'

'We caught the 8.47.'

They saw the porter and called him over. He told them, with regret, that he couldn't provide Virol and milk.

'Are you sure you don't want another brandy?' Skelton asked.

'I really think I've had enough, don't you?'

'No.'

They ordered more.

'It's poor Alan and Norah I feel really sorry for,' Skelton said.

'I thought you said they came to no harm.'

'I'm afraid their Rover Sunbeam is finished.'

'Burnt?'

'To a crisp. I'll have to buy them a new one. They have caravans with bathrooms in them these days. I'll get them one of those. And a car to pull it.'

'Can you afford it?'

'Did I read in the paper the Imperial Bauxite Company is in trouble again?'

'You hate business law.'

'I'll console myself with the thought that I'm doing it for the joy of Jesus.'

CHAPTER THIRTY-EIGHT

Skelton's hip was starting to ache more than it had for several years. If he went to the doctor, the doctor might tell him he needed an operation. The operation might go wrong and paralyse him from the waist down. Elizabeth's teeth were growing huge and crooked. Mila was having an affair with a one-legged architect. He had read somewhere that the gallows at Holloway were a double affair, built so that two women could be hanged simultaneously. Why would you want to do such a thing? Had they anticipated an increased demand? If you were hanging alone did you glance at the neighbouring rope wishing a friend could share your final moments?

At seven he heard Mrs Bartram arrive, He silently dressed and went downstairs to help her with the kitchen fire.

Skelton remembered something about Mrs Bartram's sister in Maidenhead not being well and asked after her. She told him she was much better. Mila had kindly recommended some liniment. The chemist in the High Street had had to order it in specially but she'd been able to pick it up the previous day. Skelton said he could run her over to Maidenhead in the car if her sister needed it urgently. Mrs Bartram didn't want to put him to any trouble. Skelton said it would be no trouble at all and certainly a lot less trouble than catching two buses there and two back. Mrs Bartram remembered that they'd changed the timetable for the No. 20, so there'd be no knowing. Skelton reminded her it would be running the Saturday service anyway which was always unreliable. Mrs Bartram said that, goodness knows, even that's better than the Sunday service. Mr Gore said he had to go and get some dahlia tubers a friend had promised him Sunday before last and had had to wait an hour and a half for a No. 20. Skelton wondered why he hadn't taken the train instead, into Reading and out again. Mrs Bartram asked him whether he'd ever tried that on a Sunday, and he laughed and said he hadn't.

Skelton realised that he'd got through twenty worry-free minutes and resolved to write to Dr Freud recommending a chat about somebody's sister's liniment as a cure for anxieties and neuroses.

At eight, Mila emerged, dressed for her archery class at the academy.

They had breakfast.

Dorothy, the nanny arrived to take Elizabeth to her ballet

class and Lawrence to his piano. Mila went to the academy.

By then there was warmth in the sun and Skelton thought of going for a walk, but his hip was still hurting. Some doctors recommended vigorous exercise for limbering up the hip when it got bad and others suggested complete rest. Dr Wilkins, when Skelton had been a child, used to say, 'No more football for you, young man. Not for a while anyway. You need to give it plenty of rest and let nature do its work.' Dr Wilkins was the first person he ever met who spoke posh. Now almost everyone he knew did. Even Mrs Bartram would pass for posh in Leeds.

He took a book out on to the little balcony above the veranda at the back of the house. *The Price of Things* was not one of Elinor Glyn's best. Amaryllis, the heroine, was fey and Verisschenzko, the Russian, talked too much.

Across the valley he could see there was some trouble on the building site. A group of men had gathered and were having what looked like a heated discussion. Perhaps a strike was brewing.

Eliot Dean arrived in his Lagonda. Skelton wondered whether he'd had it specially adapted to accommodate his wooden leg.

Dean's arrival calmed the men and they gathered around, submitting to his effortless authority. He took some plans from the car and spread them on the bonnet. Pointing at the plans, he explained a technical point. This, whatever it was, cleared up the dispute and the men went back to work.

Eliot rolled the plans up, leaning now to the left and now

to the right to tuck in the ends. Without his stick, on the uneven ground, this must have been quite a feat of balance.

Somebody called to him. He smiled and waved. Mila joined him. White pleated skirt, white plimsolls, sailor top, hair tucked into a sort of turban, carrying her bows and arrows in the long canvas bag.

Though they didn't shake hands or touch, there was an intimacy in the way they stood, he with his hand on the top of the car, she with her weight on one leg, one hand swinging the bag, the other easing the sailor collar from the back of her neck as if it was chafing. They didn't look away from each other's eyes, not for a moment.

In *Married Love*, one of the books he'd read in the course of his research into the more intimate aspects of the Dryden Case, Marie Stopes talked, in alarmingly mystical terms, about 'the bodily union'. Rainbows came into it somewhere, he seemed to remember, and filmy cobwebs and iridescent glories.

She also said that a man who does not feel the iridescent glories is probably suffering from a disease called 'sexual anaesthesia'.

Could a side effect of a displaced hip, he wondered, be 'sexual anaesthesia'?

He wished he'd never read Marie Stopes.

The conversation between Eliot and Mila grew serious. Mila was speaking; Eliot was nodding slowly. Were they making arrangements? Would she meet him behind the church at two in the morning while her husband lay sleeping?

They would be in London by four. Eliot would leave the car in a garage in Mayfair. Mila would send a telegram to her husband, just the barest of details so that he wouldn't report her missing to the police. They would take the boat train to Paris. There, conscious of the sexual magnetism in her, he would kiss those cherry lips and crush her in his arms until she could not breathe.

Skelton took a vow not to read any more Elinor Glyn either.

After a few moments, they seemed to reach an agreement. Mila left, again without a handshake, and Eliot walked out of sight behind a half-built wall.

Skelton felt the nervous shudder that came over him when a trial was as good as over and the judge began his summing-up. Something had been agreed between Mila and Eliot. It was out of his hands now. There was nothing he could do. He would behave like a gentleman and accept the inevitable. If Mila was in love with another man, then he would quietly defer to his changed circumstances and move immediately to practical matters of where they would live and what to do about the children.

Perhaps California was too ambitious, too exotic, too remote. He would go to Canada. The children would have just as much fun skating and sledding as they would swimming in the pool he'd planned for his Californian home and eating in the same restaurants as film stars. Police witnesses would arrive at court on their horses and sit straight in the saddle as they gave their evidence, the brims of their hats exactly horizontal, their tunics a commendable red. American cars could be easily bought in Canada. He'd turned against the Packard Twin 6 Roadster as too eccentric-looking and was veering towards the majesty of the Cadillac Phaeton. He'd seen a photograph in a magazine of a woman in beach-pyjamas standing next to a Cadillac Phaeton. It was the size of an English house and had yellow sides, a grey cloth roof and a black bonnet which, in America and probably Canada, too, would be called a 'hood'.

He waited in the drawing room for his wife to come home and the axe to fall. A casual pose was what he was after, so he spread newspapers on the floor as if he'd been browsing from one to another, put a record, chosen at random, on the gramophone and lounged in an armchair, long legs stretched, feet resting on the fender.

The record was not ideal. 'Ee, By Gum' by Gracie Fields, was a record that Ricketts, a major from the village who considered himself a great joker, had given him. 'You'll like this, coming from t'north,' he'd said in what he thought was a Yorkshire accent. Ricketts was always giving gramophone records away. His son worked for His Master's Voice and got them free.

Skelton got up to change it but heard Mila coming in through the back door so hurriedly sat down again in his casual pose.

'Why are you playing this?' she asked as she came in. She was chewing a raw carrot she had stolen from the kitchen.

'What?'

'The gramophone record. It's awful.'

'It's the one Ricketts gave me.'

'I know. It's awful.'

'I know.'

'So why are you playing it?'

'It seemed impolite not to.'

Mila took the record off. 'You should be outside,' she said. 'It's a beautiful day outside.'

'I was sitting outside but the sun got in my eyes and I couldn't read.'

'I asked Mrs Bartram to bring tea. Would you rather have lemonade?'

'No, a cup of tea would be lovely.'

Mila culled a couple of dead blooms from the arrangement on the sideboard and threw them into the fireplace. They'd probably need a fire later when the sun went down.

'I'll just have a cup of tea and then I'm going up for my bath.'

'How was your lesson?'

'The girls are tired of archery because they so seldom hit the target, so I showed them how to box.'

'Did they have gloves?'

'Shadow boxing. Well, it was supposed to be shadow boxing, but they grew tired of that, too, and started a little bare-knuckle sparring. There's a big girl called Eileen who has the makings of a champion. Very light on her feet. Excellent reflexes. Marvellous right jab, one of which sent

Pauline Bickerstaff practically flying through the air.'

'And did Pauline Bickerstaff live?'

'Nothing broken as far as I could see. No teeth missing. There might be a black eye.'

'Will there be trouble?'

'Only if Pauline or one of the other girls blabs, and Eileen said that if any of them do they'll get the same treatment as Pauline only worse.'

'Should you be encouraging that sort of talk?'

'Of course I should.'

Mrs Bartram arrived with the tea and Mila poured.

'On my way back from the academy, I ran into Eliot Dean.'

'Did you?'

'Yes. Well, I didn't run into him, I spotted his car at the building place and went in to talk to him.'

Skelton reminded himself not to lose his temper, weep, beg or do anything else that might compromise his dignity.

'There's something I think I should tell you.'

Skelton pressed his lips together. *The sentence of this court*, he found himself thinking, *is that you will be taken from here to the place from whence you came . . .*

'You see, Eliot and I have a sort of a secret and he was very keen that I shouldn't share it with anybody, only I think I should share it with you because it might be important.'

Might be important. Skelton waited.

'It's about the time I spent nursing Eliot during the war.'

They had an affair, Skelton thought, *and she thought it was*

359

all over but then when she saw him again the flame of love was
rekindled and she realised that marrying him, Skelton, had been
a terrible mistake. Or they had an affair and finished it because
she thought she loved, him, Skelton, but at the time she didn't
realise that he, Skelton, suffered from sexual anaesthesia.

'It's something that Eliot is very ashamed of now which
is why he didn't want me to tell you.'

'Yes?'

'He tried to kill himself.'

He tried to kill himself because he was so ashamed of having
an affair with a married woman? He tried to kill himself because
Mila, out of stubborn loyalty, refused to leave her husband and
he was heartbroken, but now she regretted saying that and was
more than ready to go with him to Paris?

'Why?'

'Why did he try to kill himself? Because he had lost a leg.'

And, because he had lost a leg, he feared his bodily unions
could never be filled with iridescent glories, in which case life
was not worth living.

'And because of what he'd seen, what he'd been through,'
Mila said. 'Shell-shock, war hysteria. He wept almost
constantly. He screamed and cried like a baby if his food
came a little late or if the margarine did not reach the edges
of his bread. He cried if he thought the exercises I gave him
were too hard. He cried so much in the night that he had to
be moved far away from the other patients.'

The possibility began to dawn that none of this had to do
with adultery. There was no affair. There was a nurse and a

patient, who was now ashamed because he had blubbed a lot and tried to do himself in.

'Why are you smiling?' Mila asked.

'I'm not smiling. Many chaps who came back from the war were the same, weren't they?'

'Yes, but rarely quite so childish. He has, since the war, built a considerable reputation as an architect, much of which, he is sure, depends on his war record and his VC. He knew that there had been a lot of opposition to building the houses on Tommy Northwood's farm and he was afraid that I would be among those in opposition and might bolster my case by destroying his reputation. He made me swear not to breathe a word even to you, but then something occurred to me.'

'What, that it didn't feel right keeping secrets from your husband?'

'What?'

'Are you telling me this because you think it's wrong for married couples to keep secrets from each other?'

'Good Lord, no. I think it's *essential* for married couples to keep secrets from each other. You do have to promise not to tell Eliot's secret to anybody else, though,'

'It goes without saying that Mr Dean's secret is safe with me.'

'Even in court. In the Mary Dutton trial.'

'Why would I want to mention it in court?'

'Promise first.'

'I promise.'

'Not to mention his name.'

'I promise not to mention his name.'

'He cut his throat. I found him in the bathroom.'

'You saved his life.'

'I saved hundreds of lives. We had taken away his razor before and monitored his use of glass and knives and so on because this was not the first time he had cut himself. He would make little cuts. Some of the other men did this. The doctor thought they did it because the physical pain distracted them from the mental pain. But Eliot always cut his throat. Cut it a little and then the next time it would be a little more. Afterwards the doctor said that we should have spotted that this was leading to suicide. He had seen patients like that before. Some patients flirt with suicide, wanting to try it out before they commit themselves. As if they're practising for the final act.'

'Who is this doctor?'

'Professor Andrew Walsh. I came upon a mention of him the other day. He's at Guy's Hospital.'

'I think you just saved another life.'

'Good.'

The room had been completely retiled. The shiny white ones, which gave it the atmosphere of a public lavatory, had been replaced with warm red. They had a different smell, too. Earthy. Like a greenhouse.

Mary knew already about Jessie's death. Enid Fellows had written.

'She was an unpleasant woman, but she never did me any real harm,' Mary said.

'She was very troubled.'

Skelton told her about Sammy, about Professor Needham's notions that suicide is hereditary, and Professor Walsh's theory suggesting that Ted could have 'rehearsed' the final act of taking his own life with increasing doses of the rat poison.

Mary looked puzzled. She helped herself to one of Edgar's cigarettes and had almost finished it before she said: 'That doesn't make no sense at all.'

'In what way?'

'Ted would never have done himself in.'

'Can you be sure of that?'

'Course I can. I was married to him nearly thirteen years. If he was upset about something, he'd take it out on me or one of the kids. I don't think he had the turn of mind ever to think about doing himself in.'

'Perhaps you're right, but it would be very helpful if you never voiced these doubts outside this room or ever again for the rest of your life.'

'Is that fair?'

'What?'

'People thinking Ted did himself in. It's a crime, isn't it, to take your own life?'

'I think at this point in time the matter is academic . . . it doesn't make any difference. He won't, after all, face punishment. And as for what's fair and what's not fair, I think it's fair that you are allowed out of this place and your children are allowed to have a mother.'

'But—'

'As things stand, everybody wants you to go free, Mary. All they need is a plausible reason to acquit. Ted's suicide is a story everybody can accept.'

'But it is just a story,' Mary said. 'What if they find out later it's a lie and he didn't kill himself?'

'They won't. And even if they do, you cannot be tried twice for the same crime.'

'Is there a back way into the courthouse?' Keeling asked.

'Several,' Edgar said.

'Cos the road at the front is blocked solid.'

'Mary Dutton Defence League?'

'And reporters and coppers and goodness only knows who else.'

'If the worst comes to the worst, we can use the tunnel from the Steelhouse Lane lock-up,' Edgar said.

The crowds were backed up into the Old Square as far as Bull Street. Even on Colmore Row people gathered around the car. Edgar had to close the window.

'It's him,' they said.

'Your fans are out in force, Dolores,' Edgar said, then decided it was better not to speak because preventing nausea was taking every atom of his concentration.

They went in off Newton Street by way of the coroner's court.

Skelton had arranged a meeting with Mr Justice Kirkland and Sir Rupert Mottram, the solicitor-general who was leading the prosecution. He presented his evidence that Ted had taken his own life, omitting all mention of Sigmund Freud, Ted's Oedipal tendencies or of Sir Robert Baden-Powell. He did, however, produce written testimony from the two professors, Needham and Walsh. Needham's notion, that madness and suicide can be hereditary conditions, was now well supported by the fact that there had been two other suicides in Ted's family, Sammy and Jessie. Walsh's theory, that some suicides 'practise' their final act suggested that it was perfectly feasible for Ted to have taken a series of increasing doses of arsenic over a period of time.

It wasn't a perfect defence, but it would do. Kirkland advised Skelton to make a submission of no case to answer and Mottram offered no objection.

'This is excellent work,' Kirkland said. 'Jix will be cock-a-hoop. You might actually have saved the country.'

By which he meant the Conservative Party.

'I expect Mary and her children will be fairly bucked, too,' Skelton said.

'Yes, of course. How old are you?'

'Thirty-six,' Skelton said.

'Bit young for silk, but we'll see what we can do.'

He had another quick word with Mary before the trial. She'd done her hair and looked as though she might even have got hold of some lipstick and rouge. He tried his best to reassure her.

The public gallery was, given the circumstances, subdued. There was a bit of a cheer when Mary was brought up which was quickly silenced. Six or seven women had been told to take their Mary Dutton Defence League sashes off before they came into court, but some of them put them back on again as soon as they rose for Kirkland's entrance. Kirkland saw them but made no objection.

Mottram kept his opening remarks brief, giving no more than a bare bones account of the case against Mary. Skelton rose and submitted that there was no case to go to the jury. He began his story with the discovery of Sammy and his suicide, then Jessie's suicide. He mentioned Professor Needham's testimony and was so convincing that the conclusion that Ted had taken his own life seemed inescapable. The means by which he did it and Walsh's theory were no more than interesting details.

Kirkland commended the preparation and investigation of both prosecution and defence, gave his opinion that it would not be safe for the jury to proceed further and directed them to make a formal verdict of not guilty.

There were cheers. Word was delivered outside the court and the cheers began there, too.

When Mary appeared on the courtroom steps, Lillian Gish herself could not have been greeted with more warmth and adoration. Mary smiled graciously. Skelton stepped back into the shadows to allow her moment of triumph She did not take his hand and hold it up like a boxing champion. She did not call him her saviour or her Galahad. Instead she basked alone.

Skelton tried to be glad.

He had told Mary that he had arranged for Keeling to bring the Daimler round and whisk her off to be reunited with her children in Collingford. She had told him that it would not be necessary.

A Morris Cowley appeared, nosing its way through the crowd.

Edgar joined Skelton at the top of the steps.

'The Daimler's round the back when you're ready,' he said.

'Is that Jessie Dutton's car?' Skelton asked, indicating the Morris Cowley.

'I expect so,' Edgar said. 'Billy's now. I expect he's lent it to her.'

'Is he driving?'

Edgar shielded his eyes and bent his knees to see. 'No, I don't think so. It's Enid Fellows.' With a last wave to the crowds, Mary was whisked away.

CHAPTER THIRTY-NINE

Mary's acquittal did not save the Conservative Party. Ramsay MacDonald's Labour Party took 287 seats to Stanley Baldwin's 260.

It was generally agreed that the flapper vote had swung it for the socialists. On polling day young women had queued for an hour or more to make their crosses.

Norman Bearcroft, at the Birmingham East constituency, had turned a Conservative majority of 1,248 into a Labour majority of 602. In his manifesto he had pledged to speed up the process of incorporating the Collingford Borough Police Force into the Warwickshire County Force and to bring any public official tainted by corruption to justice. And in his victory speech, he paid tribute to his friend, colleague and solicitor, Walter Critchlow, who had sadly passed away on the eve of the election. Rose was there to hear him, in her Ranger's uniform, resolutely not weeping.

She had taken up Edgar's offer of an introduction to William Allen in Bennett's Hill, but, now that her father had died, she was thinking she might move to London – where Edgar could have given her no end of introductions – or perhaps she would join an expedition being planned by the Royal Geographical Society to the Valley of the Assassins in Luristan. It was hard to decide.

The *Times* had details of MacDonald's new cabinet. By way, perhaps, of acknowledgement to the flappers, he had made Margaret Bondfield Minister of Labour, the first woman ever to hold a cabinet post.

Mila, for once, was pleased. It was a start.

May had brought what seemed like endless days of sunshine. Back from her Saturday morning class, Mila sat in the garden at Lambourn with the newspapers scattered around her.

Skelton came out to join her. He had been reading a letter from Alan. Pending delivery of their new caravan, for which their gratitude was measureless, he and Norah had moved back to their parents' house in Rhyl. Their time there was not wasted. The Angel had appeared once again to Alan and told him – the Angel was far more specific in its instructions these days than it had been when it had first appeared – to ask his father to cancel the threadbare concert party he'd booked into the Pavilion Theatre for Whit Week and instead book the Joy of Jesus Mission, four shows a day. They played to full houses. Halfway through the week they opened for early afternoon matinees – six shows a day in total and had added a novelty trombonist to the bill. The trombonist shared their way of thinking. After shrapnel had been removed from his chest, the doctors had told him that he would never play again. So, he had prayed every day for a year and swore that, if the blessing of breath should ever be restored, he would devote every note to praise. He did a stirring 'Rock of Ages' and a technically brilliant 'Sabre Dance'. When he played 'I'm Forever Blowing Bubbles', he had a little device which would make actual soap bubbles emerge from his bell.

'Listen to this,' Mila said. She was angry.

'What?'

She held up the *Mail* and turned to a photograph of Mary Dutton, her hair done and face painted to look more like a film star than ever. Above the photograph was a headline A TALK TO WIVES BY MARY DUTTON.

'I hope they paid her a sizeable fortune,' Skelton said.

Mila read extracts. '*Why I could not run away. You've got to fight for what you've got. I keep asking myself one question as I write this story. Why did I stay with Ted? And I answer: Because I loved him.*'

'Oh dear,' Skelton said.

'So speaks the murderess,' Mila said.

'You think she killed him?'

'Of course she did. Brute like that. Any self-respecting woman would have done the same.'

'You never believed the suicide, then?'

Mila folded the *Mail* and put it with the other papers. 'It's preposterous. The evidence that suicide runs in families is deeply flawed – if it happens at all it's by example not heredity, and Ted was the first suicide in the family so there was no example for him to follow. And the evidence for people "practising suicide" is entirely anecdotal. You didn't believe it, did you?'

Skelton turned his chair away from the table so that he could stretch his legs and let the sun warm his hip. 'One sort of has to when one's saying it,' he said. 'It was a good enough story to convince.'

'And that's all you need, is it?'

'It's all one can ever have.'

'What about the truth?'

'Now you're talking about areas of philosophical speculation about which I am not qualified to comment. Anyway, the truth's always messy. Stories are much neater.'

Mila pulled her chair so that she could stretch her legs too, and they lay side by side like a sire and his dame on a medieval tombstone.

'Do you think she killed him?' Mila said.

'Hard to say. I'm increasingly wondering whether Edgar might have had it right.'

'What did he say?'

'Enid Fellows.'

'Killed him?'

'Yes?'

'Why?'

'Because she loved Mary and could not stand to see her being so badly treated.'

Mila, amused, turned to face her husband. 'When you say "loved" . . . ?'

'They're living together now with the children.'

'As man and wife?'

'If you mean "Are they sharing a bed?" I'm afraid I haven't made enquiries. They get a decent living from renting out the forty acres and Billy's been very generous. He inherited Jessie's house, so he gave that to them, and he got a lot of money as well which he's possibly donated to the lepers in Kumasi.'

'Really?'

'Not really. One likes to see the good in people.'

'If Mrs Fellows really loved Mary, wouldn't she have confessed to the crime rather than seeing her friend hang?'

'This is exactly why stories are better than the truth. Stories plug all the gaps. The truth leaks like a colander.'

Parker-Ellis's majority had been reduced a little, but he'd kept his seat. He celebrated with a series of parties, one of which was at his home in Lambourn. Skelton and Mila were invited, but they were saved the irritation of attending by a previous engagement. This was not a lie. They, who went to perhaps three or four parties a year, had been invited to two on the same night.

Hannah Dryden, the heiress who had first christened

Skelton 'The Latter-Day Galahad' had wintered in Nice, Switzerland, Singapore and Jamaica. Now she had returned and was celebrating with a cocktail party at her Mayfair house, a white tie and tails affair. Mila wore midnight-blue silk, with beading and a handkerchief hem.

They drove to London in the Bentley. After driving the Daimler, Skelton had found he could not go back to the Wolseley.

'What's wrong with the Wolseley?' Mila had asked.

'It's an old man's car.'

Then Eliot Dean had come for supper and they had talked at length about Lagondas, but Skelton had decided the Lagonda was perhaps a little too showy. He was considering a Rolls-Royce but when Billy Dutton had popped into 8 Foxton Row to tie up a couple of matters, the talk had turned to Bentleys. As it happened, Billy could fix him up with a 1927 3-litre saloon, very low mileage, impeccable bodywork and it would only cost him a few pounds more than the resale value of the Wolseley.

Each time Skelton pressed the starter button of his Bentley, he felt a glow of what he could only describe as love. He didn't steer it, he swung it into corners. When he changed down and kicked the accelerator he was pressed back into his seat.

They arrived in Berkeley Square fashionably late. A flunky in bright satin livery admitted them, another took their coats, and another provided them with champagne cocktails. They smiled and nodded at no one they knew and made their way from one room to another looking for their hostess. There was an odd smell in the air, perhaps some sort of incense or exotic cigarettes. Far off, they could hear a jazz band playing.

'I think it's upstairs,' Mila said. 'I think sometimes these houses have a ballroom on the first floor.'

They went back to the hallway where they'd seen a double staircase, which Mila seemed to think was called an 'imperial staircase'. Young people, some of the men in black ties, were lounging on it, drawling and smoking. There were no ashtrays.

Being careful not to tread on any hands or thighs, they made their way upstairs. On the landing, a swarthy-looking man approached, seemed as if he was about to say something to Skelton, then moved on, muttering.

'Good Lord. I think that was Alejandro Zabala,' Skelton said.

'Who?'

'He was one of the witnesses in Hannah Dryden's defamation case. I didn't know any of them actually knew Hannah. I thought they were all invented by Maurice. Zabala is allegedly the finest swordsman in Argentina.'

'You have nothing to worry about, then,' Mila said. 'You are with the finest swordswoman in Berkshire.'

They found the ballroom. The music was very loud and the dancing very energetic. They came back to the landing. Both had finished their champagne cocktails.

'I thought there'd be food. What do you call them?'

'I don't know.'

'Not dinner. Little things to eat that you have with cocktails. Perhaps in here.' Skelton popped his head around a door and pulled it back immediately.

'I think we should leave.'

'What?'

'I just found our hostess.'

'Should we—?'

'She was with the cashiered colonel. You remember I mentioned him?'

'With the bad wig?'

'It's all he's wearing.'

AUTHOR'S NOTE

How Arthur Skelton Came to Be

When my wife Caroline's father died, we inherited his books. He was a coal miner's son, a passionate self-educator, so he had quite a lot of them.

In one of them, Caroline found a picture of Harold Davidson, the Rector of Stiffkey, a great celebrity of the 1930s, defrocked for allegedly consorting with chorus girls and the like, whose life ended when he was accidentally eaten by a lion in a circus ring. Caroline knew all about the Rector of Stiffkey. Years ago, she had worked with his son, Arnold, shared a flat with his grandson, Guy, and met his widow, Molly ('How tiresome to have one's husband eaten by a lion').

The picture drew us to the book – H. Montgomery-Hyde's biography of Norman Birkett, published in 1964. We started reading. Birkett's dangerous and disturbing world was all there on the first page, which assures the reader that the great man would be the best, indeed the only, barrister capable of successfully defending you if you ever got caught cutting up 'a lady' and shoving her remains into an 'unwanted suitcase'.

It's the word 'unwanted' that makes it special, suggesting that, having cut up the body, you'd go up to the loft space where you keep the suitcases and think, *No, not the Samsonite, I might need that next time I go to Swanage.*

The rest of the book wasn't quite up to the same standard as the first sentence – how could it be? – but still it gripped.

Norman Birkett, came from Ulverston in Cumbria and was a neighbour of Stan Laurel, of Laurel and Hardy fame, to whom he bore a modest resemblance. The son of a Methodist minister, he left school at the age of fifteen to take up an apprenticeship with a draper but carried on his studies at night school and eventually won a scholarship to Cambridge.

He became the most celebrated barrister of his day – first call for any case that was tricky, delicate or hopeless.

Those were the days when barristers didn't specialise, so on Tuesday he'd be doing a multiple stabbing, Wednesday a scandalous divorce and on Thursday he'd be unravelling the intricate shenanigans of *Consolidated Stuff vs Amalgamated Money*. It was he who defended the Rector of Stiffkey in the consistory court, who secured Mrs Wallis Simpson's divorce from Mr Simpson so that she could marry the King and precipitate an abdication without which HM Queen Elizabeth II would be a half-forgotten minor royal. He unsuccessfully defended Radclyffe Hall's lesbian shocker *The Well of Loneliness* against accusations of obscenity, and successfully saved Tony Mancini, the Brighton Trunk Murderer, from the hangman's noose. (Years later, on his deathbed, Mancini admitted he did it.)

For a couple of writers, eager for stories, Birkett's casebook was a gift. We, Caroline and I are writing partners as well as being married, filleted a dozen or so and sold them as afternoon plays to BBC Radio 4. Two series were made, the first in 2010 starring David Haig as Birkett and the second with Neil Dudgeon in 2012. Some of the plays are available as audiobooks and a lot of them have been posted, probably without permission but such is life in the digital age, on YouTube.

A few years later, Warren, the agent we've been with ever since he was in short trousers and I had hair, suggested turning some of the Birkett stories into novels.

Something approaching historical accuracy is just about possible for a forty-five-minute play. In a novel it gets tricky. I have a great deal of respect, reverence even, for Norman Birkett. What if I wanted him, for narrative purposes, to do or say something stupid or wicked? What if I wanted to put thoughts in his head about his life, his wife, politics or religion? What if I wanted him to get drunk and fall over or lose his trousers – as it happened, I did want to make him lose his trousers.

'Based on', seemed a better idea.

And so, Arthur Skelton, very loosely based on Norman Birkett, sprang into being.

There are some obvious similarities between the fictional Skelton and the real Birkett, characteristics that seemed too useful not to steal. Both have two children. Both are tall, thin and geeky. Norman Birkett married a Swedish PE instructress; Skelton a sporty one-quarter Swede. Birkett had a clerk called Edgar, although Edgar Bowker, the real one, has very little in common with Edgar Hobbes, the fictional one. I should have changed the name, I suppose, but 'Edgar' seemed too perfect to abandon.

The cases are even more fictionalised than the man. Mary Dutton's story bears some resemblance to that of Annie Pace, accused in 1928 of poisoning her husband in the Forest of Dean, but nowhere near enough to stand up to a historian's scrutiny. These alterations, too, were necessary. Real life is always far more implausible, coincidence-ridden and downright silly than you can get away with in fiction.

Take, for instance, the story about a defrocked vicar who got eaten by a lion in a circus ring. Who in their right mind would believe a thing like that?

ACKNOWLEDGEMENTS

With many thanks to librarians everywhere, particularly those at the British Library; to the late Agnes and Robert Baden-Powell and their inspiring book *A Handbook for Girl Guides or How Girls Can Help to Build Up the Empire* (1912), quotations from which embolden Rose at every stage of her journey; to Kelly Smith at Allison & Busby for her encouragement, advice and meticulous editing; to Warren and Carol who suggested it in the first place; and to Caroline, Georgia, Connie, Clemmie and Ben for everything else.

ACKNOWLEDGEMENTS

DAVID STAFFORD began his career in theatre. He has written countless dramas, comedies and documentaries including two TV films with Alexei Sayle, *Dread Poets Society* with Benjamin Zephaniah, and, with his wife, Caroline, a string of radio plays and comedies including *The Brothers*, *The Day the Planes Came* and *The Year They Invented Sex* as well as five biographies of musicians and showbusiness personalities. *Fings Ain't Wot They Use T'Be – The Life of Lionel Bart* was chosen as Radio 4 Book of the Week and made into a BBC Four TV documentary. *Skelton's Guide to Domestic Poisons* is his debut novel.

dcstafford.com   *@dstaffordwriter*